Proposing to Preston

THE WINSLOW BROTHERS, BOOK #2
THE BLUEBERRY LANE SERIES

KATY REGNERY

SPENCER
HILL
PRESS

Please visit www.katyregnery.com

First Edition: July 2015
Katy Regnery

Proposing to Preston: a novel / by Katy Regnery—1st ed.
ISBN: 978-1-63392-080-4
Library of Congress Cataloging-in-Publication Data available upon request

Published in the United States by Spencer Hill Press
This is a Spencer Hill Contemporary Romance, Spencer Hill
Contemporary is an imprint of Spencer Hill Press.
For more information on our titles visit www.spencerhillpress.com

Distributed by Midpoint Trade Books
www.midpointtrade.com

Cover design by: Marianne Nowicki
Interior layout by: Scribe, Inc.
The World of Blueberry Lane Map designed by: Paul Siegel

Printed in the United States of America

The Blueberry Lane Series

THE ENGLISH BROTHERS

Breaking Up with Barrett
Falling for Fitz
Anyone but Alex
Seduced by Stratton
Wild about Weston
Kiss Me Kate
Marrying Mr. English

THE WINSLOW BROTHERS

Bidding on Brooks
Proposing to Preston
Crazy about Cameron
Campaigning for Christopher

THE ROUSSEAUS

Jonquils for Jax
Coming August 2016

Marry Me Mad
Coming September 2016

J.C. and the Bijoux Jolis
Coming October 2016

THE STORY SISTERS

Four novels
Coming 2017

THE AMBLERS

Three novels
Coming 2018

Based on the best-selling series by Katy Regnery,

The World of...

The Rousseaus of Chateau Nouvelle
Jax, Mad, J.C.
Jonquils for Jax • Marry Me Mad
J.C and the Bijoux Jolis

The Story Sisters of Forrester
Priscilla, Alice, Elizabeth, Jane
Coming Summer 2017

The Winslow Brothers of Westerly
Brooks, Preston, Cameron, Christopher
Bidding on Brooks • Proposing to Preston
Crazy About Cameron • Campaigning for Christopher

The Amblers of Greens Farms
Bree, Dash, Sloane
Coming Summer 2018

The English Brothers of Haverford Park
Barrett, Fitz, Alex, Stratton, Weston, Kate
Breaking up with Barrett • Falling for Fitz
Anyone but Alex • Seduced by Stratton
Wild about Weston • Kiss Me Kate
Marrying Mr. English

"You're like a fairy godmother, just swooping in and making everything lovely. Wow. I'm going to start crying as soon as I stop laughing."
From the bottom of my heart,
I thank you, Carly Phillips.

xo

CONTENTS

Part I

Chapter 1

Two years ago

"Oh, my dearest darling . . . when I say that I love you with all my heart, I mean that my heart is a canyon, a cavern with hidden recesses, perilous cracks, and dark corners. And yet somehow, your love, like the sweetest and brightest light, has found every secret part of me and claimed them all as your own. Yes, my heart belongs to you, my darling, but only because I have given it to you freely—shredded, doubting, and hard, though it was—it comes to you warm and vibrant now, made whole by the force of your love, the warmth of your light."

Preston Winslow shifted uncomfortably in the narrow, stiff theater seat, unable to look away from the young woman on stage who delivered the saccharine-sweet speech like a Tony depended on it. Her costume was a white lace, high-necked Victorian dress that he suspected was quite a bit tighter over her voluptuous breasts than Victoria herself would have approved. Every time the actress gasped dramatically for breath, her flesh pushed provocatively against the straining fabric. After almost two hours of watching her breasts instead of this godawful play, Preston's seat wasn't the only thing that felt uncomfortably stiff.

"I have used you and abused you, been fickle and frivolous and flighty. But now I know, my darling. Now I see. It was—ever and always—you! Pray, tell me that there's still time to win your affection, sweet Cyril. Tell me that I haven't lost my heart's dearest wish: another chance to deserve your love!"

Cyril, who was doing as poor a job of ignoring, um— Preston glanced at the program—*Elise Klassan's* knockers as he was, lifted his glance quickly from her bosom and focused on her face.

"My dear Matilda . . ." he began, straightening his glasses and tuxedo bow tie. Preston really couldn't care less if Cyril and Matilda lived happily ever after, so it was strange that he held his breath as he waited for Cyril to give her his answer. "If you were the last woman on the face of the earth, I could not be troubled to give you the time of day."

Cyril took one last lascivious glance at Matilda's rack, then turned on his heel and exited to stage right. *Good riddance*, thought Preston. Any man who'd give up a chance to fall asleep beside those epic ta-tas—even in a high-necked Victorian nightdress—was a complete moron.

Sliding his eyes back to Elise Klassan—um, *Matilda*— Preston sat up, leaning forward, moving, almost unconsciously, to the edge of his seat.

Her face.

Oh, God, her face.

It was like watching a silent, slow-motion movie of a derelict building filled with dynamite. One moment it's standing upright, then the slow collapse, the dusty-clouded demolition, the complete destruction. And suddenly it didn't matter that the play had been terribly written and he'd been dragged to it by his on-again, off-again girlfriend, Beth, who snored lightly beside him. Preston sat helplessly, staring at Elise Klassan's desperation with a sympathy that felt profoundly . . . real.

Her face crumpled in agony, but not all at once. First blank, as though processing Cyril's rejection, her brows furrowed a little, and he saw her lip quiver. Her eyes fluttered, like they were trying to stay open, then she closed them tightly, as though the mere action of keeping them open was too painful to bear. Her hand rose slowly to her throat, flattening above her heaving chest, and the theater was so silent, he could hear his sharp gasp as a solitary tear rolled down her cheek.

"Cyril," she murmured in a lost, broken voice that sounded nothing like Matilda, and Preston's lips parted, transfixed on her sorrow.

She took a deep, jagged breath, her body swaying listlessly for a second before collapsing to the stage with one hand still on her chest and the other flung over her head.

Preston stared at her for a long moment, then lifted his eyes, his gaze darting around the stage to see if someone was coming—if stupid, pretentious Cyril was coming back to tell her that it wasn't too late and he was a jackass for letting her go. But no one came. She just . . . lay there. Unmoving. Dead? Oh, God, was she dead? Preston's heart clutched as the lights faded slowly to black and the curtain silently closed in front of her. He stared at the slightly rippling red velvet, wondering when it was going to reopen, wondering when he was going to have one last glimpse at Elise Klassan's lovely smile as she took her bow.

He waited, staring, breathless, but nothing happened.

Finally, the house lights came up, and there was a weak smattering of applause from behind him, filling the small theater with lackluster approval, and the fifty or so patrons in attendance stood up, mumbling about the show, shrugging into their coats, and shuffling from their seats to the aisles.

Beth started beside him, yawning loudly and sitting up. "It's over?"

Her voice jerked Preston's eyes away from the stage, and he stared at her like she'd appeared from out of nowhere.

"Thank God." She sighed, plucking her tan pashmina wrap from the back of her seat and wrapping it around her shoulders. "Sorry, Pres. I had no idea it would be so . . . *bad*."

He had an overwhelming urge to tell Beth that it *wasn't* so bad—even though, by and large, it *was*—because he'd been riveted by Elise Klassan. He shifted his eyes back up to the stage, focused on the curtain, as if the very force of his longing to see her one more time would be enough to make the edges suddenly part.

"Pres?" nudged Beth, her hand falling lightly over his and squeezing. "Ready to go?"

"Uh . . . yeah," he murmured, finally pulling his gaze away from the stage and looking at his date. "Why didn't they bow?"

"Huh?"

"Don't actors and actresses usually take a bow after the play's over?" he asked, gesturing at the stage with annoyance.

Beth raised an eyebrow, then made a big show of looking around the almost-empty off-off-Broadway theater before catching Preston's eyes again. "Umm . . . not if there's no one to applaud."

Giving one last troubled glance to the curtain, Preston stood up, pursing his lips. "Well, it doesn't feel like the show's over without that part."

"I doubt it'll be around for much longer anyway," she said dismissively, taking her bag from the floor by her seat and rising to her feet. "Really awful stuff."

"Not *really* awful," said Preston thoughtfully.

The material was admittedly bad, but Elise Klassan had done her best and given a performance that was sticking with him, almost like it had hitched a ride on his back and was following him up the aisle and out of the theater. There was something about her. Something . . . well, he didn't know. He couldn't put his finger on it, but suddenly he couldn't stop thinking about her.

As they neared the exit, Preston was surprised to find one last audience member still sitting in his seat, his expression a mirror of the way Preston felt, staring at the stage thoughtfully as though waiting for more, and Preston paused beside him in the aisle.

"I'm going to freshen up. Meet you in the lobby?" asked Beth. She kissed his cheek and made her way out the theater door.

The man in the last row looked up at Preston. "Is she dead?"

"Excuse me?"

"Matilda. Is she dead?"

Preston chuckled, but the man didn't.

"I don't know," he replied softly, feeling his smile fade.

"What did you think?" asked the man.

"Not good."

"Hmm. And yet you were the last to leave," observed the man.

"Actually," said Preston, looking down at him, "you're the only one still sitting."

"What was 'not good'? The play itself?"

Preston nodded.

"What about the actors?" The man opened his program. "Mark, uh, Smithson. He played Cyril."

Preston shrugged. He didn't have a good opinion about Mark Smithson's performance, and he wasn't going to make one up for the sake of conversation.

"Paige Rafferty?" He glanced down at the program again. "She played Constance."

Preston looked out the small window in the door to the lobby, but Beth hadn't come out of the bathroom yet. Again, he really didn't have an opinion of Paige Rafferty's performance other than that was sure he wouldn't remember it by tomorrow. "She was fine, I guess."

"But unremarkable."

Exactly. Preston nodded.

Up until now, the man's tone had been convivial, almost playful. But now, he fixed his dark eyes on Preston's, hawk-like and narrowed, and Preston wondered for the first time who he was. A reviewer? The director? Someone else associated with the play?

"And what about . . . Elise Klassan?"

Preston flinched. He didn't feel it coming, but he felt it happen. Then he licked his lips, which made his cheeks flush with heat, and he dropped the man's eyes in embarrassment.

"Mm-hm," rumbled the man, his voice smooth as warm honey. "Me too."

"She was good. She was . . ." Preston's voice trailed off, and he looked back at the stage for a moment, disappointed that the curtain was still closed and no longer rippled. The theater was so quiet and empty, it almost felt surreal, like there hadn't been a play at all.

What was it about it her that was affecting him so deeply?

He suspected that she was pretty under all that stage makeup, bouffant 1890s hairdo, and neck-to-ankle dress, and, as duly noted, her high, pert chest was undoubtedly a thing of beauty. But his feelings really weren't about beauty or attraction. They were about something else far less quantifiable or easily explained. The only words that came to mind? *Under his skin.* Her performance had gotten under his skin. The way her face had crumpled, the way her voice had broken when she whispered "Cyril," the profound sorrow on her face, and how terribly discomfited he felt at not seeing her alive and smiling one last time.

There was something about Elise Klassan that was special. Compelling. And she shone more brightly than hammy lines and mediocre costars. He was affected. He was moved.

He was touched. And though he knew this was the point of theater, he found he didn't like it.

When Preston turned around, the man stood, his lips spreading into a wide, satisfied smile. "You've helped immensely."

"Have I? With what?"

The man nodded, reaching down for his umbrella and chuckling softly to himself before looking back up at Preston. "I wasn't sure if I was right. But now . . . seeing you. . . . well, I know I am."

He nodded once more, as if in thanks, then he side-stepped out of his row, winked at Preston, and exited the theater.

God, it was so humiliating.

So. Dang. Humiliating.

Elise Klassan stared at herself, the bright-white, bubble-like bulbs surrounding her dressing room mirror and lighting her up like a hundred sparklers on the Fourth of July. She reached for another makeup wipe and scrubbed at her other cheek, sighing deeply.

When she had agreed to play Matilda in the off-off-Broadway world premiere of *She Loves Me Not*, Elise had read the script four times, trying to find a way to play Matilda that didn't reek of melodrama. She'd decided to play the character as a lost waif, a forgotten nobody who rises to prominence via an inheritance, though she has none of the skills necessary to negotiate her way through higher society. If Matilda could be seen as vulnerable instead of headstrong, the audience would be sympathetic to her ending up rich but alone. Instead, the director had blocked her efforts at every turn, insisting that the play was a farce with

Matilda receiving her just-deserts-comeuppance at the end and forcing Elise to overact the dramatic moments so they'd read funny.

They didn't.

They just read bad. No, not bad. Awful.

Throwing the used, light-orange makeup wipe into the garbage, she grabbed another and scrubbed at her lips vigorously, the red lipstick coming off on the small, white cloth in garish streaks. She attacked her eyes with similar gusto and her cheeks again, relieved to see her lightly freckled face finally emerge from behind the thick pancake. With impatient fingers, she pulled the hundreds of pins from her hair, neatly placing them in an empty Altoids tin. Her dirty-blonde hair tumbled in waves around her shoulders, and she drew it back into a ponytail and wrapped a gray scrunchie around it.

She'd taken off her dress and Victorian underthings as soon as she'd entered the shabby dressing room, but now she pulled on her favorite Old Navy jeans, faded and soft from frequent wear, and took a floral, long-sleeved T-shirt from the chair beside her modest dressing table. Flipping it over her head, she smoothed her ponytail again and put on her glasses before looking at herself in the mirror. She looked like herself now, like Sarah and Hans Klassan's youngest daughter, Elise, from Lowville, New York.

Staring at her pink, fresh-scrubbed, bespectacled face, she couldn't help the intense moment of self-doubt that ensued: Was she crazy for leaving her family's farm in upstate New York and coming to New York City?

Certainly her three older sisters hadn't made such a rash decision with their lives. Good Mennonite daughters, they'd all settled in or around Lowville, all were engaged or married to local men from their church, and her oldest sister, Abby, already had two babies. But not Elise.

Always considered an "odd duck" by her family, she'd been captivated by the theater in second grade when she took a field trip to the local high school to see *Finian's Rainbow*. It wasn't just the beautiful songs, like "How Are Things in Glocca Mora" or "Look to the Rainbow." No. It was the way the high school students, some of whom were friends of her older sisters, had transformed themselves into someone else. To be someone else, she marveled, looking down at her no-frills, homespun clothes, sounded wonderful.

And if the bug hadn't totally bitten her by the end of the show, the final line, "Maybe there's no pot of gold at the end of it, but there's a beautiful new world under it," certainly did. As far as little Elise was concerned, the stage was the rainbow, and the beautiful new world was a life beyond Lowville.

Turning her back on the simple life offered by her parents' tight-knit Mennonite community, Elise had applied to college in that beautiful new world. She'd put herself through the Tisch School of Arts at NYU with loans she'd be paying off for the rest of her natural-born life while she waited tables and played crappy parts in off-off-Broadway plays, hoping for her big break.

"Great life you've made for yourself here," she muttered, taking a deep breath and letting it go slowly. "Beautiful new world my . . . my . . . *foot.*"

She hung up her dress for tomorrow night's performance (ugh), put her makeup away, and swiped a paper towel over the top of her dressing table. Grabbing her backpack, she turned off the light in the tiny, grubby room and made her way down the backstage hallway toward the exit.

Incredibly tired and a feeling a little defeated, she didn't exactly look forward to the twenty-three block walk home to save bus fare, but pulling out her sofa bed and falling asleep sounded like pure heaven. Her roommate, Neve, whom she'd found via an ad in Backstage magazine, owned the apartment where Elise sublet the living room. On Friday nights, Neve bartended until after three, and Elise was fairly certain she'd sleep right through her roommate's late-night return.

"Great job, Elise!" cried Paige, bustling out of her own dressing room with a southern-cheerleader, can-do grin. "Great show!"

Sighing inside, Elise forced a smile and nodded at her costar. "You too, Paige. Great work."

It was all such baloney, but Elise said the lines with such practiced warmth and sincerity that Paige beamed at her.

"Think the audience noticed my flub in act two?" Paige asked, her elbow rubbing Elise's as they headed toward the stage door together.

"Nah," said Elise. "You covered it like a pro."

In fact, Paige hadn't covered it. Elise had. But who cared anyway? There weren't more than fifty people in the theater that held over two hundred, and she didn't believe the play would last beyond the month.

Great, she thought. *I'll be unemployed by May.*

Well, unemployed in the theater, she corrected herself. Her job at Virile Vic's BBQ wasn't going anywhere.

Literally.

"Yeah," said Paige, giggling. "Well, it sure was exciting! We're on the stage in New York City, Elise! That's what I tell myself every morning. I made it! See you tomorrow!"

Paige burst through the door to the sidewalk, waving good-bye as it slammed shut. Elise stopped short at the green-painted metal door, sighing heavily and leaning her shoulder against the cement wall to her right.

Outside the stage doors of most Broadway shows, hordes of fans stood impatiently, waiting for the stars of the show to exit and begging for the actors to sign their programs or take selfies. Although Elise, as a rule, hadn't pursued acting for fame or recognition, she still dreamed of a day when audiences would turn out in throngs to see her because she was good, and because she loved the craft of acting more than anything else in the world.

I made it!

What a joke.

Pushing open the heavy door, she was greeted with the cool, smelly air of Twelfth Street Manhattan, a wet sidewalk, a slight drizzle, the never-quite-dark skies of New York overhead, and . . . nothing else. Two men holding hands bustled by her, chatting animatedly, and a woman walked slowly toward her, talking on her cell phone, explaining why she couldn't make it out to Connecticut this weekend.

There were no fans. No well-wishers. No one.

Hiking her backpack higher, Elise turned right and started walking at a brisk pace, refusing to feel sorry for herself.

She'd been in New York for seven years, the last three of which she'd been auditioning, doing the occasional off-off-Broadway show, and wondering if she was throwing her life away. She had no important reviews of her work, her updated headshots this year had decimated her bank account, and when she called home, she knew full and well that none of her family members respected or supported her life choice, disappointment heavy in her mother's voice, especially. Friends were a luxury that rehearsals, performances, auditions, and waitressing didn't readily afford, and apart from some girls she occasionally hung out with from Vic's, she was mostly a loner. Which was fine with Elise because although she came alive on stage, most people would accurately describe her as fiercely driven but a natural introvert; she preferred to study the world in the shadows, taking silent notes to be used when she finally got the chance to channel a character.

But being an introvert didn't translate to embracing loneliness. She was lonely. In fact, she was *terribly* lonely for love. Although she'd never had a serious relationship, and didn't necessarily have the time, energy, or courage to pursue one now, she yearned for someone to love and love her back, with a constant, aching longing that was surpassed only by her single-minded determination to succeed on Broadway.

Her favorite plays—and the ones for which she was highly praised at Tisch—were all romances: traditional, heart-breaking romances like most of Shakespeare's oeuvre, of course, but also *The Importance of Being Earnest, Cyrano de Bergerac, Blithe Spirit*, and *Prelude to a Kiss*. Elise loved the language used to express love in these plays, almost as much as she loved—and feared—the idea of true love, itself.

Loved it because when it was true it sounded so perfect, so romantic. Feared it because from everything she'd ever read or watched, someone always ended up getting hurt. She yearned for the very thing that scared her, and it made no sense, but maybe that's just because her experience was so limited.

My opinions of love are all based on fiction, she thought, huffing softly as she stood at a crosswalk, a cold avenue-breeze cutting through her T-shirt and making her shiver. She was hoping to make it through spring without needing another raincoat. Hers had been stolen from Vic's one night, and she simply didn't have the means to purchase another. She rubbed her arms, reminding herself that April had just as many warm days as chilly, and hoping tomorrow would be one of the former.

But wouldn't it be heaven, mused her romantic side, as she started walking briskly again, to have her hand clasped in someone else's, someone's warm and strong fingers laced through hers as he walked her home?

Wouldn't it be lovely for him to fall into bed beside her and hold her until morning when she'd have to get up for the brunch shift at Vic's? Wouldn't it be bliss to know that he was in the audience every night, even if the play was a stink bomb from hell? Wouldn't it be thrilling to know that when she opened the stage door, he'd be standing there with roses and tease her by asking for yet another autograph?

She bit her lip, forcing such silly and useless romantic fantasies to the side. Even if she somehow managed to find someone who saw beyond her shyness and religious background, there was no room in her life for love, and that was the truth. Love was a luxury she couldn't afford. Heck, she couldn't even afford a spring jacket. And she probably wouldn't have a part in two weeks because she couldn't imagine such a bad play would demand additional performances.

Wincing at the state of her life, she quickened her pace, straightened her spine, and reminded herself as she always did of how much she'd give up for her dreams: her home and family, friends and boyfriends . . . she'd dedicated her whole life to the stage, and she was too invested to turn back now. Nobody "made it" right away. If you wanted something badly enough, you worked for it. You left your parents and sisters and home and church and took a bus to New York City without looking back. You paid off your loans as best you could, and you went without jackets and bus rides to save money. You acted in stink bombs because it was still a chance to act, and if you didn't take the part, there were one hundred other girls lined up who would. You worked long hours at Vic's only to show up for rehearsal on fumes. You accepted it when your director said there would be no curtain call because he wanted his farcical play to end on a "low" note, and you certainly didn't feel sorry for yourself when thousands of other hopeful thespians were leading the exact same life.

Besides, she reminded herself with a bit of wistful bravado, *You aren't a quitter, Elise Klassan. One day, you're going to see your name in lights. One day, the stage door will be mobbed.*

Chapter 2

Preston Winslow dreamed of Elise Klassan's breasts and woke up harder than marble in the bedroom of his posh Fifth Avenue apartment. He immediately regretted his decision not to let Beth stay overnight, which had prompted the response: "Screw you, and don't call me anymore, Pres. I mean it." Really, he couldn't blame her; she'd tried everything to get an invitation into his bed, and after asking him outright if she could stay over and being refused, she was hurt and embarrassed. But he just wasn't interested in sleeping with Beth; he was completely distracted by some unknown, off-off-Broadway actress who he'd never even met in person.

He'd been right on the money about Elise Klassan getting under his skin. As the day wore on, he found himself distracted and unable to study for either the New York or Pennsylvania bar exams he'd be taking back-to-back in July. His mind couldn't shake the image of her dead body on the stage floor, and he had this insane feeling that he'd grieve her, or *miss* her, for the rest of his life if he didn't just bite the bullet, buy another ticket, and see Elise Klassan alive and well, playing the dreadful Matilda once again.

Calling himself all sorts of a fool because the New York bar exam was one of the toughest to pass and truly required his dedicated attention, he bowed out of his study group, hailed a cab outside the New York Public Library at seven thirty, and arrived at the crappy theater on Twelfth Street twenty minutes later. With only ten minutes to spare before they raised the curtain, Preston found a seat in the third row center, noting that the theater was only slightly more packed than it had been yesterday, which still meant that fewer than half of the seats were full.

Glancing to his left, he noted with some surprise that his unlikely friend from last night had also returned.

"Back again?" asked the man, lifting an eyebrow. "And here I thought the play was 'not good.'"

"Maybe it deserves a second chance," mumbled Preston, feeling exposed and way beyond ridiculous for finding himself back in the audience so soon.

The man chuckled. "No it doesn't. But *she* does, doesn't she?"

Preston gave the man an annoyed look meant to discourage more conversation, then glanced back up at the closed curtain. He was incredibly irritated with himself for not getting off with Beth last night *and* blowing off his studies tonight. He wasn't acting like himself one bit. Yes, it was Elise Klassan's fault. No, he was not in the mood to discuss it.

"Let me give you some advice," said the man, leaning over the empty seat between them and lowering his voice to a whisper. "Remember her name after tonight. Remember Elise Klassan. Because whether you meant to or not—"

He sat back without finishing his statement as the house lights dimmed and the curtains opened to show a Victorian parlor with Cyril and Constance sitting side by side on a love seat. Preston looked away from the man beside him and braced himself for a guaranteed onslaught of dreadful overacting.

Relaxing as much as he could in the uncomfortable seat, Preston recalled that Elise wouldn't appear until the next scene, so there was no reason to pay attention now. He hadn't paid attention much to the program last night, but tonight he'd made a point to take one, and now he opened it to the Cast Bios page. Tilting the thin Playbill at an odd angle to catch the dim light in the theater as Constance tried unsuccessfully to dull her strong southern accent and Cyril continued to prove that he wouldn't be able to act his way out of a cardboard box, Preston narrowed his eyes in an attempt to read the small type.

Elise Klassan (Matilda)

Preston's eyes slid to the left where a tiny black-and-white picture of Elise smiled back at him, making his heartbeat quicken. In the photo she was wearing a white tank top with some sort of floral pattern at intervals. Her hair was back in a ponytail, and her shoulders, neck, and long arms were tan. But her face stole his breath away and made him softly gasp. She wore the sweetest, loveliest smile he'd ever seen, anywhere, at any time.

Forcing his eyes from her face, he scanned her biography:

Elise Klassan (Matilda) is delighted to be back at the Twelfth Street Rep Theater again after starring as Jenny in "By Proxy" and Francesca in "Tuscan Summer" last season. Elise holds a B.A. degree in Fine Arts from the Tisch School of Arts at NYU and was honored to train with Richard Bromberg for one semester at Julliard. Raised on a farm in upstate New York, Elise dedicates this performance to all of the little girls who dream of the big city lights. More at www.EliseKlassan.com.

It was a treasure trove of information about her, and his eyes skated swiftly back to her face as he processed the pertinent facts of her life . . . raised on a farm, dreamed of more, attended college in the city. He noted that her credits didn't include a mention of Broadway, and he wondered how she was living—if she had independent means or if she worked odd jobs to make ends meet.

And suddenly he *wanted* to know, almost like it was *important* . . . no, *essential* . . . to know how she survived, and if her life was good, and what had happened to her that made her voice break when she whispered "Cyril" before collapsing.

The meager audience clapped softly as the first scene came to a close, the lights dimmed, and Preston looked up immediately to give *He Loves Me Not* his full attention. As the lights came back up for scene two, there she was: Elise Klassan, alive and well, sitting in a straight-back chair, embroidering. He leaned forward, the Playbill falling from his lap to the floor in a whisper as he stared at her lovely face and the rest of the world slipped away.

Two hours later, Preston stared at the stage with terrible sorrow crowding his heart as the curtains closed on the life-less body of Elise Klassan. He'd paid far closer attention to her performance tonight, and though he was still distracted by her breasts, he found himself even more interested in *her*: her expressions, her gestures, the tone of her voice, the sound of her laugh. As the hours ticked by, he realized with certainty what he'd only glimpsed at the end of last night's performance: Elise Klassan was a phenomenal actress. The reason Preston hadn't been able to shake her today was because she seemed so real. Because as much as the lines were inelegant and cheesy, she still made him believe. What had the man said before the show? *Remember her name after tonight.* No doubt he would. With a bit of longing he knew he'd remember her name for the rest of his life.

He felt a little dazed and a lot bewildered. What now?

Did he just hail a cab and ride home now? Did he walk home, processing his feelings? Did he dare try to meet her? How exactly would he manage that?

Again, the final two patrons remaining in the theater, the man turned to Preston as the last straggler filed out into the lobby. "So?"

"Fantastic," murmured Preston.

"Yes, she was. I needed to be sure, but there's no doubt in my mind now. She's got *it*."

"It?" asked Preston, leaning down to pick up his Playbill.

"The 'it' factor. She's got it in spades." The man cleared his throat, picking up his umbrella and standing up. "You can't look away when she's on stage. Not even in this louse of a show. Imagine what she could do with a great play if this is what she manages with garbage."

"Yeah," said Preston, standing up. "You're right."

He slid his gaze back over to the stage longingly, then gave himself a mental kick in the ass. He didn't know this woman. She'd be beyond creeped-out if he suddenly appeared back-stage to . . . to . . . what? What would he do? Tell her he enjoyed the show? She wouldn't believe it. She had to know the show was terrible. Tell her he enjoyed *her*? Creepy. Tell her he dreamed about her last night? Serial killer creepy.

Never having experienced the sort of fan feelings reserved for young girls screaming about Justin Bieber, he felt embarrassed for himself, confused by the depth of his feelings for a woman he'd never met, never spoken to. It was unnerving, and with the bar exams bearing down on him, closer every day, he didn't have any more time to waste on this infatuation with a promising young actress.

He scoffed softly, turning back to the man. "Well, that's it, then. I guess I better . . ."

"How'd you like to meet her?"

Preston's heart tripped. "W-What?"

The man nodded, grinning back at him. "Sure. I'm headed backstage. Why don't you join me? I'll introduce you." He chuckled lightly. "You can be her first fan."

"Oh, I don't think—"

"You don't *want* to meet her?"

"Yes! Yes, I do, but—"

"So come on."

Without another word, the man turned to exit his row, and Preston followed. Who was this guy anyway?

"I hope you don't mind my asking, but what's your connection to—"

"The show? I have none. Thank God."

Preston kept following the man as he walked confidently to the stage, stepped up a small set of stairs to the left of the curtain, and pushed a red button on the wall, turning back to Preston.

"You have no idea who I am, do you?"

Preston looked closer at the man, then shook his head.

The man chuckled. "You're not a Broadway regular."

"No. My girlfriend—that is, my friend, Beth, dragged me here last night—"

He looked affronted. "*Dragged* you?"

"She's a patron of this theater and a few others."

"Oh," said the man, nodding in surprise. "I should have guessed from your Brooks Brothers shirt and pricey jeans. But you didn't seem like an asshole."

Preston was taken aback. "I hope I'm not."

Before the man could answer, a young woman peeked out from the curtain, her hair in a haphazard black bun, wearing dark-rimmed glasses and holding a clipboard.

"Yes?" She straightened her glasses, and her eyes widened like saucers. "Oh! Holy sh—I mean, oh my gosh! Mr. Durran. Welcome. I-I'm Kat Singleton, the assistant stage manager, and I'm a huge—"

"Ms. Singleton," said the man patiently. "I'd like a word with Elise Klassan."

"Of course! Oh my God—of course!" She flicked her eyes to Preston, who was watching the exchange with fascination. "Um, come with me, sir, um, Mr. Durran."

They followed Kat onto the dark stage, through a labyrinth of ropes, curtains, sets and technical boards, through a door, and into a poorly lit back hallway where various people bustled back and forth, most with headsets on, and all looking exhausted. The hallway was made of cement blocks, tight, narrow, and dirty with a strong smell of hot lights and mildew, but Preston barely noticed, wound tight with anticipation, scarcely able to believe that he'd be face to face with Elise Klassan in a matter of seconds.

Kat stopped at a nondescript door and knocked. "Elise?"

"Give me a sec, Kat!"

Kat turned to Mr. Durran, giving him a sheepish smile.

She knocked again. "Elise, it's important. Please let me in right now, huh?"

Preston heard the lock click, and Kat slipped into the room, leaving him and Mr. Durran alone in the hallway.

Elise looked up from her dressing table, where she sat in a bra and panties, her face still half-covered with makeup.

"Everything okay?"

Elise had worked with Kat a couple of times now, but they'd never been especially close, and postperformance was a busy time for the assistant stage manager, so it was unusual that Kat would come by to see Elise directly after a performance.

Stopping what she was doing and turning her body to Kat, Elise realized that Kat was panting with excitement, her bottom lip between her teeth and her eyes dancing.

"Kat? What is it?"

"Brace yourself."

Elise's heart sped up, and she placed the makeup wipe in her hand on the dressing table counter. "Okay."

Kat licked her lips, speaking in a dramatic whisper. "Donny Durran is *here* . . ." Elise felt her eyes widen as her breath caught. ". . . and he wants a word with you!"

Elise reached out for Kat's hands, clasping them as she burst into a smile, her whole body tensing with nerves and excitement. "Me?"

Kat nodded, giving Elise's hands a squeeze before releasing them. "Fix your face and get dressed quick."

"Oh my God!" Elise giggled softly and nodded, turning to grab another makeup wipe and scrub her face furiously.

"Where are your clothes? These?" asked Kat, taking the jeans and flowered, long-sleeved T-shirt off the chair beside Elise. Kat unfolded the jeans and held them open for Elise, who managed to step into them while taking off the last of her eye makeup. Kat took the dirty wipe and passed Elise the shirt. "Here!"

Elise slid the shirt over her head, and it caught on several pins. "My hair!"

Kat pulled the shirt down and plunged her hands into Elise's hair, tugging out pins right and left as Elise caught them in her fist.

"What do you think he wants?" asked Kat.

Elise had no answer. The play was terrible. She shook her head, at a loss.

"Stay still!" whispered Kat.

"I don't know what he wants," said Elise. "I'm shaking."

Kat pulled the last of the pins from Elise's hair and handed them to her, putting her hands on Elise's shoulders and looking squarely into her eyes. "Stop it."

"Okay."

"Take a deep breath."

"Right. Good."

"Do you want to put your hair up?"

Elise placed the pins in a neat pile on the table and ran her fingers through the silky waves. "No. It's fine."

"Sit."

Elise sat back down on the stool behind her, straightened her spine, and crossed her legs, facing the door.

Kat offered Elise a serene smile, pointing at it. "Smile."

Elise took a deep breath and smiled up at Kat gratefully.

"Good luck," she mouthed, as she turned to the door and opened it. "Gentlemen, allow me to introduce Elise Klassan."

Elise stood, channeling the most confident and gracious character she could imagine as she extended her hand to the most well-regarded, best-recognized casting director on Broadway.

"Hello, Ms. Klassan, I'm Donny Durran."

"Yes, I know! What an honor to meet you, sir!" said Elise, trying to keep her hand from trembling as she clasped his like a lifeline.

Out of the corner of her eye, she noted the tall, young, good-looking man standing just behind Donny, and she flicked her blue eyes to his intense, bright green. "And you are . . ."

"My new talent scout," said Donny with a light chuckle.

"That's not true," said the handsome man quickly, shaking his head, his eyes fixed on hers like lasers. "I'm not a-a scout. I'm a lawyer."

"He's a lawyer! Well, lucky for you, Ms. Klassan, because I'm thinking you might need a good lawyer very soon," said Donny.

Her smile fell. "Oh. Why? Have I done something wrong?"

Where Elise came from, you only needed a good lawyer for a couple of things—mostly foreclosures and legal defense.

Mr. Durran pulled his hand away with a yank. "Aside from almost breaking my hand? No."

"Oh," she said, shaking her head with a nervous chuckle. "Oh. That's good. I mean, sorry. I'm so sorry about your hand! I, uh, then . . ."

Mr. Durran smiled kindly at her, putting her at ease. "You might need a good lawyer to look over a contract for you in the near future. Perhaps Mr. . . ."

"Winslow," said Green Eyes, his deep, rich voice vibrating through her trembling body. "Preston Winslow."

"Perhaps Mr. Winslow could help you out with that."

Elise flattened her hand over her racing heart, looking back and forth between the two men in confusion before sitting back down on the stool by her dressing table. "A contract? What contract?"

"You know what I do, right, Ms. Klassan?"

She nodded. Everyone on Broadway knew Donny Durran—he was the best of the best. If you were discovered by Donny Durran, you'd made it on the Broadway scene. As long as you worked hard and stayed sharp, you'd have access to the very best parts in New York.

"Well, my partner and I are casting a new show. Part of the Lincoln Center summer series. It's a revival of *Ethan Frome*. You know the story?"

Know it? Edith Wharton was Elise's favorite author of all time, bar none.

"I love it," she croaked, trying not to faint, or hope too hard, or . . . faint.

"Ah, good. Always nice to find someone familiar with the material," he said to Mr. Winslow, who hadn't looked away from Elise since their introduction. As Mr. Durran turned back to her, he explained, "Garrett Hedlund has signed on to play Ethan, and Maggie Gyllenhaal is playing Zeena, but the directors specifically wanted a young unknown to play Mattie. You'll have to audition, of course, but I'm thinking . . . you."

"Me?" she parroted, trying not to hyperventilate. A lead role. In one of her favorite plays. At *Lincoln Center*? With *Hollywood stars*?

A small noise of disbelief escaped her throat—a cross between a whimper and a moan—and her heart was beating so fast she was starting to feel dizzy.

Wait, wait, wait, her subconscious intervened, strong-arming its way to the front of her brain. *This must be a joke.*

"But *He Loves Me Not* is the worst play of all time," she heard herself mumble as she exhaled the breath she was holding.

Horrified by her inadvertent disloyalty, she looked up at Mr. Durran, but was distracted by Green Eyes, who smiled at her—smiled the most sexy, beautiful smile she'd ever seen, and though it didn't make an ounce of sense, she felt like that smile was suddenly holding her up. She nodded at the hot lawyer gratefully then turned to Mr. Durran, taking a deep breath and composing herself.

"I just mean . . . it wasn't my best work."

Mr. Durran nodded. "The material's trash. But you weren't."

She licked her lips, forcing herself to stay focused on Mr. Durran, though she would have liked to see Green Eyes' reaction to such praise.

"You were quite good, Ms. Klassan. Quite good. Mr. Winslow and I caught your performance two nights in a row, and not because we found the play the least bit compelling. But you . . . well, I'll be damned if you don't have something." He reached into his pocket and pulled out a card. "I've written the audition time and place on the back. Tuesday afternoon at three. The Claire Tow Theater at Lincoln Center. You know it?"

"I know it," she whispered.

He nodded. "Well, that's fine. Don't let me down, Ms. Klassan."

"No, sir," she said, grinning up at him. "I can't thank you enough."

"You're welcome."

She felt like she should say more, so she added, "You've just made my dreams come true."

"I think you did that all yourself," said Mr. Durran, "doing the best you could with this lemon."

Elise's glance flicked to Green Eyes, who still stared at her, a teasing smile playing on his lips. "And thank *you*, Mr. Winslow."

"Mr. Winslow," said Mr. Durran thoughtfully, darting a quick glance back at his associate. "He had much more to do with this than you know, Ms. Klassan. He was . . . *captivated* by your performance."

Elise watched as his cheeks flushed and his smile faded, but he didn't drop her eyes. He stared into her, through her, like he was captivated by far more than her performance, and though some part of her knew she should find such searing attention unnerving, it wasn't. It was exciting. It was exhilarating. Unchecked it could prove . . . addictive.

"Well, I'll leave you two now. Tuesday, Ms. Klassan. At three."

"I'll be there," she murmured, dragging her eyes from Mr. Winslow to smile at Mr. Durran. "And thank you again."

Mr. Durran winked at her, then turned, exiting her dressing room and leaving her alone with the beautiful, intense Mr. Winslow.

Chapter 3

"Hi," said Preston, still stunned to find himself suddenly standing in Elise Klassan's dressing room after thinking about her nonstop for the past twenty-four hours.

It had been thrilling to see Mr. Durran offer her the chance of a lifetime—the way her eyes sparkled with excitement had made every atom of his body gravitate to her, want for her, hope for her. He'd fleetingly wondered what he wouldn't do to make them sparkle like that again.

"Hi," she answered, giggling softly as she looked down at the business card in her hands and then back up at Preston.

Her cheeks were pink and smattered with light freckles, but her lips were lush and full. Cute and sexy. A lethal combination.

"I guess congratulations are in order," he said, wishing he sounded more witty and less stiff. He'd heard of men struck by a lightning bolt of love—or more likely, by a lightning bolt of instant and intense attraction. He'd always regarded such accounts as silly . . . until now.

Elise Klassan beamed at him before lifting her backpack and hefting it over her shoulders. Her bright eyes twinkled when she looked back up, waggling a finger at him in censure. "Not yet."

"But you got an audition," he said, grinning back at her.

She gestured to the open door, and he walked through it, waiting in the hallway as she turned out the lights and locked her dressing room.

"Yes, but not the part."

"Not yet," he amended, mimicking her words. "But you will."

She looked up at him, youthful giddiness lighting her face. "You think so?"

"I know so," he answered, staring down at her from the opposite side of the narrow hallway.

She leaned against the hallway wall across from him, her soft, golden waves a lovely contrast to the drab concrete behind her. "How do you know Mr. Durran? Do you work together?"

He thought about lying. He strongly considered telling her that yes, he was an entertainment lawyer who regularly worked with Mr. Durran, because he wanted an "in" with her that badly. But he couldn't bear lying to her. Something about the openness of her face made it impossible.

"The truth is, I don't know him at all. We met last night . . . I mean, we chatted after the show, and then ran into each other again tonight."

"Again?" She laughed softly. "Why in the world would you come and see *He Loves Me Not* again?"

"For you," he answered simply, his voice low and gravelly in his ears. He cleared his throat, suddenly feeling much younger than his twenty-nine years.

"For *me*?"

He nodded as his chest tightened with some unspecified emotion. Anxious for a breath of fresh air, he gestured to the hallway. "Shall we?"

She searched his face for an extra beat before turning to the left, and Preston followed her past several closed doors, waved good-night to a crew member who told Elise he'd see her tomorrow, and stepped down three concrete stairs to a bright-green door. Elise pushed it open, and Preston was surprised to find them on a dark, wet New York sidewalk.

Elise crossed her arms over her chest and looked at him, her face uncertain and her eyes cautious. "Are you making fun of me?"

Preston leaned away from her, taken aback. "Making fun? What are you talking about?"

"You came to a bad play two nights in a row *to see me*?" she asked, her eyes challenging. "That doesn't make any sense."

"It does to me," he said. "I came last night with my . . . I mean, I came to see the show, and I admit I didn't get into it until the end, but all day I thought about you dying, and I couldn't get it out of my mind, and so I . . . I don't know, I came back to see the show again."

Her face softened. "You're serious."

"Hundred percent," he confirmed, nodding at her.

"And you don't know Mr. Durran personally?"

"Not even a little bit."

"So . . . who *are* you?"

"A fan of your work?" he asked, offering her his most charming smile.

"My *work*?" She chortled. "My excellent portrayal of Matilda?"

He sniffed. "You were better than the play. Like Mr. Durran, I'd like to see you in something good."

She swept her suspicious eyes down his blue-and-white-striped dress shirt, glancing briefly at his watch, skating down his designer jeans, and resting on his expensive leather loafers before sliding back up to his face. His body tightened at her perusal, turned on by her frank inspection.

"Are you a patron?" she asked. "Of the theater?"

He shook his head. "No. But the friend who brought me last night? She is."

"She." Elise took a deep breath, and two spots of color appeared on the apples of her cheeks. "Girlfriend?"

"No," he answered simply. *Not anymore.*

"I see," she said, releasing the breath she'd been holding, the hint of a smile warming her lips. "So, are you really a lawyer?"

"I graduated from Columbia law school last June. I'm taking the bar, well, *bars*, in July."

"Bars? I'm assuming New York and . . ."

"Pennsylvania."

She tilted her head again, scanning his face like she was trying to make a decision about him.

Before she could overthink it, he asked quickly, "Let me take you for a glass of champagne. To celebrate."

"Oh, I don't—"

"Coffee? Who says no to a cup of coffee?"

"Me, I guess." She grinned at him, shrugging her shoulders. "I don't drink coffee."

He took a deep breath, pursing his lips. Was she politely blowing him off? Probably. She didn't know him from Adam, she'd had a long day, and probably had people she wanted to call, friends with whom to celebrate her good fortune. He had no right to monopolize her, or follow her around like some stray dog looking for a home. As much as he hated to admit it, it was time for him to leave her alone.

"Well, then I guess this is good-bye," he said softly, surprised by how sad the words made him feel.

She pulled her bottom lip between her teeth, her eyebrows furrowing as she stared back at him, shifting her weight from foot to foot.

He put out his hand and offered her a final smile. "I really did enjoy your performance, Elise Klassan. I think . . . well, I think you're a terrific actress. You certainly made me believe. Good luck on Tuesday."

She looked down at his hand, but didn't offer her own, and her eyes finally glided back up his chest to his face. "By any chance are you walking north?"

His grin spread so wide that it eventually turned into a small, relieved chuckle. "Absolutely. I'm absolutely walking north."

She shrugged, smiling back at him. "Want to walk with me a while?"

He nodded, turning his body north before she could reconsider her invitation. "I'd love it."

At first, his strides were longer than hers, but almost immediately she noticed that he adjusted them, slowing down so that he didn't outwalk her or make her speed up to match him. She glanced at him as they made their way to the first crosswalk in silence. His thick, almost-black hair was just a little too long and curled slightly over his collar. He'd run his fingers through the tangle of waves once or twice, taming it back, and her fingers itched to do the same. Sliding her gaze down, she noted his jaw was sharp and strong, covered with a scruffy black stubble that was masculine and appealing. She wondered if it scratched when he kissed, or if it was unexpectedly soft, and she drew her bottom lip between her teeth as she stared at his full, sexy lips. With cheeks cut from marble, and sinfully long black lashes framing his emerald-green eyes, his beauty was startling, over-the-top, like it should be impossible.

He was—by anyone's standards—a ridiculously handsome man, and her body had been affected by him from the first moment she lifted her eyes to his, but Elise worked in the theater where beautiful men were not uncommon. She wasn't immune to Preston Winslow's beauty, per se, but she'd met enough shallow, self-serving stunners to know that it was foolish to judge a book by its cover or a person by a pretty face. As handsome as he was, his looks had little to do with why Elise had invited him to walk with her.

She'd asked him because she sensed that he was honest and kind, which was incredibly refreshing. Always having been pegged as intense and introverted, Elise had felt like an outsider for a good deal of her life; both at home where she was an actress in Mennonite clothing, and in New York City, where she was a farm girl trying to make it in a vast metropolis. But something about Preston Winslow made her feel like she belonged. There was no room for him in her life, but she couldn't help feeling drawn to him, and she just wanted to spend a little more time with him before they had to say good-bye.

"I read your bio tonight," he said as they crossed the street, "in the program."

"Oh?"

"Did you really grow up on a farm?"

She laughed softly, nodding. "I did. In Lowville, New York, which you have never heard of, right?"

"Right," he said, "though I'm not from New York, so maybe that's the reason."

"Nope. No one's heard of it. It's as dull as it sounds." She was rambling, as she always did when she was nervous. She shifted the focus back to him. "Let me guess . . . you're from Pennsylvania."

"Good guess!"

"Well, you're taking the bar there, so . . ."

He nodded, grinning down at her as they eased into a comfortable strolling pace. "What kind of farm? What did you grow?"

"Cows," she said, chasing the answer with a soft giggle. "We grew cows on forty acres, housed them in three barns, and milked them in two milk houses."

"You *grew* cows. . . ." he said, amusement thick in his voice.

"Yep. Dairy farm. Have you ever smelled a dairy farm?" She looked at his expensive clothes again. "I'm guessing no."

"So tell me about it."

"When they're out in the field? Grazing? You don't smell anything. Well, manure. You *always* smell manure, but you don't notice it if you grow up with it. And when they're corralled in the yard, waiting to be milked? Imagine a boys' locker room after a game."

Inside, she was cringing at herself like crazy. This nice, gorgeous lawyer was walking her home, and she was talking about cows and manure. She resisted the temptation to thump her forehead with the heel of her hand and stared down at the sidewalk, settling for a wince instead. Diarrhea of the mouth was not uncommon for her when she was anxious or out-of-her-element, or, apparently, walking the streets of New York with scorching-hot strangers, but this was a new low.

"Uh . . . yum," he said lightly.

"I'm nervous," she confessed.

"What? You mean you don't usually lead with manure and locker rooms?"

She stopped walking and looked up at him. "You're obviously very wealthy—"

"Why do you think so?"

She looked pointedly at his clothing. "You reek of it."

"Are you saying *I* smell?"

"Yep. Of old money," she said. "And you're ludicrously handsome, and you suddenly showed up in my dressing room out of nowhere standing next to Donny Durran and saying nice things and walking me home, and I just . . ."

She stood there helplessly, staring up into his gentle, green eyes, trying to figure out what she was trying to say, and wishing to God she had been granted just a smidge more social grace, or had had the time to channel a smooth, sophisticated socialite before meeting Preston Winslow.

"You think I'm handsome, huh?"

"It's an empirical truth."

He considered her. "You're an actress. I wouldn't expect you to be nervous."

"Why not?"

"Because it takes a lot of courage to get up on a stage and be someone else, and you do it very well."

"Actually, I disagree with you. It doesn't take any courage to be someone else. It's much scarier to be yourself." She scanned his face, wondering if she'd said too much. "Don't you think?"

"Yeah," he said softly, reaching toward her face like he was going to push a lock of her hair behind her ear and then stopping himself at the last minute. As if to control them better, he stuck his hands in his pockets, tilting his head to the side and grinning at her. "Listen, I liked your performance. I think you're intriguing. I don't have to walk you home, but I'd like to. You don't need to be nervous, because I don't expect anything from you. We can talk or walk in silence, but it's just steps. One after the other until we get to where you need to go. Nothing less. Nothing more."

She swallowed, taking a deep breath, a little swept away and a lot reassured by his short, gentle speech. Her bunched-up shoulders relaxed, and she nodded at him gratefully.

"I bet you're a good lawyer," she said, resuming their walk, inexplicably happy when his footsteps matched hers.

"I don't know yet. I was supposed to be studying for the bar tonight, but I . . . got distracted."

That made her smile, and she stole a peek at him, noting a small dimple in the cheek closest to her. It made her breath catch, and her heart hugged itself like it had just learned a new secret about something completely wonderful.

"What kind of law will you practice?"

"Sports. Well, sports *and* entertainment, technically," he answered. "I was—I mean, I used to row at school, in college. I loved it. But . . ."

"But?"

"I tore my rotator cuff," he said, a slight bitterness entering his voice. "I had surgery to repair it, but the damage was too extensive. I had to give it up." He paused, giving her a sly look. "The rowing, not the shoulder."

"I'm sorry."

"I was, too."

"It was important to you."

He nodded. "Very. I was on the national team, a few months out from the Olympic trials. Yeah, it sucked."

Her eyes widened. Rowing hadn't just been a hobby or pastime for him, but a passion, a huge commitment, a lifestyle . . . like the stage was for her. And he'd had to give it up? She didn't know how she'd survive giving up something she loved as much as acting. Her sympathy for him was sudden and enormous.

"Wow. I . . . wow. I don't know what to say."

"I was pissed for a while, you know? It was a real blow to be sidelined so close to making the Games, and I guess it didn't help that my brother's an Olympic sailor. He made it all the way, and I couldn't."

"You couldn't help it that you got injured," she pointed out.

"I could've. I was training too hard. I wasn't allowing my muscles time to repair themselves."

"You were pushing yourself to be the best. I get that."

"You do, don't you?" he said with a bit of wonder.

She nodded. "Acting's my whole life."

"And with tonight's big break," he said, "you're about to explode."

She chuckled. "Don't jinx me!"

"I don't believe in the jinx," he said. "I believe in hard work, in setting goals, and seeing them through. You're the only one who can make your dreams come true."

Elise sighed beside him, her heart fluttering as she absorbed the simple beauty of his words. *You're the only one who can make your dreams come true.*

"I love that," she said softly, goose bumps covering her arm as it brushed against his.

It was much warmer than last night, and Mr. Winslow had rolled up his long sleeves to the middle of his forearm. She looked down at the sinew of muscle, likely leftover from his rowing days. He had thick, strong arms. They'd feel like heaven wrapped around her.

"So, how did law school figure into your plan?" she asked, eager to distract herself from the nearness of him, the strange intimacy of walking side by side with him.

"I'd planned to go to law school after the Olympics. You know, win the gold, become a sports lawyer. Make millions. Rinse, repeat."

"Marketing via Olympics."

"Exactly." He sighed. "But there was no Olympics, and no gold. Just me, a washed up rower who can't row anymore."

Elise reached for his arm and stopped walking, the pressure of her fingers halting him midstride as he looked down at his arm and then into her eyes.

"You're much more than that. With drive like yours? I bet you'll be the best sports lawyer New York and Philadelphia have ever seen. You're not a washed-up anything. Know what I think? I think you're on the verge of greatness too."

Preston had meant the words "washed up" lightly, jokingly almost, except that when he talked about his failed bid for the 2008 Olympics, it felt like yesterday, not five years ago, and he couldn't help the bitterness that still slipped into his voice.

It had been a brutal blow to find out that he couldn't row competitively anymore. Not only had he wanted to follow in his older brother Brooks' footsteps, but he'd found his identity in rowing. His father, the late Taylor Winslow, had crewed in college, and Preston had felt a kinship to his father when he was out on the water, sliding down a glassy river. Losing his chance at the Olympics had been like losing his dad all over again. And though his acceptance to Columbia law school had been fast-tracked and he'd graduated Cum Laude a cool three years later, it hadn't erased the goals he'd worked so hard to achieve, and it didn't relieve the sting of disappointed dreams either.

But looking down at Elise's hand on his arm, their first skin-to-skin contact, he couldn't find any bitterness in his heart. He felt nothing but gratitude for her kindness, his heart thundering its approval for her solidarity and hope, and for the soft, warm touch of her fingers on his skin.

He looked down at her upturned face, his blood racing through his body, pounding between his ears.

"You're stunning," he whispered.

She'd been frowning with indignation at his self-deprecation, but softened immediately, her eyes widening and her lips tilting up into a sweet smile.

"Thank you."

She looked down at her hand, and he felt the slight pressure of her fingers squeezing before she pulled it away. And he was left. Missing her.

Glancing up, he realized she'd stopped them beside a deli. "Wait here a second, okay? Don't go anywhere!"

He rushed into the deli, choosing a large bouquet of light-pink roses and placing a twenty-dollar bill on the counter before rushing back outside. Elise stood where he'd left her on the sidewalk, her eyes expectant. He pulled the flowers from behind his back and offered them to her with a grin.

"You said no to champagne and coffee. But you *can't* say no to flowers."

"No," she said, her smile faltering as her lips parted and she reached for the blooms. "I can't. They're so lovely."

She raised the bouquet to her nose, eyes closing as she inhaled deeply and sighed. When she opened her eyes, they were sparkling as they had when Donny Durran handed her his business card, and Preston felt his chest swell with satisfaction and longing. Such a simple gesture, but it had made her so happy, and suddenly her happiness was like a drug, and Preston wanted more.

"Thank you," she murmured, that sweet smile fixed on her lips.

Kiss her.

The words repeated in his head on a loop, blocking out all other thoughts, all other sounds and smells and ideas and common sense. Her face was upturned, her full, pink lips slightly parted. They'd be warm and soft beneath his, and his breath hitched with yearning. Taking a step toward her, he dropped his eyes to her lips, staring at them, longing for a taste of them. He was just about to bend his head to hers when—

"Ah-hem. Sir? Your change?"

"Huh?"

"You ran out without your change."

Preston whipped his eyes to the side and found the shop owner in a white apron, holding out a dollar bill and a few coins.

"Oh. Yes. Of course, how . . . how good of you. Thanks."

He accepted the change, and Elise stepped away from him, pointing her body north again, away from him, and Preston sighed internally, simultaneously frustrated and relieved. Frustrated, because he couldn't remember the last time he'd wanted to kiss a girl so badly. Relieved because for all he knew, she would have smacked his face and run away if he'd taken such a liberty after knowing her for less than an hour.

They started walking again, their pace slower than before as Elise admired her flowers.

"This was really sweet of you."

"Well, you deserve a little celebration," he said. "You must be excited for Tuesday."

"I'm over the moon," she said. Then, with a full, delighted voice, "You know what? I'm gobsmacked!"

"Well, there's a good British word," he said with an English accent. His mother was from London originally, so he'd spent an enormous amount of time there whilst growing up.

"Wow! That's a really authentic accent!" she exclaimed. "It's hard to get it that good!"

"My mum is British."

"Is it just you and her?" asked Elise.

"Nope. Me, and her, and my four siblings."

"Four!"

"Three brothers and a little sister. You?"

"Big family, too. Four sisters, and I'm the baby."

"Like Jessica," he said, thinking of his little sister, who was in college in London. He hadn't seen her in months, and reminded himself to call her.

"Jessica's your sister, I assume?"

"Mm-hm. Brooks is the eldest, then me, then Cameron, then Christopher, then Jessica. She's in London with my mum right now. She's studying modern art."

"I approve," said Elise with an efficient nod. "I love modern art. And your dad?"

"Passed on."

"I'm sorry."

He shrugged because he didn't want to talk about it. "It was a long time ago."

"Still . . ."

"And you?" he asked, changing the subject back to her. "One of four sisters!"

"Abigail, Caitlyn, Lillian, and Elise."

"Little Elise who had big dreams," he said, nudging her gently with his elbow.

She nudged him back. "Little Elise, who, like little Preston, believed in making her dreams come true."

"And now look at you! Here you are," he said, gesturing with wide arms to Manhattan. "On the eve of your triumph!"

"Shhhh!" she hushed him dramatically. "The jinx!"

He lifted an index finger to his lips, trying not to smile.

Shaking her head at him with glee, she stopped walking in the middle of a tree-lined street, leaning against the trunk of a tree across from a brownstone apartment building.

"*Ethan Frome*," she said with longing, holding the flowers to her chest and closing her eyes dramatically as she let the back of her head rest against the smooth bark of the tree. "Can you imagine?"

"I can. And I'll buy the first ticket on your opening night."

"Promise?" she asked, peeking at him through one eye.

"I do," he answered solemnly.

Her other eye opened, and she lowered her chin, staring back at him intently, the way he might look at something he wanted, but couldn't have. Her voice was soft and wistful when she said, "Well, I guess I'll see you then."

"Then?"

"On opening night, I mean." She gestured to the stoop across the street from her tree. "This is me. Home. My apartment building."

"Oh." Preston looked up at the shabby, nondescript brownstone painted a dull, peeling goldish color. He felt sorry—*incredibly* sorry—to have to say good-bye to her. He wasn't ready to watch her walk away.

"Thank you again for the flowers," she said, stepping away from the tree.

"Of course, but I—"

"And thank you for walking me home."

"It's my pleasure. I'd like . . . I mean, Elise, wait—"

"Mr. Winslow," she interrupted, turning to face him from the bottom step. She swallowed over the sudden and unexpected lump in her throat, and ignored the painful squeeze of her heart. "I have to get ready for the biggest audition of my life in three days . . . and you have two bar exams to study for. The timing's just . . ."

". . . shit," he finished softly.

She nodded. "I was going to say 'not good,' but 'shit' works too."

"So this is good-bye," he said.

"I think it needs to be," she said regretfully, hoping she wasn't making the biggest mistake of her life.

He ran a hand through his dark hair, palming the back of his neck as he stared at her, and she somehow knew that his brain was trying to figure out an alternate solution. When he dropped his hand listlessly to his side and sighed, she knew he'd been unsuccessful.

"It was lovely to meet you, Elise Klassan."

"The pleasure was all mine, Preston Winslow."

He held out his hand, and she braced herself before clasping it. She knew her palm would fit against his like their hands had been made to hold one another, and she knew it would weaken her resolve to say good-bye. She reached forward and his hand met hers, joined with hers, melted into hers, warm and strong, pumping gently before letting go too soon.

"Until we meet again," he said, his intense, green eyes seizing hers for a long moment before he turned quickly on his heel and walked away.

Elise watched him until she couldn't see him anymore, and only when he was finally out of sight did she realize they never actually said good-bye.

Chapter 4

Preston walked the remaining thirty blocks to his apartment feeling a little dazed and not at all himself. He'd just found and lost the most amazing girl in the world, all within the course of an hour.

He'd never felt this way before, never experienced this painful pull in his heart to return to the place he'd left her and throw pebbles at her window until she came back downstairs. Preston had believed himself a pretty smooth operator before tonight, but he'd been leveled by a farm girl from upstate New York. How had it happened? And why?

She was beautiful, yes. But after walking with her and talking with her, he was fairly certain that her beauty was enhanced by something inside of her. It made her eyes shine and softened her face, it sweetened her smile and made her words sincere. There was an authenticity about her, a purity that appealed to him. She wasn't overeager or grabby with him. If anything, she was more reserved than most of the women he knew, which made him long for the thrill of chasing her, deserving her, belonging to her. It was completely absurd after an acquaintance of sixty minutes, but he couldn't help it, and he wondered . . .

Can your whole life change in sixty minutes? Can you say good-bye forever to someone wonderful just because the timing's bad? Can your head force your heart to move on when it clamors for more wet-sidewalk, misty evening, one-foot-in-front-of-the-other magic?

It was times like these that Preston sorely wished his mother lived in the States and not London, where it was three o'clock in the morning. Or—if he was truly honest with himself—it was times like these that Preston longed desperately for his father: a man who had deeply loved a woman. A man who'd listen and give him advice and wouldn't make fun of his sudden and intense feelings.

But his mother was in London. And his father was long gone. Brooks, his oldest brother, was in South Africa training the national team for their first bid as the America's Cup challenger, not that he would have been much help. His nomad ways hadn't left much room for a girlfriend over the past few years. That left Cameron, who was hot-headed and apt to piss off Preston more than help him, Jessica, who was just a kid, or Christopher, who was Preston's youngest brother, but also the most sensitive of the bunch.

He fished his phone out of his pocket and dialed Christopher's number.

"Pres?"

"Yeah."

"Hey, man . . . what's going on? It's, uh, after eleven."

"On a Saturday. Don't tell me you were sleeping."

"Nope. Definitely not sleeping."

Preston winced. *Shit.* "Forget it. I'll call you tomorrow."

"No, no, no. Hold on." Chris asked someone to "give him a few minutes," and though Preston couldn't make out her muffled reply, he could tell she wasn't happy. A few seconds later, Chris was back on the line. "Okay, well, that's that. Tell me what's going on with you?"

"You've got company."

"*Had* company."

Chris lived in DC, an intern for the junior senator from Pennsylvania, and from the stories Chris told, the female pool of Capitol Hill staffers was not immune to his boyish good looks.

"Oh, crap. I'm sorry, Chris."

"I'm not. She was cute, but *really* conservative. It was going to be a long night of rhetoric. Now I have plenty of time to catch up with my brother."

"She *left*?" Preston shook his head. He'd totally just cock-blocked his little brother from getting into some Republican panties. "Go after her. I'll call you tomorrow."

"Forget it. She's already gone. What's on your mind? How's your internship going?"

Preston worked twenty-five hours a week for one of the hottest sports lawyers in New York, an arrangement his father would have approved of. He was hoping to get a job at the same firm once he passed the bar.

"Good. But that's not why I'm calling."

"What's her name?" asked Chris after a short pause.

And *this* was why Preston had chosen to call Chris. Because he was as perceptive as a summer day was long.

"Elise."

"What does she do?"

"She's an actress."

Chris whistled low. "Damn, but you've always aimed high."

"An off-off-Broadway actress."

"Huh. Okay. Wasn't expecting that."

"Tell me about it. Nor was I."

"So, what's the deal?"

Preston told Chris all about going to the play with Beth last night, how he hadn't been able to stop thinking about Elise all day, how he'd finally gone back to the play and gotten an unexpected chance to meet her. His voice slowed down, mellowing a little as he recounted their walk to her apartment building. He told Chris how she'd grown up on a farm, how she came from a big family like theirs, how he'd blurted out his whole sad story about the Olympics, which he rarely shared. How she'd placed her hand on his arm and tried to comfort him. How she'd all but insisted they say good-bye.

He sighed as he approached his tony-doorman building on Sixty-First and Fifth that faced Central Park. From his one-bedroom apartment on the eighteenth floor, he had an incredible view of the Pond and the Zoo and was able to take a four-mile jog every morning simply by crossing the street.

But he wasn't quite ready to go home yet, so he crossed the street and sat down on one of the many benches positioned under the ancient stone wall that bordered the park. Resting his elbows on his knees, he leaned his head forward.

"I didn't want to say good-bye. I wanted to see her again."

"You barely know her, Pres. Maybe she's got a boyfriend. Maybe she's . . . I don't know, not interested in guys."

"Thanks."

"No. I'm just saying . . . aren't you a little attached for only meeting this girl a couple of hours ago?"

"I can't help it," he muttered, sitting back on the bench and looking at the couples passing by. Salt in the wound. "There was something about her. Something different. I really liked her."

"Okay . . ." sighed Chris. "Then, against my better judgment, I'm thinking that you probably shouldn't give up."

"Oh, that's really helpful, Chris. She said good-bye. She said the timing was terrible. She wasn't at all ambiguous."

"Yeah, I know. But tell me this . . . do you think she liked you?"

Preston thought about her sparkling, blue eyes when he gave her the flowers, the touch of her hand on his arm . . .

but ultimately, she'd let him go. Did she like him? The honest answer was that he wasn't sure. "I don't know."

"Oh, man!" exclaimed Chris. "That's it!"

"What's it?"

"You don't know if she likes you or not, and you can't stand it."

"That's *not* it. I really—"

"—liked her. Yeah. I know. But this has got to be the first time in your life a woman isn't throwing herself all over you. It's got to be . . . intriguing."

Intriguing. The exact word he'd used with Elise.

"It is," he confessed. "It's a little maddening."

"And she's hot."

Preston shrugged. "Not like a bikini model hot. She's classy, smart. And yeah, she's gorgeous, but she's sweet, too."

"Cute and beautiful," said Chris reverently. "A Winslow brother favorite."

Preston nodded. Damn, this sucked.

Chris took a deep breath, sighing long and hard. "Well, my brother, if she's worth it, I think you already know what you have to do."

Preston heard the take-no-prisoners lilt in his brother's voice, and he grinned. "All out?"

"All the stops. All out." He could see Christopher nodding sagely in his lonely DC apartment. "A hundred percent."

Elise couldn't help comparing Sunday afternoon's performance to yesterday evening's. And she had to confess: her heart hadn't been in it today. Not that it mattered since a good quarter of the sixty or so audience members had used the two-hour matinee to catch up on their senior-citizen beauty rest. But still . . . Elise had integrity, even when it came to *She Loves Me Not*, and today was far from her best performance.

She'd worked a half brunch-shift at Vic's from eight in the morning until twelve thirty, distracted and dreamy, going through the motions of work but forgetting drink orders and extra baskets of biscuits. Her mind wandered in an endless loop to her walk home with Preston Winslow last night.

After she'd gotten up to her apartment, she'd placed his pink roses in a plastic cup of water and carried them to the floor beside the sofa bed so she could drift away to their scent. Sleep had been elusive as she relived their conversation—the way he'd put her at ease, the story of his failed Olympic bid, and the determination it must have taken for him to pick up the shattered pieces of his life and pursue a different path. The whole evening had been like a misty-magic dream sequence: the lovely flowers, his charming smile and wistful eyes as they said good-bye. The longer she dwelled on Preston Winslow, the more she wondered if she'd made a dreadful mistake. Couldn't she have found a little space in her life for someone who seemed as wonderful as him?

"No," she said to her half-made-up, half-cleaned-up reflection. "No, you couldn't. You have until Tuesday afternoon to prepare for the biggest audition of your life. So, just stop it. No more Preston Winslow."

She tore another makeup wipe from the package, scrubbing her lips and eyes clean, then changing into a calf-length denim skirt leftover from her high school wardrobe that had been patched so many times, it wasn't even predominantly denim anymore. She slipped a modest, black T-shirt over her head, pulled the pins out of her hair, and twisted it into a bun. Plunging her hand into her backpack, she found her glasses and put them on, flicking off the dressing room lights and pulling the door closed behind her.

After a stop at the New York Public Library for a copy of the Acting Edition dramatization of *Ethan Frome* (she crossed her fingers it would still be in stock when she got there), she intended to spend the entire afternoon and evening sitting on her couch, reacquainting herself with the material, running lines, and finding a way to bring Mattie Silver to life.

And she was determined not to let thoughts of Preston Winslow break her concentration.

Which is why it was very, very inconvenient to find him waiting outside the stage door for her, holding a picnic basket, and wearing a hopeful smile that just about broke her heart.

"Hi," he said.

"Hi," she answered, her heart thundering with pleasure and relief to see him again so soon. The strength of her reaction made her breathless, made her knees weak, made her realize that—inconvenient or not—he was already under her skin much deeper than she'd suspected. "What are you doing here?"

He searched her eyes before speaking.

"It's good to see you."

And damn it, but she couldn't help responding in kind. "You too."

He cleared his throat.

"Elise, I know the timing is shit. I know that you've got an audition on Tuesday, and I should be at the library studying for the bar. And if you tell me to go away, I'll go and I'll never bother you again, I promise . . . but I can't stop thinking about you. I tried. It's useless. It's finally stopped raining for the first day in ages, and the sun's warm and the sky's clear. I have a very soft blanket and a bottle of wine and lots of food to keep you nourished. And I found this battered, old, first-edition copy of *Ethan Frome* at Baumann

Rare Books on Madison Ave, which is definitely not usually open on Sunday mornings, and I thought, or rather hoped, that you'd read it to me this afternoon and keep it for your trouble." He paused, his eyes searching her face desperately, before whispering passionately, "*Please don't say no.*"

"I don't drink," she said, her heart racing with excitement as she tried hard to reign in her runaway smile.

"I came prepared for that possibility," he said, reaching into the basket and pulling out a green glass bottle of sparkling water.

Her defenses fell, and she beamed at him, taking the red, fabric-covered first edition of *Ethan Frome* from his fingers with care. "How did you get a first edition book from a store that's closed on Sundays?"

"I tracked down the store owner at home and made him an offer he couldn't refuse."

"How industrious, Don Corleone. Did you break the law?"

Preston look affronted. "I'm a lawyer!"

"Ha!" she scoffed. "So was Tom Hagan. Lots of lawyers are crooks."

"Not this one," he said, grinning at her. "No Tom Hagan here. No laws broken. That book was purchased, paid for, and is all yours . . . on the condition that you'll read it to me."

"I can't possibly . . ." she started, teasing him with a long pause, ". . . say no."

"Phew!" He exhaled dramatically, letting his shoulders relax. "I had no more tricks up my sleeve. It was this or . . ."

"Or what?" she asked as he hailed them a cab.

He glanced back at her. "Or spend my Sunday getting nothing done while I daydreamed about you."

"What about your studies?" she asked, clasping the book to her chest like a treasure.

"They'll keep until tonight."

"You'll be up late," she worried.

"It'll be worth it," he said softly, putting his hand on the small of her back as he helped her into the back of the cab.

Two hours later, Preston lay with his head on the blanket beside her lap, the cover of *Ethan Frome* shielding his eyes from the late-day sun as Elise started reading chapter six aloud.

Her reading voice was warm and low, and she did a wonderful job bringing the characters to life. Preston had never read the novella before, and now he was rapt with attention, imagining himself Ethan, who longed so terribly for his sick wife's young cousin, Mattie, while trapped in a loveless marriage.

"*Ethan did not know why he was so irrationally happy, for nothing was changed in his life or hers. He had not even touched the tip of her fingers or looked her full in the eyes. But their evening together had given him a vision of what life at her side might be, and he was glad now that he had done nothing to trouble the sweetness of the picture*," read Elise, her musical voice softer and softer until it trailed off into silence.

A moment went by, then another and another until Preston rolled his head to the side, squinting to look up at her face, which was staring at the book, but not reading.

"Elise?"

"It's so sad, isn't it? For him to want her so terribly?"

"It's only sad if he can't have her," said Preston.

"Of course he can't," she said, laying the book on her lap with a sigh. "He's married to someone else. It's . . . impossible."

"I'm quite certain they had divorce in 1911."

"They lived in a tiny New England village. It just wasn't done."

"Then he didn't love her enough. Mattie, I mean."

Elise gasped. "How can you say that? You *know* he loves her."

"Well, I haven't read the rest of the book, but if I was Ethan and I loved Mattie like he says he does, I wouldn't let her go. I'd fight for her. I'd . . . well, I'd figure it out."

"Just like that," said Elise, her lips wobbling as she looked down at him.

"Hell, yes, just like that. What do *you* think?"

She stared down at his face, her eyes soft and gentle. "I don't think it's that easy."

"How do you mean?"

"Life throws curveballs. It's inconvenient and unpredictable . . . and loving with your whole heart might not be enough. Plus . . ." she paused, dropping his eyes, "it's risky."

"There's no other way to love." Preston flipped over onto his stomach, nudging her leg as he looked up at her. "Hey. Did someone hurt you? Were you—"

"Me?" asked Elise, shaking her head. "No."

"You sure?"

"Quite." She nodded. "I've never been in love."

This surprised him. No. *Shocked* him. She was so lovely, so innocent and honest, he couldn't imagine why some guy hadn't claimed her yet. But then he thought about her insistence on saying good-bye last night, the fear he had—at almost every moment with her—that she'd suddenly bolt and he'd never see her again. Perhaps she kept everyone at arm's length . . . which made this afternoon together all the more precious to him, because she was allowing him to get close to her.

"Then what? Why risky?"

"In every play or book I've ever read, the person who loves the most deeply ends up the most hurt."

"I don't think it's always like that."

"They wouldn't write about it if it wasn't *like that* a good portion of the time."

"So it scares you?" he asked, searching her face. "Love scares you. Being in love."

She nodded once, an almost imperceptible movement. "Very much."

He held her eyes so long that she blinked, looking away from him, and he panicked that she might jump up and run home, too discomfited by his attention to stay with him any longer.

"Okay," he said softly, knowing that he was about to lie to her, but having no better recourse. "Then I won't ever fall in love with you, so you'll never have to fear me."

She stared at him, unspeaking, and then suddenly her lips slid into that sweet grin that Preston liked so well. She giggled softly, her face brightening as she shook her head back and forth. "How do you keep doing that?"

"What?" he asked, thinking whatever it was, he'd keep doing it forever if it made her this happy.

"Saying the perfect thing. To make me say yes . . . or make me feel better . . . or make me feel . . ." She shook her head, reaching out to run her fingers through his hair, then cupping his cheek with her palm.

He reached up, covering her hand with his. Gently sliding her hand down his cheek, he twisted his neck until his lips touched her palm, and he closed his eyes, savoring every second of contact before letting go of her hand, which she drew slowly away.

"It's late," she whispered.

"It's not so late," he countered.

"You have to study, and I need . . . I need to finish reading this and then read it again. And I should find a copy of the script and run some lines." Her face was stricken, and he watched her wince as she swallowed. "Preston, I can't . . . do this."

"This?"

"You," she clarified, "and me. The timing's—"

"—shit." He looked down at the blanket, pushing at a few crumbs before sitting up. "We could figure it out," he said, using the same words he'd used about Ethan and Mattie.

Elise shrugged, closing the book and pulling her backpack from the corner of the blanket. She shifted to her knees and pulled the pack onto her back. "I don't see how. Life's just too busy—for both of us—right now. We don't need this distraction."

"I like you," said Preston, reaching out to cup her cheeks with his warm, strong hands. "I like you more than I've liked anyone, in . . . in forever. I don't want to say good-bye to you."

"I like you, too," she whispered, unable to stop herself, mesmerized by the clarity of his bright-green eyes staring deeply into hers.

His gaze dropped briefly to her lips before claiming her eyes again, and she knew that it was her cue to get up and walk home, but she couldn't. He was about to kiss her, and she wanted him to.

Leaning forward, he dropped his lips to hers, and her eyes closed as her heart fluttered madly behind the prison of her ribs. He cupped her cheeks gently, pulling her closer as his lips caught hers. As though he knew that rubbing his coarse scruff across her skin would burn, he was careful with her, his lips strong, yet soft, insistently taking hers, loving them before giving them back and then taking them once again.

One of his hands slid into her hair, his fingers fanning out in the soft tresses as he cupped the back of her head. His other hand feathered slowly down her neck, tracing her shoulder and skating down her arm before winding around her waist to draw her up against his chest.

Lifting his mouth from hers, he tilted his head, then dropped his lips again, sealing them over hers as she tangled her arms around his neck, arching her body into his.

And he kissed her.

Oh God, he kissed her.

Elise had been kissing men on the stage since she was sixteen years old, and many times the touch of someone else's lips on hers had stirred a feeling within her, whether she actually liked her costar or not. But never—not with her meager list of ex-boyfriends, or with any man she'd ever kissed under the hot lights of the theater—had she experienced the sort of chemistry she now shared with Preston Winslow.

His tongue, hot and velvet, slid against the length of hers, and she moaned softly from the back of her throat, a hum of pleasure as his fingers curled into a fist on her lower back, pushing her body closer to his. His hair, soft as silk through her spreading fingers, teased her skin as his lips continued their gentle invasion.

And then, as quickly as it had begun, it was over. Preston rested his forehead against hers, his sigh hot and sweet against her lips as his chest pushed forcefully into hers with every deep breath he took.

Just another second, her heart whispered. *Keep your eyes closed and memorize this. This. Him. Now.*

"Elise," he murmured, and she heard the question in the sound of her name—the plea, the supplication, the permission to keep going, to take more.

For years, she lived her life for one reason: to be a successful stage actress. She'd sacrificed, suffered, and labored toward that goal single-minded, poor, and lonely, but always grounded in the belief that if she let nothing get in her way, she would eventually make her dreams come true.

Now? Here? With Preston Winslow's arm around her, his breath warming her skin, his fingers wound in her hair, the low sound of his voice like precious music to her ears, she began to understand the magnitude of the threat he posed to her ambition. She'd sensed it the first night she met him, as his eyes dove into her very soul, that Preston Winslow unchecked in her life could become an addiction. And here she was, limp and languid against him, her heart begging for one more perfect moment before the brutal ache that would start when she walked away from him yet again.

Before she lost every shred of strength she possessed, she pushed at his chest, leaning away from him. He dropped his hand from her hair and unfurled the fingers that had been resting in a tight knot against her lower back.

"Elise?" he asked, his eyes searching hers.

"I have to go," she said, standing up quickly before she lost her will.

"No," he said, kneeling on the blanket, looking up her. "Come on. Stay for a few more minutes. I won't kiss you again."

"I can't," she said firmly. "And . . . I can't see you again."

Her eyes burned, and she blinked them to ward off tears. She'd done it a million times on stage—brought herself to the brink of tears, then held them back for effect. But that was only acting. This was one hundred times harder.

"Today was perfect." She swallowed the lump in her throat. "I'm sorry."

He sat back on his heels, looking down and nodding. "Well, I tried."

"You did," she said softly.

He didn't answer, just looked away from her, out over Sheep's Meadow toward the setting sun.

"I shouldn't keep this," she said, amazed that her voice didn't break as she held the book out to him.

He finally looked at her, and though it would have been easier if he was angry with her, he wasn't. Instead, he smiled, his beautiful lips tilting up just enough to soften his face and break her heart a little more.

"Yeah, you should. I got it for you. For luck."

She straightened, clasping the book tenderly against her chest. It was time to go; another moment and she would either burst into tears or fall back into his arms.

"Preston—"

"Good luck on Tuesday, Elise," he said, his voice still managing to be warm, though his eyes were profoundly sad. "You're going to be great."

"Thank you," she somehow managed, raising her hand in farewell.

He nodded once, then turned his face toward the sunset again.

And though she looked back at his solitary figure several times as she took steps—one after the other—farther and farther away from him, it hurt more than she ever could have guessed that he never once looked back to watch her go.

Chapter 5

Elise had been to many auditions in her twenty-four years.

In the small town of Lowville, New York, where she grew up, she'd auditioned for every church play and high school show, even driving her father's beaten pickup truck an hour each way to Utica every day one summer to be in a larger, more professional show.

At Tisch, she tried out for every part she was remotely qualified for, and since graduating from college, she went to every open audition she could find. She'd sat for hours at the Actor's Equity building in Manhattan, her number in hand, waiting to be called, only to be dismissed after a five-second look. More than anything else, she likened the New York stage audition process to a meat market, and if you weren't the cut they were looking for? You were out.

Today she finally understood there was a whole other world when it came to auditioning. Never having been to an agent submission audition like today's, she couldn't help but draw comparisons. At an open call audition, better known as a "cattle call" to those who, like Elise, were one of hundreds who showed up to audition, there was no guarantee you'd be seen, and the chance of getting a callback was about two percent. Here? At Lincoln Center? She arrived early and gave her name to a receptionist in a neat, quiet, air-conditioned office. She had a place to sit while she did her breathing exercises and ran Mattie's lines in her head, and when it was her turn to audition, she was escorted to a small practice stage where she personally met the director, casting director (not Mr. Durran but his associate), and several other people attached to the production.

"Elise Klassan," said the director, squinting at her from a long table in the second row of the small theater. He looked down at the table where she noticed her black-and-white headshot in front of him.

"Yes, sir," she said softly, offering his bent head a small smile, such that she imagined Mattie Silver would employ.

"Donny raved about this one," said Max Schofield, Mr. Durran's partner and a casting director just as respected as Mr. Durran.

"Well, we'll just have to see, won't we?" The director looked up again. "I'm Harold Fischer, the director. That's Mr. Schofield, our casting director. Heidi Lyons, our stage manager, Steve Smith, our assistant stage manager, and Frank Coletti, one of our three producers. Welcome. Thank you for coming."

"Thank you, sir," she answered, channeling Mattie Silver with every cell in her body.

She'd worn a long, white skirt—gauzy and prairie-style— not unlike the skirts she'd worn to church on Sundays at home. She'd found it at a street fair last summer on sale for five dollars, and she liked the familiar, traditional, feminine lines of it. On top, she wore a gray-cotton peasant blouse, ruched around the collar and short-sleeved. She hoped to convey a country-girl look; with limited resources, it was the best she could do.

"Let's get right into it, shall we? Steve, can you get up there and read for Ethan?" Mr. Fischer turned to Elise. "Garrett's in LA. He'll be here for rehearsals the last two weeks in May."

"Ah," said Elise, nodding in understanding, but feeling far out of her depth when Hollywood actors were referred to by their first names.

Steve, the assistant stage manager, hopped onto the stage and pulled a folded copy of the script from his back pocket.

"Assuming you know the lines?" asked Mr. Fischer, a slight challenge in his voice. "We only have a month to workshop this."

She'd only had two days to learn them, but damn if she didn't memorize them as fast as she could. Being off-book for this audition had been imperative for her.

"Yes, sir."

"Huh," he chuffed, obviously impressed. "Someone who actually came prepared. That's refreshing."

"Donny knows his stuff," commented Mr. Schofield.

"Indeed," replied Mr. Fischer, turning back to Elise. "I want the scene toward the end. Ethan is driving Mattie to the train at Zeena's request. They're both heartbroken, but they're also trapped. I want to feel your frustration, Miss Klassan. I want to feel Mattie's desperation. *Here.*" He thumped once on his chest, over his heart, for effect.

"I understand."

"Steve, we'll start with Ethan's line, 'Matt, what do you mean to do?' and go from there. Got it?"

Steve nodded at Mr. Fischer, then turned to Elise. He had kind, brown eyes and winked at her, offering her an encouraging smile before asking, "Ready?"

She took a deep breath. This was it—the biggest audition of her life. Was she ready?

"Yes."

Steve waggled his head from side to side, loosening up as he opened his script to a dog-eared page, and looked at Elise.

"Matt," he asked. "What do you mean to do?"

Elise swallowed, hearing the twang of a New England Mainer accent in her head and focusing on it before answering softly, infusing her voice with heartache, "I'll try to get a place in a store."

"You know you can't do it. The bad air and the standing all day nearly killed you before."

"I'm a lot stronger than I was before I came to Starkfield," she insisted.

"And now you're going to throw away all the good it's done you!" exclaimed Ethan.

Elise looked up at him, surprised that he no longer looked like Steve, the assistant stage manager, but like Preston Winslow, dressed in a homespun, band-collar shirt, his thick, black hair hidden under a wool-felt-brimmed farmer's hat. Her heart leapt, making her pulse race as she dropped his eyes.

"Isn't there any of your father's folks could help you?" asked Ethan.

She shrugged. "There isn't any of 'em I'd ask."

"You know there's nothing I wouldn't do for you if I could."

Her heart caught, and her voice broke just a little. "I know there isn't."

"But I can't. Oh, Matt," he broke out, his green eyes desperate as he reached for her, then pulled away, just short of touching her, "if I could ha' gone with you now I'd ha' done it—"

"Ethan," she said, pulling a paper from the warm skin between her breasts and unfolding it slowly, her eyes beseeching his. "I found this."

Ethan knew what it was: a letter he'd started writing to his wife, to tell her that he was leaving with Mattie. And Mattie knew why he'd never sent it—because Ethan was too good and too honorable to leave his invalid wife behind.

"Matt," he cried, "if I could ha' done it, would you?"

"Oh Ethan, Ethan," she sobbed, pressing her palm to her forehead. "What's the use?"

"Tell me, Matt! Tell me!"

She gulped, her hands balled into fists at her sides.

"I used to think of it sometimes, summer nights, when the moon was so bright I couldn't sleep."

"As long ago as that?" asked Ethan, his face hopeful, his green eyes thick and glassy with longing.

"The first time was at Shadow Pond."

"Was that why you gave me my coffee before the others?"

She giggled softly, recognizing the sad, foreign sound as her own sorry voice. "I don't know. Did I? I was dreadfully put out when you wouldn't go to the picnic with me; and then, when I saw you coming down the road, I thought maybe you'd gone home that way o' purpose; and that made me glad."

He reached for her hand, clutching it in the warm strength of his. Her hand molded perfectly to his just like she knew it would—like they were made for each other.

"I'm tied hand and foot, Matt. There isn't a thing I can do."

She pulled her hand away, because his touch didn't belong to her, and it burned her skin. "You must write to me sometimes, Ethan."

"Oh, what good'll writing do? I want to put my hand out and touch you. I want to do for you and care for you. I want to be there when you're sick and when you're lonesome."

Her heart clutched, but she mustered her strength to reassure him. "You mustn't think but what I'll do all right."

"You won't need me, you mean? I suppose you'll marry!"

She gasped, the terribleness of another man but Ethan ever touching her almost making her sick. She belonged to *him*. She was *his*. "Oh, Ethan!"

"I don't know how it is you make me feel, Matt. I'd a'most rather have you dead than that!"

Face to face with losing the sweetness of him in her cold, bleak life, she wondered if death would be better than any life that didn't include Ethan. With sudden clarity, she knew it was true.

"Oh, I wish I was, I wish I was!" she sobbed, watching his face turn away to look out over a meadow, toward the dying light of the setting sun.

"Don't let's talk that way," he finally whispered, reaching for her arm.

Her voice was low and destroyed, a sob and moan and keening desperation rolled into broken words. "Why shouldn't we, when it's true? I've been wishing it every minute of the day."

"Matt! You be quiet! Don't you say it."

"There's never anybody been good to me but you," she murmured, feeling lost, feeling bereft.

"Don't say that either, when I can't lift a hand for you!"

She looked up into his bright-green eyes, longing to run her fingers through his black, silky hair all over again.

"Yes," she sobbed in a whisper, her decimated heart breaking into a million pieces behind the prison of her ribs. "But it's true just the same."

"And, cut!"

Elise started, blinking madly at Ethan—no, Preston—no . . . it was Steve, the assistant stage manager, who stared back at her, his mouth parted open, his eyes wide.

"Wow," he murmured, nodding with respect and admiration in his kind, brown eyes.

Elise took a deep breath and swallowed, feeling Mattie Silver let go of her and start to fade away, back into the vapor of hot lights, seeping into musty, velvet stage curtains until Elise needed to call her back again. She turned to look at Mr. Fischer and the other production folks, still seated at the long table, staring at the stage in silence.

Mr. Fischer's eyes were wide and thoughtful, before raising his elbows to the table and breaking into slow and deliberate applause.

Most evenings, Preston liked the New York Public Library.

No, he more than liked it. He *loved* it.

There was an austerity to the exterior of the building—a
European-style grandness that he respected, and inside, it
was both beautiful and functional. He loved the white marble lions that guarded the front doors, the sturdy wooden
tables and chairs with brass reading lights, and murals of
the sky on the ceiling of the Main Rose Reading Room.
He loved the smell of books, the hushed shuffling of feet
on burgundy-tiled floors, and the whisper of pages being
turned. His favorite place to study was the Map Division, a
smaller room on the first floor that housed several globes
and stacks of maps on the perimeter of a gilt-ceilinged room
with arched windows and plenty of light. Once upon a time,
it had been his father's favorite place to study too, and Preston often imagined him here—imagined that he was sitting
in the same chair his father had used, studying at the same
table, looking out at the same view.

He usually found peace here.

But not yesterday. And not today.

He sighed, looking out the window before him, distracted
from his studies. The sun was starting to set. It would be
dark soon. And he'd barely gotten anything done.

All day, he'd wondered about Elise, hoping that she'd
nailed her audition with the same deep well of sensitivity
and authentic emotion that he'd witnessed in her portrayal
of Matilda. After she'd left him on Sunday, he'd packed
up the picnic basket and blanket with a heavy heart, gone

home, and purchased the e-book of *Ethan Frome* for his Kindle, only to go to bed beyond depressed because it was, quite possibly, the saddest, most hopeless story he'd ever read. Everyone ended up suffering, unfulfilled and unhappy, and his heavy heart felt heavier still.

Picking up his cell phone from the table, he briefly considered calling Beth and asking if she wanted to grab a drink. He'd smile and say he was sorry, and she'd accept his apology and invite him over. They'd have decent, but predictable, sex, and then he'd head home, but something inside of him knew that fucking Beth wouldn't exorcize Elise. He just wished he knew what would.

He'd thought—more times than he cared to admit—about showing up at her apartment or the theater, but after she'd rejected him not once, but twice, stalking her was too high on the Creepy Meter for Preston to consider. He needed to respect her wishes, no matter how much it hurt or frustrated him.

He placed his phone back down on the table and conceded defeat. Tonight would just be another wasted evening of no studying as he stared out the window, trying to figure out another angle toward winning more time with Elise Klassan . . . but he'd be damned if it wasn't the last. He packed up his books and slung his leather bag over his shoulder. He'd walk home, change into sweats, and head to the park for a long, hard sunset jog. And hopefully, once he'd sweated for an hour or so, he'd be in a better place to knuckle down and get some work done.

He left the Map Division and headed down the white marble stairs toward the exit, pausing to admire the brass chandelier above his head. Maybe he'd pick up some sushi, too. There was a decent place around the corner from his apartment. And after tonight, he'd put the Kibosh on further thoughts of the elusive Ms. Klassan. Three days was long enough to mourn a beautiful, interesting woman and one soul-bending kiss, wasn't it?

Hell, yes, he answered himself resolutely.

Pushing open the glass doors, he took a deep breath of fresh air and stepped down the first set of marble stairs, under the high marble arches, making his way to the second set of stairs, which he stepped down quickly.

"Preston!"

He stopped in his tracks, his head whipping around, his eyes searching for her on the crowded steps. And then he saw her about ten feet away, sitting in a white skirt and gray shirt, her backpack beside her, her face golden from the light of the setting sun. And for a moment—for just a split second—he wondered if the sheer force of his longing was tricking him into believing that she was here. He squinted, taking a step toward her, finally blocking the sun as he stared down at her, and she lowered her hand from over her eyes, locking her gaze with his.

"Hi," she said.

"Hi," he answered, his heart hammering with happiness and relief as she smoothed her skirt and started to stand.

"No," he said. "Don't get up. I'll sit."

She settled back onto the marble step, and he dropped his leather bag between them as a little wall, lest she worry he'd try to kiss her again. He didn't want her to leave. Feeling almost as if these were borrowed moments, precious and rare, he didn't want to do anything that might cut them short.

"So?" he asked, turning his face to hers once he was seated. "How'd it go?"

She smiled, then started laughing, and she looked so beautiful, his heart pounded and fluttered, making him breathless. She'd gotten the part, just like he'd known she would.

"You did it!" he exclaimed, beaming at her.

She nodded, looking up at him. "I did it."

"They offered it to you on the spot?"

"Mm-hm," she said, her grin splitting her face. She pushed her hair over her shoulder, and Preston's fingers twitched, longing to feel the softness of it against his skin once again. "They said I was perfect. I guess I was the last audition of the day, so they could compare me to the rest of the actresses, and . . ."

"And you were the best."

"The best for the part." She shrugged. "I guess."

"You guess," he muttered, shaking his head at her modesty. "You got it, didn't you?"

"I did. I'll be Mattie Silver in *Ethan Frome* at Lincoln Center from June first to July thirtieth."

"I'm happy for you, Elise," he said, and he was, truly, but he was also confused by her sudden appearance. Twice now she'd told him to back off, and both times he'd lost concentration, lost focus, lost part of his sanity thinking about her. He didn't know how many more times he could do this: put himself out there only to watch her walk away.

He glanced at her. "Can I ask you a question?"

"Sure," she said softly, looking straight ahead.

"I'm just . . . you were pretty clear with me on Sunday night that—"

"I know. I insisted we say good-bye." Her smile faded, and she bent her head, scratching the back of her neck and peeking at him through long, brown lashes. She sighed, and he noticed the slight tremor of her breath as she exhaled. "The truth?"

"Yeah. Please."

"While I was auditioning, I couldn't . . . I mean, I couldn't stop thinking about you. I've never had a muse, but . . . it was almost like you were there with me, Ethan to my Mattie."

"Saddest story I ever read," he said softly, wishing he could ease the fierce hammering of his heart as he processed her words.

"You finished it?"

"I had to find out what happened." He paused, massaging his jaw with his thumb and forefinger. "Almost wish I hadn't, though."

"Because it was sad?"

"Because it made me miss you."

She raised her eyes to his, and the nakedness he saw there, the truth born of struggle, took his breath away. He held her eyes, noticing her tongue dart out to lick her lips only peripherally, but his body tightened in response to the slight action.

"When I got the part," she murmured, her blue eyes focused on his, "the only person I could think of . . . I just . . . the only person I wanted to tell . . . was you."

His breath caught, and he looked away from her to hide how much her words meant to him. He rested his hand on the top of his bag, his heart soaring when she took it, lacing her fingers through his.

"So I came here and made a deal with myself," she continued. "I'd sit here and wait until closing, and if you walked down the steps, it meant . . ."

"What?"

"I don't know. Maybe that I'm supposed to give this a chance."

"This," he whispered, holding his breath.

"You and me."

His heart thundered with excitement, but common sense intervened, refusing to let him throw caution entirely to the wind. "But the timing's still shit."

"Yep," she agreed. "I'm about to be in my first real show, and you're taking the bar in a few weeks."

Unwilling to drop her hand, he reached over his body with his free hand, pushing his bag down to the next step and sliding closer to her, because he couldn't bear having her so far away anymore.

"Then again, I can't stop thinking about you," he pointed out, "and you can't stop thinking about me."

She nodded, then scoffed softly and shook her head, giving up her internal struggle and letting her head fall wearily to his shoulder. Preston decided that the soft weight of her burdens resting gently on his destroyed shoulder was a pleasure, and he had a quick thought that that small, broken part of his body belonged to her now. She would always be welcome there—always, no matter what, for the rest of his life.

"Maybe we can . . ."

". . . figure it out," finished Preston, dropping her hand so her could put his arm around her shoulders and pull her closer.

"Yeah," she said, sighing like she was done fighting something that had proven it wasn't going away.

He took a deep breath, his chest swelling with emotion—with relief, with hope, with attraction and affection, and the first real stirrings of love he'd ever known.

"Okay." He rested his lips on the crown of her head, feeling a profound sense of gratitude for third chances at new beginnings. He grinned against her hair. "So, does this mean I can take you out to dinner tonight?"

"I'd love that."

With enough words exchanged to know where they stood, they sat in silence as the sky changed from yellow to gold to violet to blue.

Chapter 6

Unsurprisingly, *He Loves Me Not* only lasted another week, which worked out perfectly, because as much as Elise despised playing Matilda, she would have felt bad leaving the play in the lurch to do *Ethan Frome*.

The first two weeks of May were a whirlwind. Elise quit her job at Vic's and found a waitress position at a small French bistro near Lincoln Center, so she'd be closer to the theater. Because they only had four weeks to workshop the show, her rehearsals were six days a week from nine in the morning until six in the evening, and Sundays from one in the afternoon until six in the evening. She worked with the understudies for Ethan and Zeena, as Garrett and Maggie wouldn't arrive until May twentieth when they'd have only ten days to rehearse before their first performance. On Mondays, Tuesdays, Wednesdays, and Thursdays after rehearsal, she worked from seven until midnight at Bistro Chèvrefeuille, which, she learned on her first day with some delight, meant "honeysuckle."

She didn't make as much in tips as she would if she worked on weekends, but she was making good money doing *Ethan Frome*, and besides, Friday and Saturday nights belonged to Preston. As long as she didn't *have* to work, she couldn't bear to give up the evenings they'd agreed to spend together.

Every Friday and Saturday evening at 6:15, he was waiting for her by the Lincoln Center fountain with some new plan for exploring Manhattan together: a horse and carriage ride through Central Park, a visit to the top of the Empire State Building, a drink at the rooftop bar at the Metropolitan Museum . . . which had prompted him to ask, as he handed her a cup of sparkling water, "Why don't you drink?"

"I was wondering when you'd ask me that," she said, following him to an empty bench where they had a knockout view of the New York skyline. "Does it bother you?"

"Nope." He looked down at his gin and tonic. "Does it bother you that I do?"

"Not at all," she said, grinning at him. She served alcohol regularly to the patrons at Bistro Chèvrefeuille, and as long as a drinker practiced moderation, which Preston seemed to, it didn't bother her at all.

She knew it was the right time to tell him about growing up in a Mennonite family, but before continuing, she paused. Would he think her old-fashioned? Unsophisticated? Naïve? She supposed she was all three on some levels, but she wouldn't want it to impact their blossoming relationship. Still, it was a part of who she was—an important part of her history and a latent part of her present. If he rejected her for it, she supposed it was better to know now than to fall for him any harder and find out it was a deal-breaker later.

"Elise," he said, interpreting her silence for reticence, "it's your personal business. I didn't mean to pry. Forget it."

"No, I want to tell you," she said, offering him a brave smile. "Actually, it's because . . . well, I was raised Mennonite."

"What?" His eyes searched her face with surprise.

"My family. The farm in upstate New York? They're Mennonite."

Coming from Pennsylvania, where there were so many Mennonites, she wondered if he had some knowledge of her religion. But then, he wasn't from Lancaster, he was from Philadelphia, so it didn't necessarily shock her when he asked, "Like, horse and buggies? And no electricity?"

She shook her head with a soft chuckle. "That's Amish."

"Oh, right! Sorry. Mennonite." He sucked his bottom lip into his mouth. "Is it terrible that I know nothing about your . . . um, culture? Religion?"

She shrugged. "Why would you? It isn't exactly mainstream."

"Tell me a little about it."

"Hmm." She sipped her seltzer, picturing her mother, father, sisters, brothers-in-law, and two nephews last Christmas. "Well, they live a simple life, and the church is the heart of the community. My family is modest, but not plain. The Amish are plain. My family is Conservative Mennonite. That means they don't wear the traditional Mennonite clothing. They dress in normal clothes, though my mother always insisted we took care not to be too flashy or revealing. Um, they *don't* drink alcohol. They *do* use modern technology in moderation. They're pacifists, of course. And . . ." Suddenly her cheeks felt terribly hot as she realized what she was about to say: . . . *they don't practice premarital sex.*

She caught herself just in time.

Sex hadn't come up in conversation yet; she'd never invited him up to her apartment after a date, no matter how steamy their good-night kisses, and though he'd invited her over several times, she'd always demurred, saying she had to be up early to study her lines or get to an early rehearsal. It's not that she didn't want more of him—she did. She longed to feel her skin pressed against his, his hands exploring her body, his lips touching down on her most shocking places, but she wasn't ready to move their relationship to the next level yet, and after waiting so long to share her body with someone, she wanted to be sure Preston was the *right* someone.

And yes, she worried for the day that she'd finally have to tell him that she was a virgin. What would he say? Would he be turned off by her inexperience? Her heart clenched as she imagined him rejecting her, walking away from her—

"And . . . ?"

"Oh, uh . . ." She shook her head quickly. "N-Nothing."

"What?" he asked, smiling at her, searching her eyes with his crystal-clear, beautiful green. "Let me guess . . . they don't date Lutherans?"

She grinned at him. "Not usually."

He dropped his lips to hers, and she could taste the alcohol on them, but it didn't bother her.

"You've never mentioned going to church. And the way you talk about your family . . . it sounds like you've placed some distance between your upbringing and your life here."

After seven years in New York with a trip home only at Christmas every year, she was a lapsed Mennonite, at best.

"Believe it or not, there *is* a Mennonite church in Manhattan, and I've gone a few times, but besides the fact that the services conflict with my work schedule . . . I don't know. It just doesn't feel like me anymore. Frankly, I don't have a problem with flashy clothes, though I don't have many. I don't even really have a problem with drinking, I just never started and figure there's no reason to start now."

"Would you *call* yourself a Mennonite?"

A hot-pink, neon sign that read "V-CARD" flashed obnoxiously in her brain.

"It'll always be a part of who I am. But no, I wouldn't call myself a practicing Mennonite anymore. I think I'd just call myself . . . someone who hopes she's a good person."

"You *are* a good person. You know that, don't you?"

She bit her lip, thinking about her mother's disappointed, disapproving face when Elise shared that she'd be attending theater school in New York City after high school graduation. It had hurt her deeply that her parents couldn't support such an important decision in her life. It wasn't like acting was immoral, and Elise was careful about the roles she accepted. No nudity, nothing really foul-mouthed or erotic. Still, it didn't matter. They would never leave Lowville to come and see her in a play. She had long since recognized that her parents would never accept her for who she was, and she'd had to make her peace with it.

"A good daughter would have stayed home on the farm," she said, careful to keep the bitterness from her voice, but unable to hold back the sorrow. "My parents and sisters don't really understand what I'm doing here."

"Well, I do. And I think it was incredibly brave of you to leave your home to follow your dream," he said firmly, pushing her hair behind her ear and putting his arm around her shoulders to draw her closer.

She leaned into him, amazed that for the first time in longer than Elise could remember, she didn't feel alone. It made a well of gratitude swell deep within her, and she was determined not to take his strength and warmth for granted. Not today. Not ever.

"From the time I was a little girl I knew the simple life wasn't for me. I wanted something so different from that life. I wanted so much more."

"And you made it happen," he said, "all on your own. I'm blown away by you, Elise Klassan."

Preston wasn't entirely surprised to learn that Elise had been raised Mennonite.

From the first moment he met her, he'd sensed an otherworldliness to her, an old-fashioned modesty, an uncommon reserve. It made sense on one hand. And yet, her chosen profession—acting on the stage—couldn't be more incongruous with his (possibly inaccurate) understanding of her childhood faith and culture. He thought he'd had a good understanding of the scope of her ambition, but now he realized it was far stronger and wider than he'd originally guessed. To leave her family's farm and come to New York was impressive enough for any young girl. To leave a—what had she called it?—*simple* life for an acting career in New York, totally unsupported by her family, would have taken staggering amounts of courage, drive, and ambition.

Preston knew something about drive and ambition; he'd started training for the Olympic team when he was in high school and hadn't let go of the dream until his torn cuff and two surgeries had finally closed the window on a gold medal. But he'd had the support of his mother and older brother, *and* his father's legacy to open doors for him. Not to mention, he had a trust fund at his disposal for every expense. He couldn't imagine how much strength and determination he'd have needed to go it alone.

Squeezing her closer and dropping his lips to her head, he realized again how spectacular and singular she was . . . and how hard he was falling for her, which made his body long for her in ways that were sharp and aching and constant.

Although their standing Friday- and Saturday-night dates had enabled him to regain focus on his studies and internship, he still thought about her endlessly. And after two weeks of dating, he had to admit: he was starting to feel just a little bit impatient for things to move along a little bit faster. He wasn't necessarily talking about sex. Even before tonight, he knew she wasn't the type of girl who was going to sleep with him immediately, but he felt drawn to her with a strong, ceaseless magnetism. He wanted to see her more than two evenings a week. He wanted her to spend time at his apartment, to feel comfortable there, to throw on his sweat shirt when she was chilly and put her girly things in his bathroom cabinet. He wanted constant evidence of her in his life—a script left open on his coffee table, her shoes on the mat just inside his front door, her favorite yogurt stocked in his refrigerator door.

But mostly—more than anything—he wanted her in his bed, in his arms, sleeping beside him . . . even if it didn't lead to sex for a while. He wanted to know the sounds she made while she slept. He wanted to bury his face in her hair as he drifted off to sleep and the smell of her shampoo seeped into his pillowcase. He wanted to feel her heartbeat under his arm as they spooned on a lazy Sunday morning. And he wanted for hers to be the first face he saw every morning when he started his day.

His emotions were getting all mixed up with the yearnings of his body.

In other words, he was falling in love with her, and physically, he wanted more.

But this new revelation about her background threw a figurative bucket of cold water on his literal lap as he let the information sink in. Likely she hadn't slept in many men's beds, if any. Though she kissed like a champion, he wondered how experienced she was at everything that came after kissing, which—oh God—led him to one very important question:

Was it possible that Elise was still a virgin?

His mind sluiced fluidly to something she'd said when she was reading to him from *Ethan Frome* two weeks ago: They'd been discussing the risks of falling in love, and she'd shared with him that she had never been in love before.

Synapses in his brain fired, and suddenly Preston knew the answer to his question beyond a shadow of doubt. He didn't have to wonder, and he didn't need to put her on the spot by asking her. He knew in his heart that she wasn't the sort of woman who would have sex without love, and since she'd never been in love, that meant . . . she was definitely still a virgin.

Silent for too long and anxious that she not feel uncomfortable for sharing her personal history with him, he took her hand and suggested they walk the perimeter of the roof garden to check out the 360° views of New York, and Elise seemed eager to join him.

Later, after walking her home and taking a cab back to his apartment, he turned his mind to her virgin status with conflicted feelings. Preston hadn't *been* with a virgin since he *was* a virgin, and he'd lost his virginity at sixteen. Not that he'd come close to being a manwhore—rowing had eaten a lot of his twenties, after all—but he'd certainly had his fair share of lovers since then. Would it bother her to know that? Would his experience lessen his value in her eyes or make her pull away from him?

He flinched, narrowing his eyes, suddenly regretting that he'd engaged in casual sex over the years and wishing his history was more defendable. Because he didn't want for her to pull away. In fact, despite the fact that they'd only been dating for a few weeks, he couldn't imagine losing her. Every moment he spent with Elise, his feelings for her grew—he admired her, he loved spending time with her, he was so damn attracted to her, every time he touched her or kissed her, his blood raged for more. His shower setting was permanently set to cold.

If he liked her less—if his heart hadn't already been touched by the sweetness of her smile, her playfulness and intense determination—he might actually think about moving on, because he refused to pressure her, and patience wasn't Preston Winslow's strong suit. But moving on never even crossed his mind. He would slow down. He would temper his expectations. He would follow her cues and be respectful of her virtue. And someday—oh God, please— maybe someday, if he was patient, he would deserve her . . . and all of Elise would belong to him.

"Pres," she murmured against his neck, her lips brushing against his hot skin, her nipples sensitive and beaded inside her bra, under her T-shirt, pushing against the hard wall of his chest.

Preston dragged his lips over her collarbone, and Elise stepped closer to him so she could feel the hard outline of his erection pressing against her pelvis. No, she couldn't do anything about it tonight, standing on the sidewalk before her apartment, but she wanted to know that he desired her—she needed to know that his body reacted to her touch.

Since their talk at the Met last night, she'd sensed a subtle difference in him. He still reached for her, and he'd kissed her passionately last night when he walked her home, but he hadn't invited her over to his place again this weekend, or jockeyed for an invitation to hers. And when he kissed her, he was more careful, like she was fragile or breakable. He was holding himself back, and she didn't like it. Wanton that she was, she longed for more.

Still holding her in his arms, he took a step away from her so that his erection wasn't pressing into her anymore, and she twitched her lips in disappointment. No, she wasn't ready for sex, but she was invested enough that she didn't want him to pull away from her either.

"Kiss me again before you go," he whispered, his voice deep and drunk.

She raised her head, nailing him with her eyes, and stepped into him again, deliberately, pushing against his sex and watching as his breath hitched and eyes darkened. Her chest rose and fell double time into his as she felt his hardness twitch against her lower belly under his khaki pants. Understanding that her actions were intentional, he exhaled on a low groan, crushing her lips with his, tightening his arms around her as she arched against him.

Leaning up on tiptoes, she wound her arms around his neck, and he drew her closer to him, plunging his tongue into her mouth where she welcomed it with hers. She moaned softly as a million butterflies beat their wings against the walls of her chest, and deep inside she felt a gathering, a liquid heat as her muscles contracted and released, preparing for more, priming themselves, letting her know that someday soon they'd be ready.

"Elise," he murmured, pressing his lips to her cheek, then sliding them to the soft skin under her ear, which he nipped and kissed, his teeth taking the lobe of her ear gently as his hands slipped under her shirt to flatten against the warm skin of her back. "What are you doing to me?"

She took a deep, ragged breath, closing her eyes as his lips rested on her throat, her fluttering pulse beating against his lips, telling him that everything he felt, she was feeling too. He backed her up two steps until the tree across from her brownstone was behind her, and his soft, black hair rested against her cheek. He traced a trail with his lips from her pulse to the base of her throat, kissing her softly as she let her head fall back and eyes open.

Through the branches of the tree overhead, she could see the lights on in her apartment, and her heart plummeted. Neve was home. She sighed, spreading her fingers in Preston's hair and feeling sorry for herself. If Elise had to say good-night to her delectable boyfriend, she'd rather go nurse her loneliness in dark peace and quiet. The last thing she wanted to do was make small talk with a roommate she never saw and barely knew.

"Good luck this week," he murmured close to her ear. "Knock 'em dead, okay?"

"I hope so," she said.

Tomorrow Elise would be meeting Garrett Hedlund and Maggie Gyllenhaal for the first time and running through the show with them, and yes, she was nervous, but she knew the show cold, and over the last twenty days she had become very comfortable at Lincoln Center and with the cast and crew.

"You have to kiss him tomorrow?" growled Preston softly.

Elise grinned against his shoulder. "Are you jealous?"

"Hell, yes. I don't want some damn movie star touching my woman."

My woman. Her heart sang at his words, at the possessive edge in his voice. She *wanted* to belong to him. She *wanted* to be his woman.

"You don't have to worry. There shouldn't be any kissing tomorrow," she said, turning her neck to smile against the skin of his throat, before pressing a tiny kiss against his pulse, delighting in his reflexive shiver. "It's just a table read and a blocking walk-through."

"Okay, then." He relaxed, leaning into her, resting his forehead on her shoulder. "I hate saying good-night."

"Me too," she said, cradling the back of his head and nuzzling his ear.

"You could . . ." he started, then stopped, sighing deeply. He raised his head and lowered his arms from her waist, then stepped back from her, looking frustrated, but determined.

There it was again—Preston pulling away from her. She didn't like it, but she didn't know what to do about it either.

Even though she'd "played" sexual tension on stage, she finally understood it on a level she hadn't before. It was when you were a magnet to another person, but you had to somehow keep yourselves from colliding.

"I could . . ." she prompted, almost wishing he'd ask her to come stay with him tonight. Would she go? How many more times could she bear to say no to him?

"Nothing," he said softly. "Nothing. Do great tomorrow, huh?" He leaned forward and kissed her cheek gently. "I'll see you Friday."

"Okay," she said, fighting herself not to loop her arms around his neck and pull him back against her body.

She saw it in his eyes, how much he hated to go, but he offered her a small smile before turning around and walking away from her.

"Pres," she called after him, the word bubbling up from a place of want, a place of need, a place of new and uncertain and unexplored affection.

He turned to look at her, though he didn't step closer.

"Someday soon . . . I will," she said softly, feeling her lips tilt up into a smile as he stared at her intently from under a streetlamp six feet away.

He licked his lips, a grin spreading across his face as he nodded. "I can't wait."

Neither can I, she thought as he winked at her, then turned and started back toward the corner at the end of her block where he could catch a cab.

She sighed, hopping up the brownstone steps and turning the downstairs lock. For the first time since she realized the lights were on, she wondered *why* Neve was home. Neve was never home between six thirty at night and three in the morning, unless it was Monday. Today was Saturday. On Saturdays she often didn't come home at all, opting to stay at her boyfriend's place downtown instead. She worked an eight-hour bartending shift six nights a week at a popular club, and during the day, she and her boyfriend practiced with their band.

Walking into the apartment, it felt different immediately and not just because Neve was home. In addition to Neve, her boyfriend, Frank, and their bassist, Chou, were in the living room, surrounded by brown boxes, Styrofoam packing eggs, and masking tape rolls.

"Oh," said Neve, looking up as the door slammed shut behind Elise. "You're here. Good. We need to talk."

"What's going on?" asked Elise.

"Chou got us a gig."

"That's great," said Elise, gesturing to the boxes and repeating, "but . . . what's going on?"

"We're relocating, Elise. *I'm* relocating. The gig is a three-month, sixty-stop tour, all in the Pacific Northwest. Seattle, Portland . . . far-the-fuck-away from Manhattan. Doesn't make sense for me to keep this place. I paid up my share until the end of May, and the landlord said you're more than welcome to take over the lease."

"Take over . . . you mean, the whole thing?"

Elise paid Neve $600 a month to sleep on her sofa bed and share the bathroom and kitchen. She knew for a fact that Neve paid $1,200 for her private bedroom, which meant that Elise would have to come up with $1,800 a month to stay. Even with the extra *Ethan Frome* money, $1,800 a month was a fortune, an impossible sum.

"I can't," she said, searching her roommate's eyes with desperation.

"Well," said Neve, having the decency to look uncomfortable, "I always said it was a month-to-month sublease. I was clear about that. I mean, I knew I needed to keep my options open. Plus, come on. You have ten days. It's not *that* bad. I'm sure you'll figure something out. We'll, uh, we'll move this stuff to my room so you can go to sleep."

"Neve . . ." she started.

"I'm sorry, Elise. It's a done deal. I'll be gone in the a.m. You can, um, you can have my room until you move out." Neve turned to the two men awkwardly watching the exchange and gestured to the boxes. "Grab this stuff. Let's finish up in my room."

Feeling dazed, Elise lowered herself to the sofa, staring at the empty bookcase across from her where Neve's books used to reside. She'd lived in this apartment for over a year, and it wasn't much, but it was her home. Neve had left a gaudy pillow bedazzled with the words "Staten Island" on the couch, and Elise grabbed it, hugging it to her chest.

How in the world was she supposed to find a new apartment and move her meager belongings into it when she had nonstop rehearsals from now until June? Between rehearsals, Bistro Chèvrefeuille, and weekend nights with Preston, something was going to have to give so she could devote some time to an apartment search and get herself moved . . . and her heart ached because it only took an instant for her to know which of the three she was going to have to sacrifice.

Chapter 7

Preston had to run the last four blocks to Lincoln Center because it was already six o'clock, and he didn't want to be late for Elise. It was Friday night. *Her* night. He didn't want to miss a minute of his time with her.

It had been an extra long six days this time, and twice Preston had considered "stopping by" Bistro Chèvrefeuille for dinner, just to see her, but they were taking things slowly, and stopping by her place of work uninvited didn't feel appropriate quite yet. He knew that she essentially worked from nine in the morning until midnight from Mondays to Thursdays; he couldn't ask for more from her. And yet, he missed her. After three weeks, Friday- and Saturday-night dates just didn't feel like enough.

Running up the steps toward the Metropolitan Opera House, he scanned the crowd around the fountain to be sure she wasn't waiting for him. He didn't see her, so he took his usual seat and caught his breath, reviewing the plan for tonight and hoping that she wouldn't feel uncomfortable. He'd hired a personal chef to make them dinner in his apartment, and of course he would walk her home after dinner if that's what she wanted, but last Saturday when she'd said, "Someday soon . . . I will," his heart had leapt at the idea of them spending an entire night together and not having to say good-bye. Ergo, dinner at his place to possibly pave the way, with a chef in attendance to act as chaperone, so that she wouldn't be completely alone with him . . . at least, not at first.

Checking his watch, he saw that it was just six and watched concertgoers bustle in and out of Avery Fischer Hall, which was hosting a jazz concert tonight. Some evenings, he actually heard music coming from one of the elegant buildings in the complex, but not tonight. He kept his eyes trained on the northeast corner of the Hall, knowing that Elise would walk around the corner any minute, coming from the Claire Tow Theater, and he tried to ease the thumping of his heart as their reunion grew closer.

Generally, he saw her first—saw her break through the crowd, beelining for the spot where he was waiting for her. The first weekend, they stood awkwardly in front of each other with huge smiles before he took her hand and guided her back down the steps. Last weekend, he'd opened his arms, and she'd hurtled her body into them both evenings, greeting him with a full-body hug and deep sigh of contentment. Tonight? He was hoping that she'd fall into his arms again, but that she'd tip her face up to his to start their evening with a kiss before he told her where they were going for dinner.

He was so distracted by his daydreaming, he missed her.

"Preston?"

He jerked his head up to find her staring down at him and felt his face explode into a smile as he jumped to his feet. But one look at her kept him from reaching for her. She had her arms crossed over her chest and stood back about a foot from him, her eyes searching his face with . . . with what? *What emotion was that?* he wondered, panic seeping lightly into his blood. She glanced down at her shoes, drawing her bottom lip into her mouth. Why wasn't she making eye contact with him? What was going on?

"Hey," he said, reaching out to touch her arm. She didn't lean away from him, but she didn't step forward either. "Are you okay?"

"Yeah," she said, though she clearly wasn't. "I just . . . I can't hang out tonight."

"Oh." He pulled his hand away and let it drop uselessly to his side. "Um, what's going on?"

"I just have things I need to do," she said softly, looking down again.

Hell, no.

Was she breaking things off? Was she dumping him? Had he done something wrong? He thought back to last weekend, but he couldn't think of anything. He'd picked her up on Saturday, they'd ridden the Circle Line boat around New York City, and he'd walked her home later, sharing twenty minutes of scorching kisses on her sidewalk before leaving her. What the hell had happened between then and now?

"Are they things I can do with you?" he asked tightly, determined to keep the pleading he felt out of his voice.

She looked up at him, and he locked his eyes with hers, refusing to let her look away. And for the first time he realized that her eyes were tired, with dark circles under them, and unless he was mistaken, they were worried, too.

"I don't think so," she said quickly, stepping away from him and dropping her gaze again.

Without a word, he reached forward and took her elbow, pulling her gently behind him, grateful when she matched his stride and followed him without pulling away. He walked purposefully between the opera house and Avery Fischer Hall, headed for the Millstein pool and terrace. Not stopping until he reached the low wall across from the pool, which was far quieter than the popular fountain up front, he sat down, with Elise standing in front of him with downcast eyes. He dropped her arm.

He tried to keep his voice gentle, but damn it, if she was running away from him again, this was the last fucking time, and he'd need to make that clear . . . right after he tried his best to convince her not to.

"What's going on?"

Her bottom lip quivered, and her mouth turned slowly into an almost-perfect inverted U. She dropped her chin, and he realized that she was holding her breath because her chest wasn't moving, but her body was trembling. *Oh my God*, she was trying not to cry.

He stood up immediately, pulling her into his arms, relieved beyond measure when she didn't fight him. She sobbed, then took a deep, strangled breath and proceeded to cry very softly, her body wracked with grief as she leaned wearily against him.

"Sweetheart," he whispered, sitting back down and pulling her onto his lap where he wrapped her arms around his neck, and then gathered her against his chest. She clasped her hands, leaning her cheek on his shoulder with her face turned toward his neck so he could feel her shudders and sobs against his throat.

"Please tell me what's going on," he said close to her ear, a note of desperation in his voice. Had something happened with the show? Or—God forbid—with her family? What would make his strong girl feel so overwhelmed? So terribly sad? His heart raged with its need to help her, to comfort her, to do whatever it would take for her to smile at him again. He waited, worried and upset, holding her tightly, until her sobs subsided and she took a deep, gasping breath.

"You're scaring me to death," he murmured. "Please let me help you."

"I'm—" she started.

"Sick?"

She shook her head.

"Your family?"

"They're fine," she gulped.

"The show?"

"No," she sobbed, sniffling pathetically. "The show's good. I mean, I'm tired, but it's not that."

"I give up," he said, stroking her back as she stayed nestled in his arms. "You're going to have to tell me, or I won't be able to help you."

"I'm . . . I'm h-homeless!"

She started crying again, and he leaned back from her, capturing her face between his palms and forcing her to look up at him.

"You're not dying?"

"N-No," she said.

"No one you love is dying?"

She shook her head and sniffled, looking red-nosed and miserable.

"You're completely exhausted?"

A tear streaked down her cheek as she closed her eyes and nodded.

"How long were your rehearsals this week?"

She opened her weary eyes, tilting her head to the side. "Th-they were inc-creased to fourteen hours. Six a.m. to eight p-p.m."

"Please tell me you went home right after and got some rest."

She shook her head, looking miserable. "I can't lose my job. I have l-loans."

"So you waitressed every night after rehearsal for what? Four hours? Six?"

"F-Four." She sniffled again, and more tears streaked down her face.

He did the math . . . that meant she was awake at five, at rehearsal by six, and at Bistro Chèvrefeuille until midnight.

No wonder she was so drained. That was a ridiculous schedule for anyone, even his determined, go-getter girlfriend.

"And now something's happened with your apartment?"

Her face crumpled, and she leaned her forehead back down on his shoulder like the effort of holding up her head was simply too much to bear. Her shoulders sagged and shuddered, and his shirt became wet with her tears. Preston silently thanked God that he'd spent enough time with his little sister Jessica to know that when a woman was totally overwrought and exhausted, she was also in desperate need of some good, old-fashioned TLC.

"You're coming home with me," he said softly, brushing her hair from her face as she nestled into his neck, finally catching her breath in jagged gasps. "I'm going to feed you, and tuck you into my bed, and then I am going to kiss you good-night and go sleep on the couch. And nothing— *nothing* is coming between you and sleep until five forty-five tomorrow morning, when I will wake you up and have a car waiting downstairs to take you directly to the theater, tricked out with a fresh croissant and a hot cup of tea waiting."

She leaned back, looking at him, her eyes red-rimmed and watery, but soft with wonder or admiration or some other awesome emotion that he'd never be able to get enough of because it made him feel mortal and godlike, invincible and vulnerable, like he would take on the world for her no matter what the cost. He never, ever wanted to look away.

"You don't have to—"

"Elise," he said, seizing her eyes with his. "I'm crazy about you. I *need* to. And I need you to let me."

He leaned forward and pressed his lips to hers, tasting the salt from her tears as he took her bottom lip and squeezed it gently between his before letting it go.

"What do you think?" he asked, his lips nuzzling hers with feather strokes as he spoke.

With her arms still looped around his neck and her tears drying, she leaned back and gave him a small smile, and he felt it deep in his core where secret, important things were stored forever—the certainty that there was nothing sweeter to his eyes or more necessary to his heart than the sight of Elise Klassan smiling at him.

"I think yes. I think thank you. I think . . ." She paused, and her small smile grew wider. "I think I'm crazy about you, too."

Then she leaned forward and kissed him.

An hour and a half later, Elise sat in luxury on Preston's brown leather couch, her belly full of perfectly grilled steaks, a baked potato loaded with sour cream, a fresh green salad, and vanilla-flavored seltzer water that she'd drunk from a wineglass.

Preston sat with one bare foot on the living room floor and the other stretched out along the back of the couch, and Elise sat between his legs, her back to his front, leaning against him with her legs stretched out next to his, and his arms around her middle. She closed her eyes and sighed. She hadn't felt so safe and comfortable in . . . well, in forever.

She'd left the theater heavyhearted, knowing that she needed to tell him in person that she wouldn't be available tonight or tomorrow night because she needed to search for a very cheap apartment or somehow find a new roommate to take over the lease at hers. But he was so beautiful, sitting there by the fountain, and she was so glad to see him, the thought of walking away from him had made her feel suddenly bereft. And she was so very tired, averaging three or four hours of sleep a night after being on her feet all day and walking home from Bistro Chèvrefeuille after midnight. For as much as she didn't feel alone when she was with Preston, she hadn't seen him since Saturday, and her worries about her apartment had become unbearably heavy. And suddenly there he was—jet-black hair, caring, green eyes, sweet, sexy smile—and it hurt to tell him she couldn't spend time with him. She loved *Ethan Frome* and didn't mind the hard work of waitressing, but Preston was becoming her peace, her acceptance, her sense of belonging, her happiness. Depriving herself of him, even for a night, felt unbearable.

And once the tears had started, she couldn't stop them. She was tired and worried, and he was so strong and seemed to care about her more every time she saw him. An ounce of sympathy is all it takes, sometimes, to make someone crumble, and crumble she had, weeping all over the shoulders and front of his fancy, blue, buttoned-down dress shirt. But Preston had borne it with sweetness and care, spiriting her home to his beautiful apartment, and not letting her lift a finger as a private chef made their dinner and they sat outside on his balcony relaxing. He made her tell him all about what had happened with Neve, and offered to set up an appointment for tomorrow evening with a realtor he knew. In an instant, she didn't feel alone and frightened anymore, and the tension eased from her body as she gratefully accepted his kindness.

And now here she was, cuddled up against him on the couch, her fingers entwined with his, some soft classical music playing from the stereo in his kitchen and French doors to the balcony letting the lullaby of city noises glide into his beautiful apartment on a late-spring breeze. Goose bumps popped out on her arm, and she snuggled back into him, resting her head on his shoulder, sighing deeply when she felt the soft touch of his lips on her neck.

"How're you feeling now?" he asked.

"Much better." She sighed. "So much better."

He squeezed her fingers, readjusting his so that they were perfectly braided together.

"I meant what I said before when you were so upset. I'm crazy about you, Elise."

"I meant it, too," she said, shifting in his arms just a little so that his lips touched down on hers. A brush. A caress. A soft and loving touch.

"I have an idea."

"About what?"

"You and me," he said, and she could hear the tentativeness in his voice. She wondered at it, but only for a moment because she realized that she trusted him.

"Tell me."

"Well," he said softly, pausing for a moment before continuing, "you could move in here."

"What?" She dropped his hands and turned in his arms, shifting to kneel between his legs and face him with wide eyes.

"Don't freak out," he said quickly, still lounging on the couch before her, though she perceived a stiffening of his posture like he'd jump up and run after her if she suddenly bolted. "Hear me out."

He was right. She *was* freaking out a little. She'd never lived with a man before. Heck, she'd never had a *boyfriend* as serious as Preston. Move in together? She knew it wasn't a shocking offer for the 2000s, but old sensibilities were hard to shake, and she couldn't help the way his suggestion made her nerves sit on edge. But under the nerves—and not too far under, either—was a sense of rightness, of excitement, of . . . maybe.

"I just . . ." He reached up and scrubbed the back of his neck with his hand, dropping her eyes for a second before leveling with her. "Listen, you have to be out by Tuesday, and you have rehearsals every single day between now and then. You would need to find a place tomorrow night, sign the lease, write checks, pack, and move. Tomorrow. I just don't—I don't see how you can do that. I mean, I get why you were so worried. Your life is too crazy to add a housing issue to the pile right now. You seriously *don't* have the time for this."

He was making a lot of sense, but she still felt an old sense of propriety holding on to her, so she was silent, waiting for him to say more that would somehow make it okay with her conscience for her to consider his offer.

Preston took a deep breath, reaching for his wineglass and taking a long sip as he looked at her over the rim. He placed the glass back down on the end table and rubbed his jaw with his thumb and forefinger.

"Elise. You don't have a place to live. But you have me. And I want to help you. I would love to have you stay here with me for a while."

"For a while?" she asked.

She saw something pass over his eyes, but he blinked it away and nodded at her. "A little while. A long while. As long as you need."

"Like, maybe just until *Frome* is up and running. Then I'll have time to find a place of my own."

"If that works for you, that's fine with me."

"So, it would just be temporary," she said. "A week or so. We're not *moving in* together."

He shook his head. "Nope. Just a temporary solution to a big problem."

"And you wouldn't mind?"

"Mind . . . ?"

"Having me on the couch?"

His eyes widened, and he started to speak, then stopped himself. A hint of an ironic smile graced his lips, but he straightened out his mouth and he sighed.

"No girlfriend of mine is sleeping on my couch. You'll take my bedroom. I'll take the guest room."

"I can't—"

"Yes, you can," he insisted. "It's just for a little while, remember?"

Her eyes flooded with tears from his goodness and kindness and the way he showed sensitivity for her outdated sensibilities. Her feelings for him were growing a million miles a minute, doubling and tripling and quadrupling, and he was becoming like air or water to her . . . something that— very soon, if not right now—would make her feel like dying were she deprived of it, of him, of his steady, patient, loving presence in her once-so-lonely life.

There were no words to express the depth of her gratitude, the breadth of her relief. She reached for his face, pressing her palms to his stubbly skin as she leaned forward to drop her lips to his. He reacted immediately, his arms encircling her waist, sitting up and moving forward as he lowered her onto the couch and settled his body on top of hers. He kissed her longingly, his tongue breaking the seal of her lips, slipping between her teeth, exploring the hot, wet recesses of her mouth. Sliding his against hers, they tangled together, hot silk gliding against each other as a whimper of "more" escaped from the back of her throat.

She arched her body upward, into the hard, hot muscle of his chest, feeling his erection, thick and long, through his pants, sliding against her thigh and pelvis as he thrust lightly against her, still kissing her breath away. His hands skated up the sides of her body, bracketing her breasts, which knew little of a man's touch, but her nipples beaded from the contact, pressing against his pecs and making her ache with desire.

The heels of his hands pressed into the sides of her breasts as their legs tangled together on the couch and his tongue continued stroking hers. She was liquid and desperate for more, moaning softly when he finally drew back, resting his elbows on either side of her chest and looking down at her with dark, wide eyes.

He was out of breath, and each time he inhaled it was jerky and deliberate, his eyes searching her face as he sucked his bottom lip between his teeth.

"You're a virgin," he said softly.

Heat flooded her cheeks, and she clenched her jaw in embarrassment and surprise, staring back at him.

"Sweetheart," he prompted. "We need to talk about it . . . just for a minute. We need to set some . . . some ground rules."

"Okay," she whispered, dropping his eyes. It was too humiliating, his body on top of hers, her breasts peaked and taut for something she'd never experienced before. "Yes, I'm a virgin."

"Then this needs to be said before you come stay with me: You set the pace. You, Elise. *All* you. You say 'stop,' I stop. You say 'slow down,' we slow down. I follow your lead. Clear?"

She looked up at him, nodding. "Clear."

His hardness pressed insistently against her thigh. She knew exactly how much he wanted her—it was obvious—but he was letting her be in charge, and it made something in her heart burst with happiness and joy with the sense that as long as Preston was beside her, she'd always be safe.

He was staring into her eyes, his lips tilted up into a small, sassy grin.

"So, Elise Klassan," he said wickedly, "tell me what you want."

"A little more," she murmured, closing her eyes as she laced her fingers around his neck and pulled his lips back down to hers.

Elise slept for ten hours on Friday night, and just as he'd promised, Preston slept in the guest room and arranged for a car to take her to Lincoln Center at five forty-five a.m. with instructions for hot tea and a croissant waiting in the back seat.

"Give me your keys," he said, nuzzling her neck as he said good-bye on the sidewalk in front of his apartment building, still barefooted, wearing pajama bottoms and a T-shirt.

"Why?" she asked, leaning back, but staring at his lips. He almost chuckled. He loved how much he affected her.

"Because I'm going to go get your stuff and bring it to my place today so you can come home and relax after rehearsal."

"Home?" she asked, grinning up at him, her blue eyes sparkling.

"Temporarily," he said quickly, smiling back.

He hated saying it, but he had the feeling that she wouldn't have been able to accept the arrangement if there was anything permanent about it. For her to feel okay about it, he needed to be helping her out of a temporary jam. But with any luck, she'd never leave. He crossed his fingers behind her back.

"Pres," she said, shaking her head, "that's just weird. You're going to go pack my underwear and stuff? No. Not happening. We'll do it together after rehearsal. Besides, you need to study today."

Hmmm. Her underwear. He hadn't given it a lot of thought, but this moving thing was going to be a lot more fun than he'd originally thought.

"I'll study tonight while you're sleeping, and I promise to close my eyes when I pack your underwear," he said, holding up three fingers like a boy scout. "Come on. You said that movers came for everything except the bed and couch and that the rental place where Neve got them is picking them up on Tuesday. That leaves . . . what?"

"My books and clothes. Toiletries. A few groceries."

She shrugged, and he knew she'd listed the extent of her belongings. It didn't sound like much, and that made him feel a little bad. She had so little that belonged to her.

"Doesn't sound like much in the way of heavy lifting," he said, winking at her so she'd relax. "Let me do it. Please."

Her shoulders slumped in defeat, and she rooted around in her bag for her keys, holding them out to him with a slightly worried look.

He grinned. "I'll close my eyes."

"Promise?"

"No."

Taking the keys from her before she could pull them away, he pressed a kiss to her nose, then helped her into the cab.

"I'll be at the fountain at six," he said.

"It's my favorite time of the day."

"Kiss me," he said, reaching for her soft cheeks and leaning down to capture her lips with his.

After she was moaning and breathless, he let her go, stepping back onto the curb and slamming the cab door. He waved as it pulled away from the sidewalk, his heart hammering with the strength of his growing feelings.

Last night when he'd asked her to move in, he didn't think there was much of a chance that she would say yes, but from the moment he understood the problem she was facing, it was the solution that had made the most sense, and although sleeping in the guest room while she was sleeping in his bed was torture on one hand, he'd also felt a profound peace last night knowing that she was so close. She was safe and sound, sleeping in his bed. She was allowing him to take care of her, and it moved him in ways he didn't expect. He felt protective of her and possessive of her, but he also really liked her, and having her in his space felt so right, he also just felt . . . good.

It had been hard stopping their make-out session last night, but after a while, it had started to become painful. He wanted her so badly, and she was so hot and needy beneath him, rising to meet his instinctive thrusts, moaning as he pillaged her mouth and molded the soft flesh of her breasts with his palms. At one point, he'd brushed his thumb over the stiff point of her nipple, and she'd gasped and whimpered into his mouth, bowing her back so he'd have better access to her. She was so innocent, but her body kept meeting his, cradling his, seeking his—she welcomed his tongue into her mouth, his touch through her T-shirt. He didn't want to push her, but what he knew (and she didn't) was that if—or when—they ever made love, their chemistry ensured it would be nothing short of combustible. Once that thought had entered his brain, he'd been unable to evict it, and he'd finally had to roll off of her, regretfully making his way into the guest bathroom where he took a miserable, long, cold shower.

When he came out, he'd peeked in his bedroom, only to find her snuggled under his covers, her cheek on his pillow, her tired eyes closed as her chest rose and fell with sleep. He'd brushed the hair away from her forehead, kissed her tenderly, and pulled the door closed. She needed to sleep, and he was grateful to provide her a place to catch up.

And today she'd be moving in with him. He told himself that asking her to move in with him was an opportunity for him to prove that his feelings for her weren't based on their sexual chemistry. Having her in his space wasn't just about getting in her pants (though he'd be a big, fat liar if he said he wasn't hopeful), but more importantly, about letting her know how desperately he was falling for her and solidifying his place in her heart.

Chapter 8

After four weeks of whirlwind rehearsals, opening night finally arrived, and Elise stretched languorously in Preston's bed. She didn't have to be up for hours, but she was too excited to go back to sleep.

Last night, the dress rehearsal had gone past midnight, and Preston, who waited up for her every night, was asleep in an easy chair with his Kindle on his chest when she finally got home.

She'd stared at him, at his tousled, dark hair, stubbled jaw, and pillowed lips. His coal-black eyelashes were impossibly long, resting on the tan skin just under his eyes, and his long legs, clad in old, comfortable jeans, were stretched out on the ottoman before him. Elise had knelt down beside him, looking at his face in repose, unable to stop the fierce surge of love that made her breath catch.

For a week she'd lived with him.

It had been—without any shadow of doubt—the happiest week of her life.

Last Saturday night he'd picked her up at the fountain and brought her "home," stopping at a Chinese place on his block to pick up dinner. He had cleared out two drawers for her and half his closet, moving a lot of his things to the guest room so that she wouldn't have to walk down the hall to get dressed in the morning. Her suitcase had been packed with care, and the rest of her things were neatly organized in three moving boxes at the foot of his bed. His thoughtfulness and care staggered her, and when they'd started making out on the couch after dinner, it had been even harder to stop than it had been the night before.

Preston had slipped his hands under her shirt, resting them on the skin of her back, and she'd known that he was asking permission to keep them there. In response, she'd kissed him harder, and his hands had skated up to her bra, his fingers resting on the clasp. When she'd slid her tongue deliberately against his, sinking her fingers into his hair, he'd unsnapped it, letting his hands glide softly around to her breasts. As he cupped her virgin flesh gently, lightly, her erect nipples had strained against his palms. She'd gasped when his fingers grasped the sensitive points, rolling them between his thumb and forefinger, making darts of sharp pleasure shoot unerringly to her sex, which clenched and tightened. She writhed, pushing against him, wanting more and beginning to understand for the first time in her life the profound pleasure that a man could give a woman.

But as she was whimpering and practically begging for more, her mother's face had flashed suddenly in her mind, and she'd frozen, pulling away from him. He'd held her eyes, drawing his hands away from her breasts, refastening her bra and smoothing her shirt back down, before kissing her lightly on the lips and putting his arm around her shoulders. They didn't talk about it. They didn't need to. She'd pulled away, and just as he'd promised her, he respected her wishes immediately and without exception.

Since then, they'd made out several more times—on Sunday afternoon and evening, and again on Tuesday when she'd gotten home from work and fallen into his arms on the couch—but he hadn't reached for her breasts again.

Although her body ached for his touch, Elise still struggled with the matter of propriety. She was living—however temporarily—with a man she wasn't engaged or married to. Even though they weren't having sex, she was sharing parts of her body with him, and she needed a little time to reconcile her inbred modesty with her growing desire.

She trusted Preston. She was definitely falling in love with Preston. But Preston wasn't her fiancé or husband, and the girl inside of Elise who'd been raised by strict Mennonite parents had trouble marrying her present decisions with her careful upbringing. She *wanted* to give herself to Preston, and every day her body yearned for his a little more . . . but she just wasn't ready yet.

That said, her feelings for him, the growing love she felt for him, multiplied daily as he showed her how much he cared for her in small and touching ways. She found her favorite seltzer flavors lined up like soldiers in the refrigerator, and an old sweat shirt she'd left on the couch folded carefully and left in the hallway outside her bedroom door. He taped sweet notes to the apartment door for her to find as she left for rehearsal every morning, and he picked her up at the fountain almost every evening after work to bring her home.

After a lifetime of feeling like a misfit, she finally felt like she belonged somewhere. Aside from giving her a place to stay, Preston was the first person in her life who'd accepted her for exactly who she was without reservation. He took the multiple dichotomies of who she was in stride, making her feel like less of an oddball and more confident in herself. After all, if a man such as Preston Winslow could see the quirky combination that was Elise Klassan and want her in his life, it made her feel like anything was possible.

The only other place she'd ever felt that level of acceptance was on the stage, in the synergy between the audience and performer. It was part of the reason she'd become so fixated on becoming an actress: because strangers with wondrous smiles looked up at her with respect, acceptance, and admiration. It didn't matter that she was a farm girl who'd been raised in a strict and obscure religion because she *became* Juliette or Ophelia or Roxanne or Mattie Silver. And through that brief transformation, she belonged. Now she felt that she belonged somewhere else, too: with Preston Winslow.

She glanced at the alarm clock on Preston's bedside table and sighed. Her call today wasn't until two o'clock, and the performance was at eight o'clock tonight. It was only six a.m., but she was so excited for Opening Night, she didn't know how to go back to sleep.

Getting out of bed, she padded over to the door in her pajamas then opened it to the smell of coffee wafting down the hallway. Making her way to the living room, she peeked around the corner to see Preston in the kitchen, his back to her, humming along to classical music as he—from the smell of it—fried himself some eggs. His back was broad in a white dress shirt, and his hair was still damp from the shower he'd probably taken after his run this morning. She suppressed a whimper. Her heart clenched. Her muscles bunched. Her fingers trembled by her sides, wanting to touch him, wishing that he didn't have to go to his internship and could just stay home with her all morning.

Leaning against the living room wall, she realized that she'd heard the same piece of classical music several times over the past week. It was lyric and lovely, if a little sad, but she'd never been much for classical music and didn't know the name of it.

Walking stealthily across the living room, she pulled out one of the stools arranged under the kitchen bar and sat down, fixing a bright smile on her face. When he plated his eggs and turned around, he jumped, then grinned at her, surprised to find her sitting there.

"Where'd you come from?"

"My boyfriend's bed."

His eyes dipped to the front of her T-shirt, and he pulled his bottom lip into his mouth before lifting his eyes to hers.

"Did I wake you up?" he asked, a little extra gravel in his voice.

"No. I'm too excited to sleep. What are you listening to?"

"Beethoven. It's called 'Für Elise.'"

"For Elise?" she asked, feeling delighted.

He nodded, grinning at her.

"You listen to it a lot."

"Mm-hm," he murmured, "I've always liked it, but it has new meaning for me lately."

"I think you're wonderful," she said, putting her elbows on the counter and leaning over it to kiss him good morning. His mouth tasted like mint and coffee, which shouldn't have been such an arousing, delicious combination, but Elise found that it was. She reached up to brush her fingers through the wet curls on the back of his neck, grinning up at him when she finally pulled away to eat his breakfast.

"I think you're amazing," he said, caressing her face with his dark eyes.

"You're sinfully handsome."

He raised an eyebrow. "You're scorchingly sexy."

"You're ridiculously sweet."

"You're . . ." Suddenly he looked down at his eggs, biting on his bottom lip again. When he looked up at her, he searched her eyes before saying, "I have a present for you. I was saving it for tonight, after the show, but . . . want it now?"

"A present?" She giggled softly in surprise. "You didn't have to do that!"

"I wanted to."

"Sure, I'd love it now," she said, and he rounded the counter, planting another kiss on her lips before heading to the back hall that led to his bedroom, the guest room, and his office.

When he returned, he held out a small, robin's-egg-blue box that she was positive read *Tiffany & Co.* in white lettering on top.

"Tiffany's?" she gasped.

He shrugged, placing the box on the counter in front of her. Fishing a fork from the silverware drawer, he stood across from her and speared a piece of egg before looking up at her.

"It's just a little thing. To say congratulations and . . ."

She untied the white ribbon carefully, then opened the box to reveal a sterling silver keychain decorated with a simple silver heart engraved with the date and the words: *Tonight it begins . . .* On the keychain were four keys.

She looked up at Preston, her voice breathy with emotion. "And?"

"Stay," he whispered, searching her eyes like they were a lifeline. "*Please* stay."

Touched beyond words, she looked back down at the bright-blue box as one plump tear splashed to the marble countertop. She reached for the key ring with shaking fingers and took it from the box.

"At least until the show's over," he said, resting his palms flat on the counter, his breakfast forgotten. "I like having you here. I don't want you to have to worry about finding a place. I don't want you to leave."

"What are they for?" she asked, her voice breaking a little as she held up the fresh-cut, shiny keys which jangled lightly as she held them.

"This building. This apartment. My car. And the apartment I own in Philly."

"In Philadelphia?"

He cleared his throat. "In case you were ever there and needed a place to stay."

She winced—a slight movement indicating the pain that comes from pleasure—and dropped his eyes, more tears joining the first. With one sweet and simple gesture, he was inviting her into his life officially and without reservation. She understood this, and it made her heart swell with love for him since belonging *to* him and *with* him was something she so desperately wanted.

"Why are you crying?" he asked, coming around the counter but stopping just short of reaching for her.

"Because you're so good to me," she choked out, clasping the keys in her hand.

All of her worries about propriety sailed out the window as she let herself be surrounded by his kindness and goodness, his thoughtfulness and understanding.

Two fingers landed under her chin, and he tilted her head up gently. His green eyes were fierce, but still somehow tender.

"I'm falling in love with you," he whispered, his eyebrows furrowing with uncertainty. "I know your career is important to you, and I respect that. So much. But if you stay here, I get to see you more, and now that I know what that feels like, I don't want to give it up. I-I just want you in my life. As much as possible. Please say you'll stay."

Overcome with emotion, she whimpered, slipping off the bar stool and flinging her arms around his neck. As she pressed her body against his, he wrapped his strong arms around her, holding her tightly. A moment later, his palms landed on her cheeks, and he tilted her head back so that his lips could fall flush onto hers.

She didn't say yes.

She showed him yes instead.

Preston felt like he was on top of the world. Although he still wasn't sleeping with her, or even sleeping *beside* her, his girlfriend was moving in with him at least for a little while, and knowing that she wouldn't surprise him with a sudden "I found a new place and I'm moving out" announcement lifted an enormous weight from his chest. He had made peace with moving slow, but if she moved out, it would change the pace of their relationship from slow to molasses, and he didn't know if he could stand that big a step backward. He didn't want to get in the way of her ambition, but he wanted them to keep growing—for their relationship to deepen and blossom—and they needed to spend time together for that to happen.

As Preston walked to work, his phone buzzed in his pocket, and he took it out, smiling instantly to see that his older brother, Brooks, was calling.

"Brooks!"

"Pres!"

"Hey, man! This is a surprise. What time is it there? Afternoon?"

"Nope," said Brooks. "It's about seven a.m."

"What?" Preston stopped walking for a second. "But it's seven *here* . . ."

"That's right. I'm in New York, little brother. Just for two days."

"Hey! That's great! Why didn't you tell me you were coming?"

"I didn't know until a couple of days ago," said Brooks. "PBS asked me to record a voice-over for a documentary about sailing, but they somehow managed to get a few other guys from the Olympic Team together and asked if they could interview us together in New York. So . . ."

"So you're here! You need a place to stay?"

He had to ask, even though the timing wasn't perfect. Aside from his short conversation with Christopher several weeks ago, he hadn't talked about Elise with any of his brothers. Until they were a solid thing, he didn't want to introduce her to them. Not because he was trying to hide her, but because if things didn't work out for some reason, he wouldn't want for his brothers to ask about her or have memories of her. It would be bad enough for Preston to have his own memories.

"Nope. They're putting me up at the Waldorf. But I do have time for dinner tonight."

Tonight. Opening Night.

"I can do dinner," he said, "but I have plans at eight. Can't get out of them."

"No problem," said Brooks. "Six-thirty? You choose the place and text me the details. I have to go through Customs now. See you later, okay?"

"Yeah," said Preston. "Looking forward to it!"

Eleven hours later, Preston looked up from his seat at Bistro Chèvrefeuille to see Brooks walk in. Per usual, every set of female eyes in the small café looked up to admire his ex-Olympian brother, but Brooks waved at Preston, all but oblivious to the attention.

"Hey!" said Brooks, enveloping Preston in a big bear hug and slapping him enthusiastically on the back. "You look good, bro!"

"Yeah? You too! Damn, you're tan!"

"The South African sun," said Brooks, taking the seat across from his brother and ordering a gin and tonic from the waiter. "So, what's up? How's the internship? You ready for the bar?"

As the oldest of the Winslow siblings, Brooks had taken on the role of head of family at a very early age, and all four of his younger siblings still looked to Brooks for support and advice in varying degrees. For Jessica and Chris, Brooks was almost a surrogate father. For Preston? His very best friend in the world.

"Internship is good. They haven't made me an offer yet, but I think I'm a lock for a full-time job if I pass the bar." He took a sip of his drink. "And yeah, I'll definitely be ready. I got a little distracted for a while there, but I've got plenty of time to be sure I nail it."

"Distracted?" asked Brooks, waggling his eyebrows in a way that was truly annoying. "What's her name?"

Preston sighed, bristling at his brother's lascivious tone. "It's not like that."

"Not like what? This chick doesn't have you wrapped around her"—he cleared his throat for effect—"little finger?"

"I mean it," said Preston, raising his eyes to Brooks and warning him with a narrow-eyed stare. "We're not talking about her like that."

Brooks sat back, his eyes wide with amazement. "You're not—Jesus, Pres, you're not *in love* with her, are you?"

Preston didn't answer, just stared back at his brother, daring him to say another word.

Brooks held his hands up in defeat. "Okay. I get it. She's different."

"She is. She's special."

"Clearly," said Brooks under his breath, finishing his drink. "So? What's her story? What does she do? Where's she from?"

These weren't easy questions because Elise Klassan was very different from the girls that the Winslow brothers generally dated. She wasn't a debutante, or a sailor, or a DC intern. She wasn't part of the upper crust of Main Line society, into which the Winslows were born, or model or a businesswoman in Philly. Preston wasn't lying when he said she was different, and he found it was hard to describe Elise in a nutshell.

He started with: "She's an actress."

"What?" blurted out Brooks. "An actress?"

Preston nodded. "Yep. She's in a show at Lincoln Center right now. I'm headed there after dinner."

"I didn't even know you were into the arts, Pres."

"Beth took me to see a show she was in a few weeks back . . . I-I don't know . . ." He shook his head. "There was something about her."

"Beth Atwell? I didn't realize you two were still a thing."

"We're not anymore. She noticed I was into Elise and told me to fuck off."

"Felicity, Hope, and Constance will be delighted to know that you slighted their cousin," said Brooks.

"Like I care," mumbled Preston, thinking about the annoying trio of sisters he and his brothers had grown up with in Haverford.

"So, you're dating this Elise."

"She's not 'this Elise,' first of all. She's Elise, and yeah, we're dating. In fact, she's kind of . . . living with me."

"She moved in? Already?" snapped Brooks, eyes wide and disapproving. "How long have you two been together?"

"Over a month," said Preston defensively.

Brooks sighed. "You've got it bad."

"You have no idea," said Preston, finishing his drink.

"Okay," said Brooks, like he was heading into a gauntlet. "When do I get to meet her?"

"You don't," said Preston. "Tonight's her opening night on Broadway, and she's got two shows tomorrow and another two on Sunday."

"Sounds like a busy schedule."

"It is," said Preston, suddenly wishing they could talk about something else. He heard the skepticism in Brooks' voice, and it bothered him. He wanted Brooks' approval, not his advice to move slow and be cautious.

"Does she have time for you?"

"She *lives* with me," said Preston, signaling the waiter for another drink.

"I bet her career is really important to her."

"It is. She gave up a lot to make it here."

"I guess we know how it feels to be that ambitious, huh?"

Preston nodded. Although only one of them had actually made it to the Olympics, yes, they'd both had the dream, the determination, and the drive.

"Not a whole lot we wouldn't have given up when we were in the thick of it," said Brooks carefully, looking at Preston with worried eyes.

Preston understood his brother's meaning precisely. It was at the heart of Preston's concerns for a possible future with Elise. When push came to shove, he had a feeling she'd always choose the stage first. And although he admired and respected her ambition, he wanted to know that eventually his place in her life would be a priority, too.

"It's not an issue yet."

Yet. The word sat thick and heavy between them as Brooks nodded once before picking up his menu.

"Brooks, can you just be happy for me?" asked Preston, feeling very much the little brother to his big brother, and wishing, as he had countless times before, that his father was still alive for conversations like this one.

Brooks, who'd come through for his siblings their entire lives, looked up from his menu and forced his lips into a neutral smile.

"Of course." He lifted his glass. "Good luck, brother. May she break a leg tonight, but never break your heart."

They clinked their glasses together and segued easily into a conversation about Christopher's recent conquests at the

Capitol and Jessica's upcoming graduation from college, but there was a vague melancholy that had taken up residence in Preston's heart, near the spot that belonged to Elise.

Not a whole lot we wouldn't have given up . . .

Turning his head to the business of their siblings, Preston said a quick and fleeting prayer that the day never came when the thing Elise needed to give up was him.

So this *is how it feels!*

On the cab ride home, Elise clutched Preston's hand, staring out the window and beaming as she recalled the first standing ovation she'd ever received. It had been an almost-unreal joy to hear the roar of applause when she, Garrett, and Maggie had taken their bows together, watching as the audience leapt to their feet before them.

Afterward, she'd attended a backstage reception, comforted by the light pressure of Preston's hand on the small of her back as various theater critics, fellow actors, and other theater big-wigs complimented Elise on her portrayal of Mattie Silver. Her heart had swelled with pride, and it had been all the sweeter for having Preston by her side and knowing that she didn't celebrate her success alone, that he was proud of her, too.

Wasn't he?

Of course he was.

But then, he'd been very quiet at the reception and now in the cab. As she started coming down from her high, she realized that he hadn't said very much since they'd left the theater. She turned to him.

"Hi," she said.

"Hi." He had been looking out the window, but now he turned to her, squeezing her hand and smiling. "You were brilliant."

His smile was genuine, but it didn't quite reach his eyes. "Are you sure?"

"I am. And so was everyone else in attendance, or did you miss that standing ovation?"

"Nope," she said, searching his face. Come to think of it, he hadn't kissed her since the play either. Was something wrong or was she searching for problems where none existed? "I noticed. It's burned on the happy side of my brain."

"It was well deserved," he said, squeezing her hand again before turning away to look out the window.

"Pres," she said, "is everything okay?"

He turned to her and nodded. "Absolutely."

"Are you sure?"

"Yes. You were epic, Elise. Really. You blew me—and everyone else—away."

He turned to look out his window again, and so she did the same. They were still holding hands. He was saying all of the right things. So why couldn't she shake the feeling that *something* was wrong?

The cab stopped at his apartment, and Preston dropped her hand to pay the cabbie, sliding out of the back seat and holding the door open for her. As the cab pulled away, he took her hand and pulled her toward the building, but she stayed rooted on the sidewalk until he turned around to look at her.

"Are you coming inside?"

"As soon as you tell me what's going on," she said softly, giving him the no-nonsense look her mother used to give her and her sisters when she was waiting for an explanation.

Preston stared at her for moment in surprise, opened his mouth like he was about to say something, thought better of it, then pursed his lips together.

She tilted her head to the side, still holding his hand but refusing to move or say anything else until he was straight with her. Preston didn't know this about her yet, but Elise was good at patience. She was very, very good at waiting and had every confidence that she'd eventually outlast him.

They stood on the sidewalk, staring at each other for a good two or three minutes before Preston finally dropped her eyes and bent his head forward, muttering softly, "I'm an idiot."

"I don't think so," said Elise, "but if you insist, maybe you could explain why."

"I'm a selfish prick."

"Hard to believe since you're one of the most selfless people I know, but again, I'll reserve judgment if you want to make your case."

"Can you just let it go? I'll get over it without infecting you."

"You may be underestimating me. Perhaps I have a natural immunity to whatever's ailing you." Her teasing grin dimmed, and she shook her head sadly. "No, I can't let it go, Preston. I could only let it go if you were less important to my heart."

"You mean that?" he whispered, taking a step closer to her.

"You doubt that you're important to my heart?"

"You kissed that guy three times tonight," he blurted out. "Three. The third time with tongue. And you looked like . . . damn it, it looked like you *enjoyed* it, Elise," he said, wincing as he looked down at the sidewalk.

"Oh." Elise took a deep breath and let it go slowly. "This is about jealousy."

He nodded, refusing to look at her.

"I see," she said, then, "Come on."

She tugged on his hand, walking into the building as the doorman swept the door open, but refused to look at him as they waited for the elevator. She kept her chin high and her eyes forward. He needed to sweat this out a little. He needed to remember what she was about to tell him, and he'd remember it better if his feelings were feverish by the time she started talking.

As the elevator rose slowly, Preston cleared his throat. "I said I was an idiot. I didn't want to tell you. I didn't want to ruin your Opening Night because it really was amazing, Elise. It was so great, and now I'm wrecking it with this stupid—"

She turned to him and placed her finger over her lips, telling him to shush, then turned her eyes forward again. When the doors opened, she pulled him out of the elevator, took her new keys out of her purse, and opened their apartment door. Placing her purse on the table in the front hallway, she didn't let go of his hand. She led him through the living room, then opened the French doors to the balcony, and he followed her outside.

"Preston," she said, "look at me."

He did, and the expression in his eyes made her breath catch: guilt, shame, anger, jealousy, frustration . . . they were all there staring back at her from deep, dark pools of green.

Letting go of his hand, she reached for his cheek, smoothing her palm over the black stubble.

"This morning you told me that you're falling in love with me."

"I am," he whispered, before closing his mouth and frowning at her as he tightened his jaw.

"I'm an actress. Occasionally I kiss people. Occasionally I kill them. It doesn't mean I actually love them or actually hate them when I do these things. It's pretend."

"I know. I just—"

She placed her finger over his lips and shook her head back and forth slowly to hush him.

"It's pretend," she said again, taking a step closer to him so that her breasts grazed the stark-white cotton of his tuxedo shirt. "Do you want to know how I'm so certain that it's only pretend?"

"Yes," he said, his breath audible as she leaned into him.

"Because the only way for me to kiss him like I love him is for me to imagine that he's you."

He flinched, the slightest movement of eyes narrowing before widening as he grasped the full intention of her meaning.

"What are you saying?" he rasped, holding his breath.

"That I'm falling in love with you, too," she said, flattening her hands on his chest as his arms came around her like bands of iron.

"Really?"

She nodded, grinning at him, trying to be brave. "I'm afraid so."

"Afraid?"

"I told you . . . that day in the meadow as I read *Ethan Frome*? Love scares me."

"And I promised you that I wouldn't fall in love with you. I'm sorry for breaking my promise. I couldn't help it. You should have been less awesome."

She laughed softly, staring up at him in the moonlight, at his dark eyes which focused on hers unceasingly.

"Are you still afraid?" he asked, taking a deep breath, which made his pectoral muscles swell against her palms and reminded her of how her nipples had felt between his fingers last weekend.

She glanced down at her hands on his chest before looking back up at him. "A little."

"Don't be," he said, his voice heartbreakingly earnest. "I won't hurt you. Not ever."

"I believe you," she said, tilting her head back as she wound her arms around his neck and pulling him down to kiss her.

Chapter 9

With a rush of breath, his lips were on hers, hard and demanding, taking what was his and offering what was hers in return. His hands slid up her back, cupping her head as he sucked her tongue into his mouth. As hers glided against his, he finally gentled, trusting the feeling of her in his arms, trusting her amazing words, trusting that even though she'd kissed a movie star tonight, she *belonged* to him.

He leaned back to look at her, at her sparkling, blue eyes, which were dark as they met his gaze.

"Take me to your bed," she whispered.

All of the air was sucked out of the room.

"My bed?"

"I'm not ready to . . ." she swallowed.

"I know," he said, his body tightening with the thought of them together in his bed, regardless of what they were doing there. "We'll go as slow as you want."

"I just want to be with you," she said, her fingers playing with the waves that curled on the back of his neck.

He nodded, taking her hand and leading her back through the apartment to his bedroom. Without turning on the lights, he dropped her hand to close the door, then turned to look at her. It only took a moment for his eyes to adjust to the low light of New York City, which filtered into his dark room, and he stood with his back against the door, waiting for her to tell him what she wanted. In the meantime, he admired the view.

She was wearing the simple, black cocktail dress she'd changed into after the play, and flattened her palms on her thighs nervously as she stepped out of her high heels and stood before him. He could make out the swell of her breasts, the sharp rise and fall of her chest in the moonlight.

Watching her, it occurred to him that it had probably taken a terrible amount of courage for her to invite him to join her here, to take this next step with him. Desperate to make things easier for her, he took two steps toward his bed, holding out his hand to her. After only a moment's hesitation, she stepped forward and took it, leaning into him, letting him enfold her in his arms.

"We won't do anything you don't want to do," he said softly near her ear, letting his lips graze the soft, hot skin with a feather touch. "You have my word."

He pushed her hair off of her shoulder and dropped his lips to the bare skin there, sliding one hand from her lower back to the top of her zipper, then pausing for a moment, waiting for a sign that she wanted him to undress her. She tilted her neck to the side to give him better access to her throat, and he dropped his lips to her pounding pulse as he pulled the zipper down, the soft hissing noise making his blood flood south where an eager part of him stiffened in anticipation.

They wouldn't be having sex tonight. Even if she offered it, he would gently—and dolefully—refuse, because he didn't want her to give away her virginity impulsively and regret it later. He wanted her to be sure, even if it meant depriving himself for a little longer.

Sliding his lips over the skin of her throat, he pushed the dress over her shoulders and down her arms, listening for the elusive whisper of fabric pooling around her feet. When he heard it, he raised his head to look at her, cutting his eyes to hers and holding them as he found her fingers by her sides and lifted them to the lapels of his suit jacket. Understanding what he wanted, she pushed the jacket from his shoulders, and it slipped down his arms to join her dress on the floor.

Answering the question in her eyes, he looked purposely down at his shirt, reaching for her hands again and placing her trembling fingers on the first button, which she unbuttoned carefully.

Step by step, he taught her how to undress a man, how to bare his body to hers. It was simultaneously terrifying and deeply arousing to take the lead with her tonight. Terrifying because it was so much responsibility to be someone's first everything, and arousing because he *was* the first. She'd never been with anyone but him, which was so hot he had to force himself to stop thinking about it or his body would have expectations that their relationship wasn't yet ready to meet.

As her finger trailed down the length of skin between the first and second buttons, he gasped softly, holding his breath, watching as her lips swept upward with a small, teasing grin. He'd been undressed by dozens of women in his life, more times than he could count. But Elise's inexperience made tonight feel different. Hyperaware that everything was new for her, he found his own senses were sharper and his skin more sensitive—almost like it was his first time too, by proxy.

Reaching up, she smoothed his shirt over his shoulders, her palms gliding over the muscles in his arm and sending goose bumps down his spine. His shirt caught on his wrists, and he reached to unbutton it, but Elise intercepted his hand, pressing her lips to his fingers before unbuttoning the cuff on one sleeve and then the other. His shirt whooshed softly to the floor, and unable to wait any longer, Preston let his eyes fall to her breasts.

Covered only with a black, satin bra, the demi-cups over-flowing with her flesh, which was white in the moonlight, his chest clenched with something profound—something like pain or wonder, or pure, undiluted gratitude. Sliding his eyes back up to hers, he reached around her back and unclasped her bra, but left it in place so she could decide if she was ready to let him see her.

Breathing audibly in soft, quick pants, she dropped her eyes to his chest and reached forward to press her hands to his pecs, which he flexed reflexively. As she touched him, her bra straps drooped down her arms, catching in the pocket of her bent elbows. The black, satin cups clung precariously to her breasts. Slowly, and with as much respect and gentleness as possible, Preston reached for the straps and smoothed them the rest of the way down her arms, watching as her breasts were revealed in the moonlight—perfect, white globes with dark-pink areoles and taut, puckered nipples.

She dropped her hands from his chest to her sides so that the lingerie fell soundlessly to the ground, then raised her eyes to his. Even in the dim light, he could see a mix of emotions in them—her bravery, her fears, her arousal, her need for reassurance.

"Sweetheart," he murmured, lifting his eyes as he cupped her face with his hands. With one step he was close enough to feel her nipples graze his bare chest, and his voice was raspy and low as he murmured, "You're so beautiful, Elise. So, so beautiful."

Her lips tilted up just a little at the corners, and a small, soft sound of pleasure escaped from the back of her throat as he leaned down to kiss her, pulling her flush against him, the warm, pliant flesh of her breasts flattened against his chest for the very first time as his tongue slipped into her mouth. With his hands on her hips, he backed up to the foot of his bed, lying back and pulling her down with him.

She covered his body with hers, their lips still intimately connected as their tongues tangled, her breasts against his chest, her flat tummy pressed again his tight abdominal muscles, and the softness of her sex cradling his erection from above. Without releasing her lips, he scooted them both back and rolled her onto her back, lying on his side next to her and kissing a path from her lips to her neck. Sliding his lips to the valley at the base of her throat, he rested them against her as he lifted his hand to caress the side of her breast, then paused, waiting to be sure that she welcomed his touch.

With a soft, impatient whimper, she slipped her hands into his hair, her fingers flexing as she bowed her back and raised her breasts to him. Gently grasping the soft, supple skin, he plumped her breast with his hand before lowering his mouth to one straining nipple. His tongue circled the puckered bud, and she gasped, the raw sound of pleasure making his eyes flutter closed as his lips sucked on her tender, rigid skin. Her fingernails razed his scalp as he shifted to her other breast, lapping at the stiff, pink flesh until she was writhing beneath him.

"Preston, I . . . I . . ." she moaned, panting between strangled sounds as he smoothed a hand over the warm, velvet skin of her belly, slipping under her black panties. He rested his palm over the soft thatch of curls, trying to steady his own breathing as he sucked her nipple back into his mouth and slid one digit between her soft, wet folds. She gasped, a sound of surprise and pleasure ending in a panted whimper as he circled her slick clit with his finger.

"Is this okay?" he whispered.

"Mm-hm," she murmured, arching her hips just a little.

Preston licked his lips, sealing his mouth back over her nipple, unable to contain his own groan of satisfaction as he latched onto her sweet-smelling skin. He licked and stroked her in perfect harmony, trailing his lips through the valley of her breasts and sucking her nipple between his lips as his finger glided across the hot, slippery bud of her clit, his tongue above matching the rhythm of his finger below, stroking and licking until Elise was arching her back off the bed.

"Pres, help me . . . I can't—" she cried, clutching at the sheets by her hips and twisting them in her fists.

Still rubbing her sensitive flesh with his finger, he raised his head to look at her face. Her head was thrown back into his pillow, her bottom lip caught between her teeth, and tears escaped from the corners of her eyes.

She was unbelievably beautiful, trusting, and responsive, and as much as he wanted her in every possible way, he reveled in this moment of bringing her to her first climax. Releasing her breast, he smoothed her hair from her forehead, leaned his head forward, and whispered close to her ear, "Sweetheart, just let go."

As if she'd been waiting for permission, her entire body tightened, crested, her hands reaching for his head and guiding his mouth to hers as a primal cry broke from the back of her throat. He swallowed the sound, stroking her tongue with his as she bucked against his hand. Her body trembled and shuddered beneath him, and he gentled their kiss, brushing her lips tenderly before finally releasing them. She panted beside him, her chest rising and falling with the force of her orgasm, the rest of her body limp and sated.

"Pres . . ." she moaned, the sound luxurious and deep, ending with a melodic sigh and soft, broken words she said over and over again. "I didn't know. I didn't know. I didn't know . . ."

Sliding his hand from her panties, Preston wrapped his arms around her, pulling her against his chest and dropping his lips to the back of her neck.

"Thank you for letting me be the first," he murmured, his heart swollen with love for her.

Her breathing was slowing down, but he felt her heart under his arm where he held her tight. It still fluttered wildly, and he felt the slight jerk of aftershocks as she settled in his arms, snuggling back against him.

"Preston," she whispered, sniffling softly. "That was so beautiful."

"*You* were so beautiful. I could watch you a million times."

"Stay with me tonight?" she asked him, placing her hands over his, just under her breasts. Just when he thought she was asleep, she whispered on a sigh, "Stay with me *every* night."

His eyes closed. Slowly. As they would at a long journey's end or when something he'd desperately hoped for against odds was finally his. For the foreseeable future, if not forever, he would hold her in his arms, his breath against her neck, the scent of their lovemaking surrounding them, and the strong beat of his heart binding her body to his.

Eight weeks later, *Ethan Frome* was a bona fide smash, but the play's two-month run was coming to a swift close. With only two shows left, Elise found she both mourned and celebrated its imminent end. Mourned because *Ethan Frome* had been her big break, and she would always cherish the memory of working with Mr. Fischer, Garrett, and Maggie, from whom she'd learned so much. But she celebrated its close because her future in the New York theater scene suddenly seemed so bright and promising—she couldn't wait to see what happened next.

She had signed with Mr. Durran's agency, and he assured her that when *Ethan Frome* folded next week, he'd have dozens of upcoming opportunities for her to choose from. In fact, just yesterday, he'd left a message that *Our Town* was going to be staged at the Barrymore in September and he'd already pitched her for the part of Emily Webb. Much like the part of Mattie Silver, Emily was a beloved American character that Elise had played before and knew very well. She'd whooped and hollered when she heard the message, committing to giving the best audition possible and excited beyond belief to have the possibility of another amazing role to look forward to.

Elise wasn't the only one with good news, either. Preston had come home last night to say that he'd been offered a conditional position at the law firm where he was interning, Mulligan & McKee. As long as he passed the New York bar when he got his results in November, the job was his, and until then, he'd be paid on the assumption that he'd already passed. Suddenly he wasn't a student and intern anymore—he was a junior associate at the hippest, most in-demand legal firm for athletes in New York City.

"I was sure they'd wait to offer me something in November!" he'd said, his eyes bright and alive with excitement.

"Nah!" she said. "They know talent when they see it, Pres!"

He'd kissed her, swinging her around the living room with glee. "We're on top of the world, sweetheart. I'm taking you out to dinner tonight!"

Grinning at him, she'd slipped out of his arms and sprinted to their bedroom to change from her lounging-around sweats into a dress.

She'd stopped working at Bistro Chèvrefeuille about two weeks ago. Preston refused to take a dime for rent, and without the additional expense, her salary from *Ethan Frome* could tidily cover her loan payments with some leftover.

Leaving her night job had the added benefit of allowing her more time with Preston. On Wednesdays, Fridays, and Saturdays, she wasn't home until after the show at eleven, but every other night belonged to him. Her heart belonged to him. Her body—almost all of her body—belonged to him, and every morning she woke up in his arms.

No, they hadn't had intercourse yet, but his fingers had reverently touched every plane and valley of her body, learning about her, discovering the newness of her, teaching her how a man loved a woman as he caressed the secret depths of her sex and brought her to unimaginable pleasure. And Elise was his grateful and willing student, tentatively learning about him too, remembering a touch that made him groan softly or clench his jaw with pleasure. A feather touch below his waist that would make him roll her to her back and kiss her ruthlessly like he'd never get enough of her. And when she flexed her hips, arching them into his, he would pant into her neck, whispering how much he wanted her, how much he cared for her, how wonderful and beautiful she was.

And yet, despite their growing passion, he had never pressured her or tried to guilt her into moving faster. Sex was something she'd always imagined she'd save for her husband, for her one and only, before the eyes of God. Lapsed Mennonite or not, it was the hardest line for her to cross, and she still felt a hint of panic when she contemplated it. Even though she'd started taking birth control—just to be careful—she wasn't quite ready yet to actually do the deed. And Preston, her patient angel, was gentle with her, careful, almost reverent with his touch, ever seeking her permission to move forward, never wanting to cross her unmarked boundaries without her consent.

She loved him for it. She loved him more every day. And though they hadn't actually exchanged the words yet, she was sure that he loved her, too. Never having been in love before, she understood the part of Mattie Silver better than she did the day she'd taken the role. She wasn't acting anymore. In her heart she knew the all-consuming, glorious burn of falling in love with someone for the first time. Off the stage, she was being swept away by love, and on it, she used her newfound passion to bring her character to a level of realism. In the words of one *New York Times* reviewer, ". . . rarely seen in the hallowed halls of Broadway."

When she looked at Ethan, she saw Preston. As she fell in love with Ethan, she was falling in love with Preston. While kissing Ethan, she was really kissing Preston. And when she said she'd rather die than live without Ethan, a part of her acknowledged that her feelings for Preston were surpassing everything else: her upbringing, her conscience . . . everything but her ambition, which kept a steely eye on the future but bent its neck in a whispered confession that losing him might break her.

The day of Elise's final performance as Mattie Silver dawned dark and gray, raining cats and dogs over the island of Manhattan. Compounding her melancholy over the end of *Ethan Frome* was the fact that Preston was headed to Philadelphia to take the Pennsylvania bar exam and wouldn't be back in New York in time to catch her final performance. Lying on her side, in the safe, warm cocoon of his arms, she stared balefully out the floor-to-ceiling bedroom window across from the bed, watching the raindrops slide down the glass in rivulets.

"I'm going to stay," Preston said, his lips moving softly on the back of her neck, his warm breath at once soothing and arousing. "I'm not going to miss your big night. I can take the exam next year."

"Absolutely not," she replied.

"Elise, I already took New York, and I'm sure I did well. I already have the job. It's done. I can take Pennsylvania next year if I still want to. But really, what's the point? We both work here in New York. There's no need for me to take the Pennsylvania exam now, and besides, it's your last—"

She flipped over, lying flat on her back and looking up at Preston who was propped on his elbow hovering over her.

"No," she said firmly, nailing him with her mother's no-nonsense glare. "Now stop."

He rolled his eyes, exasperated. "Why can't we talk about this?"

She reached up and palmed his cheek, forcing him to look down at her. "I'm not here to ruin your plans . . . or change them. You wanted to be able to practice in New York and Pennsylvania. That was your plan. That *is* your plan. You're taking the test."

He dropped his elbow and fell onto his back beside her, huffing softly. "It feels wrong not to be there for you tonight."

"Well, it's not wrong," she said, leaning up on her elbow now, distractedly tracing words in his chest. **Elise. Loves. Pres**. "I would never dream of standing in the way of your career."

He was silent for a long moment before looking up at her, a small, tender smile playing on his lips. "Me too."

"You too . . . what?"

"I love you, too."

Her finger stilled, and she flattened her palm over his heart, her eyes suddenly glistening as they locked with his. "I do. I love you."

"I know." He grinned at her, reaching up to brush her tears away. "You just wrote it on my chest."

"I would write it in the stars," she murmured, stroking a rogue black wave from his forehead, "so that every night when you looked at the sky, my love would shine back at you."

His jaw worked as he swallowed. "What's that from?"

"A play I did in college," she said, laughing softly as she wiped away another happy tear.

"Marry me," he whispered in the same low, passionate tone that had beseeched her *Please don't say no* at the stage door when he surprised her with a picnic, and *Please stay* when he gave her his keys.

His eyes, green and clear, held hers with the same tenderness that had become so familiar and yet still so precious to her. Their short courtship flashed before her eyes: Preston walking her home from the theater and buying her flowers, Preston waiting for her every evening at the fountain, Preston giving her a place to live, Preston teaching her heart— and her body—how to love.

In all the world, there would never be anyone who loved her as he did. She knew this. She knew it like she'd known, as a small child, that God had created the world and the heart in her chest and the mind in her head.

Staring back at him, at the face that she'd grown to love so quickly over the past couple of months, she heard herself whisper, "Yes."

His eyes flashed open with surprise. "Yes?"

"Yes," she said again, laughing at his shocked face as she leaned down to press her lips to his. He groaned with pleasure, rolling her onto her back and covering her body with his.

An impromptu marriage proposal! It was so passionate, it felt almost unreal—like a wonderfully dreamy scene from a beautiful movie.

"Tomorrow," he rasped, his eyes searching hers desperately, his breath quick and panting against her cheek. "When I come home. Just you and me. Let's just do it!"

Tomorrow?

Tomorrow felt so soon. And yet . . .

. . . they loved each other, right? And they lived together, for all intents and purposes. What was the point of waiting?

Swept away by the romance of the moment, she grinned up at him. "Tomorrow?"

"Just you and me," he repeated, leaning back to look into her eyes.

"But your family . . ." she started, real life intruding. He had family. She had family. Oh God, her family . . .

He read her face like a book. "I don't want my family there if yours won't be there, and I'm guessing that they wouldn't come if you married a Lutheran, right?"

Feeling bad and hoping the truth didn't hurt his feelings, she nodded.

He kissed her. "It doesn't bother me, sweetheart. We can tell our families later. Tomorrow will just be about us."

He was so good to her. She didn't know what she'd done in her life to deserve him, or what debt she would owe in accepting him, but how could she say no?

"Is it possible to get married that quickly?" she asked, the excitement of his proposal overtaking any real-life concerns.

"Sure. The Manhattan Marriage Bureau only requires twenty-four hours."

She beamed at him. "How do you know that?"

"I'm an entertainment lawyer! Do you know how many athletes and actors do quickie weddings?"

"A lot?"

"Tons," he said. "We'd do the paperwork this morning before I head to Philly . . . and we'll go back tomorrow afternoon to say . . . I do." He kissed her lips quickly, then rolled off of her, swinging his legs over the bed and striding purposefully to his closet. He rifled through a few suit jackets before turning back to her with a wobbly smile.

Circling back around the bed, he knelt down on the floor beside her. Snapping open a small, white box, he looked at the brilliant diamond ring for a moment, as though to ensure it was still there, before lifting his eyes to hers. She scrambled to sit up, covering her breasts with a sheet and gazing down at him with tears streaming down her face. When did he plan this? For how long? It was so romantic, tears sprang to her eyes.

"I love you, Elise Klassan." He stopped speaking for a moment and blinked, clenching his jaw once before continuing. "And I want to spend the rest of my life with someone as brave and talented and surprising and loving and . . . *amazing* as you."

She swiped at her tears, holding out her trembling hand so he could slip the giant diamond onto her fourth finger. He leaned forward as she reached for his face, her tears and laughter mixing as she kissed him. Rolling back onto the bed, he planted his elbows on either side of her shoulders and hovered over her, his face a study in happiness.

"You're going to marry me tomorrow," he said, brushing her hair from her forehead before kissing her tenderly. When he drew back, his smile was dazzling.

"Yes," she said, smiling back at him. "I am."

Chapter 10

It wasn't an especially romantic service, though Preston had picked up an enormous bouquet of white flowers on his way home, from which Elise plucked three blooms to hold. She wore a simple, white sundress from her closet, and Preston wore a suit and tie. They held hands as they walked up the steps of City Hall and sat side by side on a green leather couch, holding the license as they waited for their names to be called.

It wasn't how Elise had pictured her wedding day in her dreams—surrounded by strangers in a civic building—but Preston's proposal and her daring acceptance had packed enough romance to imbue the afternoon with a sense of genuine excitement. Not to mention, marrying Preston served another purpose for Elise; it severed her last ties to her past. Today she would marry a Lutheran and change her name to Winslow. With her first Broadway show closing to a fifteen-minute standing ovation last night and her wedding today, Elise's transformation from Mennonite farm girl to big-city actress was complete.

After an hour wait, they were ushered into a small, pink-walled room with a podium at the front. Standing across from one another, they said their vows, pledging to love, honor, cherish, and protect each other, forsaking all others and holding only unto themselves forevermore. They were familiar words, comfortable lines that Elise had said on stage many times, and she grinned at Preston, her comrade in this adventure, as he slipped the gorgeous engagement ring back over her finger.

That her fingers trembled didn't bother her, though it did—for a moment—blur the line between the daring romance of a whirlwind marriage and the very real life commitment she was making. And just for that moment, she felt a stab of something like unease, like uncertainty.

"Please continue holding hands," said the older gentleman officiating the service, "and look at one another."

Preston's eyes slid easily to hers, open wide and brimming with love and confidence. She offered him a small smile but noticed the quickening of her heart, the niggling doubt that made her stomach flurry.

"Preston and Elise, as the two of you come into this marriage uniting you as husband and wife, and as you this day affirm your faith and love for one another, I would ask that you always remember to cherish each other as special and unique individuals, that you respect the thoughts, ideas, and suggestions of one another. Be able to forgive, do not hold grudges, and live each day that you may share it together, as from this day forward you shall be each other's home, comfort, and refuge, your marriage strengthened by your love and respect for each other."

These words were new, not lines she knew by rote like their vows, and she listened to them carefully as she stared back at Preston.

Respect, forgiveness, comfort, refuge, and love. Big words. *Forever* words that felt—if she was honest—just the slightest bit *too* big, and more than a little overwhelming. Elise repeated the words to herself, her heart thundering as the magnitude of today started sinking in. This wasn't just a romantic adventure, and these weren't just lines in a play. This wasn't a scene; it was a marriage between two consulting adults . . . and these words were vows, like the ones her parents had once traded. She had just legally and spiritually bound her life to Preston's.

Looking for a safe harbor from the sudden storm of her thoughts, she focused on Preston's eyes shining with love as he smiled down at her, and she knew in her bones that his commitment to her was absolute and strong. He was here for all of the right reasons. The question was . . . was she?

She breathed deeply, willing away her jitters as the officiant continued.

"Just as two threads woven in opposite directions will form a most beautiful tapestry, so too can your two lives merged together make a beautiful marriage. To make your relationship work will take love. This is the core of your marriage and why you are here today. It will take trust, to know in your hearts that you truly want the best for each other. It will take dedication, to stay open to one another and to learn and grow together. It will take faith, to go forward together without knowing exactly what the future brings. And it will take commitment, to hold true to the journey you both pledge today to share together."

Holding onto Preston's eyes like a lifeline, Elise saw every good quality commended to them shining back at her: love, trust, dedication, faith, and commitment. From the beginning, Preston had offered his love unconditionally to her, learned to trust her with her costar, been dedicated to her happiness, had faith in her talent, and showed a commitment to her comfort and care from the moment they started dating.

She dragged her bottom lip into her mouth, dropping her eyes to his chest. Was she able to offer the same to him?

Did she love him? Yes, she did, but she acknowledged that it was a new love, predated years by her love for the stage.

Did she trust him? In many ways, she did. She trusted him not to hurt her. She trusted that he cared deeply for her. But if she was honest, she'd admit that she trusted herself more. She'd been her own guide, her own counsel, for years, and she wasn't sure she was ready to turn over that trust, or any part of it, to someone else yet.

Could she be dedicated to him? Above all other men, yes. No problem. She didn't want anyone else. But not above all other *concerns*. Her dedication to her career had shaped her entire adolescent and adult life. It was a driving factor in every decision she'd made since she was sixteen years old. Was it possible to shift that sort of dedication to her marriage just because they'd exchanged vows today?

Did she have faith in him? In them? No matter what the future had in store for them?

Her mind whirled, and because she didn't have answers, she stopped answering the questions as a heavy weight settled in her stomach. Preston squeezed her hands, and she looked up, offering him a wobbly smile and swallowing over the lump in her throat.

For most of her life, she'd been so focused on one goal, she hadn't left time for love. Honestly, she'd never seen him coming. He'd suddenly appeared in her life, fully formed, ready for love . . . and everything between them had moved so fast.

Had they moved *too* quickly? Were they ready to be married? More specifically, was *she* ready to be married? The judge's words about "two threads woven in opposite directions" stuck and stuttered in her mind, making her feel uncomfortable.

They didn't have very much in common. What if they not only moved in opposite directions, but were opposite *threads*? Or *incompatible* threads? What if they didn't form "a most beautiful tapestry?" What if they had been swept away by love and romance, but hadn't truly considered that marriage meant a merging of two lives into one life? Was she ready to merge her life? To make sacrifices for him? To trust and have faith and hand over some of the control she'd fought for so desperately in her life?

The officiant cleared his throat meaningfully, and Elise snapped her head up, her thoughts scattering as Preston squeezed her hands and grinned expectantly.

"In as much as Preston and Elise have this day consented together in the state of matrimony and have pledged their faith to each other, by virtue of the authority vested in me by the State of New York, I now pronounce you husband and wife. Preston, you may kiss your bride."

Pulling Elise into his arms, Preston searched her eyes for a long moment before whispering, "I love you, Mrs. Winslow," and lowering his lips to hers.

Mrs. Winslow.

Elise Winslow.

She'd expected to feel relief and excitement to be called something other than Elise Klassan, but she didn't. She felt uneasy. She felt uncertain. She felt unworthy of the title and terrified that she'd said yes to something as enormous as marriage. It made her heart flutter uncomfortably as she nodded at the officiant in thanks and let Preston pull her from the room, through the building, and down the steps of the civic building.

In the cab ride back to their apartment, Elise sat with her back against Preston's chest, trying to find comfort in the familiar—his arm around her shoulders, the delicious scent of his starched shirt and mild aftershave. This was Preston, not some anonymous stranger. Preston, whom she loved. Preston, who took care of her, and was kind to her, and supported her ambition.

She tried to talk herself out of her misgivings, making a list in her head of why marrying Preston today was the right decision for her life. Topping the list was her genuine love for him and his devotion to her. So, why was she worried? What was making her feel uncertain and introspective rather than confident and excited?

"I can't wait to get you home," he whispered close to her ear, his lips grazing her skin and making a heavenly shiver run down her back.

Sex.

Her mind sputtered to a stop.

She was about to have sex.

Hmm. Maybe *that* was it.

They were going back to his apartment . . . as husband and wife. There were no more barriers between them. No moral conundrum. No further fit of conscience. In the eyes of God and man, she was his wife.

Which meant she was about to have sex for the first time.

Her body relaxed against his as she considered this.

Was that it then? She wondered with a growing sense of relief. Was sex the source of her uncertainty and sudden jitters?

Without giving herself time to weigh the thought in her mind, she quickly decided it was. Of course it was.

It made perfect sense. She wasn't worried about their whirlwind courtship, or the fact that they'd never met each other's families, or the fear that their marriage would somehow interfere with her career, or the reality of meshing her wildly dissimilar life with Preston's . . . no. She was simply apprehensive about what they were about to do in his— *their*—bed. That was it. That *had* to be it.

Except, whispered the no-bullshit part of her brain, *you don't seem very uneasy about sex. In fact, for the first time since saying "I do," you seem . . . like a bride. Excited.*

But she was already so focused on the fact that she was about to lose her virginity, the stark, intimidating realities of merging their lives together were blessedly pushed to the wayside. And as she shifted her thoughts, the knots in her stomach unwound and the lump in her throat relaxed. The tension that had been building up in her body over the last hour disappeared, and her belly started fluttering with excitement.

Eager to stay in the moment and avoid any more troubling thoughts, she turned in his arms and said, "Kiss me."

Preston licked his lips before sealing them over hers and plunging his tongue without warning into her mouth. He tightened his arms around her when she sucked on it strongly, shifting in her seat until her breasts were crushed against his chest. She wasn't sure how he managed to pay the cabbie without releasing her mouth, but they ran into his apartment building still kissing frantically.

Preston backed her up against the wall of the elevator, grasping her backside and forcing her pelvis against his as he groaned into her mouth. She stood on her tiptoes, her arms wrapped around his neck, the sensitive points of her breasts longing for the wet heat of his mouth licking and sucking on her. The very idea was so erotic, she rocked her hips into his, meeting his tongue with frantic caresses while strangled sounds of pleasure that sounded nothing like her normal voice escaped from her throat. She raked her hands through his hair, frustrated that they were still technically in public and she couldn't get closer to him.

Still kissing her, he unlocked the apartment door and pulled her inside, kicking it closed behind them and pushing her up against the back of the door. Elise kicked off her heels and slid her hands under his jacket to shove it to the floor. His fingers moved nimbly to the zipper at the back of her dress, releasing it in a quick, smooth *whoosh* and pushing the straps down her arms.

Drawing back to look into his beautiful eyes, she grinned at him, dropping her fingers to his shirt and unfastening the buttons as quickly as she could. As Preston shrugged it over his shoulders, Elise reached back and unclasped her bra, letting it fall to the ground on top of his discarded shirt.

"The bed," she panted.

Preston lifted her into his arms, claiming her lips with his as he strode from the living room into the back hallway, kicking open the door to their bedroom. He placed her gently on the bed, and Elise rose onto her knees, reaching for his belt, surprised when she felt his hands cover hers. She looked up in question.

He smiled, laughing softly. "Not that I don't love every minute of this, but let's slow down a little."

"Why?"

"Because there's no rush." He leaned down and brushed his lips gently against hers. "Besides, it's not just your first time, it's also our wedding day, and I-I mean, I want this more than I've ever wanted anything, but—"

The doubts she'd successfully banished when they started kissing began to encroach again, so she grinned up at him, working his belt open, even though his hands were still pressed over hers.

"Less talking, more undressing," she said, tilting her head back. "And more kissing."

He kissed her again, his tongue gentler than it had been in the taxi or elevator. She slid her tongue against his, wanting urgency and heat more than tenderness. She popped open his pants' button, unzipped his fly, and tried to push his pants and underwear over his hips, but his boxers caught. Preston groaned softly as she tried to push them down again, and she broke off their kiss to look down.

Until now, she'd only touched his naked penis by tentatively slipping her hand into his underwear, but she'd never seen Preston completely naked. She leaned back and looked down at his tented boxers, slipping her thumbs into the waistband so she could pull them out and over his erection.

She heard a gasp—a short, ragged sound pass from her own lips—as she stared at him with the tiniest bit of fear and reached out to grasp him with her hand. It was big. And thick. And it throbbed with his pulse—tiny, almost imperceptible pumps of blood making it harder and wider as she held him. Drawing her bottom lip into her mouth, she glanced up at Preston for reassurance. And he was there for her, smiling with a mixture of love and amusement.

"I promise it'll be okay," he murmured. "But it'll *feel* better if we slow down a little and you let me . . ."

"Let you . . . ?" she asked, swallowing, the hot weight of him heavy against her palm.

He loosened her hand with a low groan, then pulled her off the bed to stand before him. Reaching for her panties, he slid them down her legs without dropping her eyes. "I'd rather show you."

She nodded, knowing that she could trust him and wishing she felt as certain about their marriage as she felt about everything that was happening between them right now. It made her heart soften and surge to put her pleasure in his hands. Why couldn't she do the same with the *rest* of her life?

His gaze slid down her naked body for the first time, and when she heard his panted sigh, her mind went blank of any other thoughts except what was happening between them right now.

"Lie down," he said, his voice low and tight.

She sat down first, then lay back, leaving her bare feet on the floor, and Preston dropped to his knees, spreading her legs and leaning forward.

He flattened his hand over her curly mound, as he had dozens of times before, and Elise, primed for pleasure, took a jagged breath and closed her eyes as his finger slipped between her folds.

"My God," he groaned, "you're so wet, sweetheart."

His fingers spread her lips, and she felt the cool air of their bedroom on her sensitive skin, making it pucker and throb. Leaning his head forward, he flicked his tongue over her clit.

Elise whimpered, clutching the sheets in her fists and throwing her head back into the mattress. He licked her again, slower this time, and just as she started to understand what he was doing, she felt his finger enter her body, and she practically bucked off the bed, straining up as his mouth latched back onto her tingling, aching flesh. Another finger joined the first, pressing against the wall of her sex as his mouth circled and lapped, sucked and licked.

A divine swirling started in her lower belly, rising higher and higher, until she could barely draw breath. Her muscles tensed until they trembled and shook, her fingers twisting into the sheets until she exploded into a million pieces, her body gyrating against his mouth and convulsing around his fingers. She heard herself scream his name, the sound echoing in her head like a prayer, and she crested, riding the wave of pleasure with her eyes clenched shut, barely aware of the world around her.

As she returned to earth, her body still jerked lightly as Preston crawled up the bed, pulled her up beside him, and wrapped her in his arms.

And Elise promptly started crying.

Tears streamed down her cheeks as she dropped her forehead to his chest, burrowing into the strong, solid warmth he offered. She felt confused and overwhelmed, cherished and terribly in love, frightened for the future but comforted by the kisses he pressed to her head, by his soft murmurs of love.

"Are you okay?" he asked, stroking her hair away from her forehead.

No, I'm not. I'm a mess. I love you so much, but I'm afraid we made a mistake today.

"Preston . . . everything happened so fast," she blurted out.

His hand on her back paused. "What do you mean?"

I mean I should have stayed your girlfriend for a little longer. I'm not ready to be your wife. I got swept up in romance and fantasy, and now I'm scared that it all moved too fast.

But how could she say any of this to him? How could she make him understand her fears without pushing him away? She didn't want to lose him, she just wished they could go back to yesterday. She took a ragged breath, closing her eyes against the maelstrom of her thoughts.

He pulled her tighter against him, stroking her back with long, soothing strokes, and it gave her the courage to say, "It feels like we just met."

"It feels like that to me sometimes too," he said. "But we love each other. I can't imagine my life without you, Elise."

The truth? She couldn't imagine her life without him either. But wanting him and making room for him were two different things, and one felt organic while the other felt frightening.

"I don't know how to be a wife," she said, her tears returning as her memories flashed to her mother doing the house chores as her father tended to the farm.

Her example of married life was based on manual labor, traditional gender roles, a shared religion, and very little obvious friendship or passion. That's not what she wanted. Not at all. As she pictured her parents, sitting across from one another in silence at the dinner table, the lump in the pit of her stomach swelled tenfold, and she clenched her eyes shut, holding on tighter to Preston.

"I don't know how to be a husband," he said. "How about we figure it out together?"

"I'm going to disappoint you," she said, sniffling.

"I don't think so," he said, pressing his lips to the crown of her head. "Today was the happiest day of my life, sweetheart."

The happiest day of *his* life, and one of the more troubling for *her*.

And yet, in that moment, she made a decision to keep her true feelings to herself today. If she was honest with him and told him how she really felt, she'd ruin today for him. She'd tarnish it. And Preston didn't deserve that from her. And besides, the deed was already done. For better or for worse, they were married.

She took a deep breath, inhaling the scent of his skin, comforted by the warm, solid strength of his arms. Maybe if she gave herself a little bit of time to adjust to marriage, her uncertainties would dissipate, and she'd feel more confident and secure in the role of wife. She knew that Preston would be patient with her. Their marriage didn't have to be like her parents' marriage. It could be whatever they wanted it to be. Today, the judge had said, *It will take faith, to go forward together without knowing exactly what the future brings.*

Tomorrow Elise would start working on her faith in them as a married couple, and—gulp—she'd start that journey by being honest with him about her doubts and worries. She knew him well enough to know that he would listen attentively, and they could start figuring out how they wanted their marriage to look. They were goal-oriented people who would set objectives and work together to achieve them in their marriage as in their careers. She had faith that they loved each other enough to figure this out together.

Tomorrow. Tomorrow they could start putting the work into the journey they'd started today.

Feeling marginally better, she pressed her lips to his chest and wiped her tears away.

Because it was so much easier, she concentrated on the feeling of his body next to hers instead of the worrisome feelings she wouldn't be able to sort out today. It felt like heaven to be clasped against him, flesh to flesh, though she felt empty, too. She wanted him. She wanted him to fill her. She wanted him to fill her so deeply that there wasn't room left for the thoughts in her head or the doubts in her heart.

She took a deep breath, pressing her lips to his chest. "Pres?"

"Hmmm?"

"Make love to me," she said.

His hand on her back froze.

"Are you sure you're ready?"

"Mm-hm," she murmured, leaning back so she could look at his face. "I want you. I need you. It's time."

Preston meant to go slow.

He had promised himself that he wouldn't have any expectations and if she still wanted to wait, that he would be patient with her. But hearing permission tumble from her lips ground his good intentions to powder, and he reached for her face, dropping his lips to hers. He kissed her passionately and *finally* with abandon, rolling her onto her back to cover her body with his.

Cradling her face with his palms, he drew back to look at her slick, rosy lips, moving his erection intentionally against the damp tangle of curls between her thighs that he'd just loved with his mouth. She flinched, clenching her eyes shut and biting her bottom lip as his cock slid into the damp valley rubbing back and forth against her aroused clit.

"Open your eyes," he said.

She did, and they were dark blue and glassy, full of rolling emotions. He read love and uncertainty, devotion and fear, trust and need . . . he saw it all staring back at him—the multiple facets of the woman he now called his wife, and it made his heart swell with tenderness to fully realize what she was giving to him today. Her heart, her life, her body. In every possible way, she would belong to him.

"I love you," he breathed, positioning himself at her opening.

"Me too," she sobbed, her breathing shallow and ragged. "Please, Pres. Please."

As he entered her, her eyes widened with surprise. Holding her gaze, he inhaled and held his breath, trying not to cry out in pleasure as he moved past her lips into her tight, wet, silky heat.

"Okay?" he gasped.

"Okay," she murmured, giving him a small smile as her fingers caressed his back from shoulder bone to hip, digging in a little where they rested over his ass.

"More?"

She nodded, her dark eyes sparkling with something undefinable and new that belonged only to him.

He allowed himself to surge forward a little more, feeling the soft ridges of her sex clinging to him as he slid deeper, his fingers dropping from her face to fist in the sheets on either side of her head.

He stayed as still as he could, giving her a moment to adjust to his size and width before he finally pushed through the thin barrier that would join them completely together.

He didn't expect her to suddenly arch her back, thrusting her hips toward him, and his eyes rolled back in his head as he glided the rest of the way into her with a low, satisfied groan. Surrounded by her soft, wet, trembling sex, he opened his eyes as he drew back and plunged forward again.

Bending back her neck, she arched up again, sinking her head into the pillow and pulling her bottom lip between her teeth. He withdrew again and surged forward, watching her face for any sign of fear or pain, but saw only pleasure in the fluttering of her eyes, in the clenching of her jaw and moans of "more."

"Pres, how do . . . how do I . . . ?" she whimpered, her fingers digging into his lower back as she started meeting him thrust for thrust.

"You let go, sweetheart. I've got you. I'll be right behind you."

As he slid into her again, her eyes opened, and she locked her gaze with his. "I'm so glad . . . it was you." Then she closed her eyes and cried out his name, her whole body tensing beneath him before convulsing into the most beautiful fucking orgasm he'd ever seen in his entire life. Her skin flushed pink and glistened with sweat as his name fell from her lips over and over again like a litany or prayer or promise, and though he wouldn't have believed it possible, he swelled inside of her, pulling out slowly, then pressing in deep.

As she pulsed around him, he felt the intense gathering, the pressure in the pit of his stomach, the tension that made his breathing so ragged and fast, he knew he couldn't hold back a moment longer. Throwing back his head, he bellowed "I love you!" and let go, flooding his wife's body with his life force and love and his most devout promise of a happy forever.

Chapter 11

The early-morning sunshine was dazzling against her eyes when she opened them several hours later, taking a deep breath and stretching. She felt Preston's warm, naked body behind her and smiled.

From the moment she'd asked him to make love to her, they'd both been ravenous for each other—greedy, urgent, and demanding, and after having sex the first time, they'd made love all afternoon, into the night, only stopping to nap before reaching for each other again. They'd barely talked, engaging in a marathon of sex that had finally left them both exhausted.

Elise moved gingerly against him, not surprised to find she was tender between her thighs. Knowing that Preston's body had used hers to aching was so sexy, it made her want him all over again. She was an addict, she thought with a saucy grin, addicted to her husb—um, to Preston.

"Are you awake?" he whispered.

"I am now," she purred, snuggling into him, sighing with anticipation when she felt his erection straining against her backside.

"How are you feeling?" he asked her, his breath warm on the back of her neck.

"Amazing." She turned onto her back so she could look up at him. "Good morning."

"Good morning, wife," he said, grinning at her. "I love you, Mrs. Winslow."

Her smile wavered because she couldn't ignore the unexpected clench of her gut. It was panic, setting in as swiftly as it had yesterday at their wedding ceremony. She'd been distracted by amazing sex for the past twelve hours, but suddenly she was right back in City Hall with a dozen uncomfortable questions circling in her head that she simply couldn't answer.

"Mrs. Winslow," she murmured, wishing that the title of "wife" felt as effortless as "lover."

"That's right," he said, his eyes twinkling with happiness. "You love me?"

She did. She loved him very much, which made her doubts about their marriage infinitely more confusing.

"So much," she whispered, her heart acknowledging the pure truth of her words, despite the way it had clutched a moment ago when he'd called her "Mrs. Winslow."

He dropped his lips to hers, kissing her gently before leaning back. "I'm going to make you so happy."

"Speaking of happiness," she said, determined to be honest with him and start a healthy dialogue about their marriage, expectations, and future. She took a deep breath. "Maybe we could go to the park today . . . and really talk. About getting married, and what we want, and where we're going . . . my career, your career . . . everything."

"Yeah," he said, kissing her again. "Sounds good."

Just like that, her stomach unclenched. "Really?"

"Absolutely. A marriage summit. To get things off on the right foot."

She grinned at him—the first genuine smile she'd been able to offer him since leaving City Hall yesterday—and it felt divine.

"Exactly," she said, laughing softly as her body relaxed.

"So noted. A marriage summit on the docket for later today . . . but for now, Mrs. Winslow? More sex," said Preston, kissing her again.

"You're insatiable," she said, ignoring the uncomfortable new title as her body responded to him instantly. She twined her arms around his neck and slipped her tongue between his lips.

Preston rolled on top of her, the hardness of his erection pushing into her thigh as his hands skimmed down her arms and—

Her phone buzzed loudly on the bedside table, and she froze.

No one ever called her. The only people who had her number were Preston, her parents and sisters, who never called her, and Donny Durran.

Preston's hands continued their leisurely exploration of hips and belly as his lips pressed tiny kisses to her neck. She wiggled away from him just enough to free her arm and reach for her phone.

"It's Donny," she said, looking at the screen over his shoulder.

"Call him back later," suggested Preston, glancing up from the valley between her breasts.

"It could be important. It could be about a part."

"It's Sunday. The part will still be there tomorrow." Preston sucked her nipple between his lips, and her back arched reflexively, but she pushed at his head.

"Stop, Pres. Stop. Seriously. I have to get this."

He sighed, rolling onto his back, and she pulled the sheet over her breasts as she answered the phone.

"Hello? Donny?"

"Elise. You're up. Are you sitting down?"

She sat up straight, glancing at Preston, who grinned at her, sliding his palm across her belly.

Stop! she mouthed. He moved his hand away, pouting.

"Uh, yes. I'm sitting down."

"This is big, Elise. *Way* bigger than *Our Town*, honey. This is huge. Are you ready?"

Her breath caught. "I'm ready."

"It's Hollywood."

"What?" she gasped.

"Yep. Turns out Jack Mosell was in the audience on Friday night, and he loved you. I mean, he *loved* you. And he's one of the best casting directors out in LA. Well, he got back to LA yesterday, and it turns out that Diana Agron has pulled out of playing Edna Pontellier in *The Awakening*."

Her heart was racing so fast she could hardly speak. "By K-Kate Chopin?"

"Yeah. Period piece. Anyhow, they've already started production on the picture, and now they're at a standstill until they can find a fast replacement for Diana. So, Jack tells them about you. And get this, Elise . . . he called you 'the American Keira Knightley.' Can you believe it?"

"The American Keira Knightley," she repeated dumbly.

"So Jack went on and on about you. Then they called me to see if your schedule's free, and I said it was. And, well, they're in such a jam, they asked if you could go out there and screen-test today, and as long as they liked what they saw, you're in."

"I'm . . . in?"

"You're in! Listen, I booked you on the ten o'clock American flight out of LaGuardia, and I'll have a car there to pick you up in thirty minutes. Jack will meet your flight and take you right over to MGM. Elise, this is the big time, kid. Are you ready?"

"I'm—I'm ready," she squeaked.

"Pack a bag. The car'll be there soon," he said. "And Elise? Congratulations. You did it."

"I did it. Th-thank you, Donny."

The line went dead, and she clicked the end button on her phone, turning to Preston. "Oh my God!"

"Is everything okay?"

She started laughing, almost hysterically, as the news settled in. "Pres! They want me in LA! Donny set up a screen test!"

"Wait. What?"

"Hollywood!" she cried. "I'm going to be in a movie!"

"Elise . . . wait, wait, wait, wait. Sweetheart, what are you doing?" Preston asked, watching his wife jump out of bed, pull on a T-shirt she found on the floor, and run to his closet. She turned around a moment later with a duffel bag, unzipped it, and plopped it on the bed.

"Packing!"

"Slow down a sec. What do you mean?"

She looked up at him, a beaming smile on her face. "Donny reserved me a ticket on the ten o'clock American fight to LA. I have to pack. Oh my God, this is so exciting!"

She leaned forward and pressed her lips to his, then turned and beelined to the bathroom.

"Elise?" he called, sitting up in bed and pulling the sheet to his waist. "Can we talk about this?"

"Huh?"

"Sweetheart, can we talk about this?"

She peeked out of the bathroom. "Pres! There's a part for me in Hollywood! For *me*!"

"Okay. I get that. But you picked up your phone, had a five-minute conversation, screamed that Donny set up a screen test in LA, and now you're packing. My head's spinning."

"He's sending a car in"—she peeked out again and glanced at the clock on his bedside table—"twenty-five minutes."

Preston whipped the sheet off his body, pulled on some boxers, and crossed the room to lean on the wall just outside of the bathroom. "Can you stop for a minute?"

"I have to pack," she insisted, glancing at him before grabbing her toothbrush and squeezing it into her toiletry bag.

She was packing. She was leaving. The panic in his chest ratcheted up.

"You've never even mentioned an interest in movies."

"Pres, this is *The Awakening* by Kate Chopin." She zipped the small pouch closed and snapped her head up to look at him. "They called me the 'American Keira Knightley.' Do you have any idea what this could mean for my career? I could pay off all my loans. I could—"

"Is that what this is about? Money?" He reached out and placed his palms on her shoulders, relief sluicing through his veins like Valium. "Oh, sweetheart, you don't have to take this job if it's about money. Listen, we haven't talked a lot about finances yet, but I'm not just comfortable . . . I'm loaded. I mean, I can write you a check from my account today, and we'll pay off every cent of your loans."

"You don't even know how much I owe," she murmured, pausing in her haste to stare up at him.

He shrugged. "Is it less than thirty million dollars?"

"Yes," she squeaked.

"Then we're good."

Her blue eyes widened, searching his for a moment as if trying to figure out if he was telling the truth or not. Finally, she sucked her bottom lip into her mouth and ducked away from him, back into the bedroom, where she put the toiletry bag in the duffel bag on the bed.

"I can't accept your money."

"*What?*" He leaned against the bathroom doorway, that terrible, panicky feeling crashing over him like a wave. She'd been acting weird—a little off—since they'd returned to his apartment yesterday. Sexually, she'd blown his mind, but emotionally, she'd been a little distant. He'd chalked it up to a combination of new-bride jitters and losing her virginity, but now he was starting to worry. "Why not? I'm your husband."

She looked up, clenching her jaw once before turning to the bureau that held her underwear and opening the top drawer.

"Because it's not about the money, Pres. It's about the job. *The Awakening*! My big chance. This is it."

"I thought *Ethan Frome* was *it*. Plus, I was under the impression that you were a *stage* actress." He licked his lips, recalling her very words. "The audience? The synergy? The—"

"I'm an *actress*," she said, glancing at him before packing her lingerie, then whirling back to the bureau. She opened the second drawer, pulling out a small pile of T-shirts and shorts before closing it. "Stage, screen, TV . . . whatever. I go where the work is. New York. LA. Wherever there's a part that needs me."

I need you . . . playing the part of my wife. You can't just leave.

The panic inside of him was whirling like a tornado now, growing by the moment; he wasn't getting through to her. She needed to stop packing for a minute so they could actually talk about this.

He crossed the room and reached for her from behind, wrapping his arms around her. She didn't protest as he sat down on the bed and pulled her onto his lap. "Please talk to me, sweetheart. We live *here*. We work *here*. We're married, and you're going to do Broadway shows, and I'm going to work for Mulligan & McKee. I mean . . . how does going to LA to be a movie star fit into this?"

Though she stayed in his arms, her posture was rigid. "I'm not going to be a movie star, Pres. It's one role. But don't you see? It could be my big break. This is what I've worked for my whole life. This. Right now."

"I know that, but what about us?"

"I'm not going to LA forever. It's just a little break," she said, turning in his arms to look at him. "Maybe while I'm out there, you can come and visit me."

A little break? Did they need a little break? And she was suggesting he "visit" like some long-distance boyfriend? He didn't want to "visit" his wife. He wanted to live with his wife—sleep next to her, wake up next to her, make love to her every night and every morning.

He tried to swallow past his disappointment. "Is this really what you want?"

"Yes." She nodded, offering him a small, hopeful smile. "It's so important to me, I can't even tell you. I never, ever, not in my wildest dreams, let myself imagine Hollywood. Please wish me luck. Please don't be angry with me."

"I'm not angry with you, I'm trying to get my head around this. We got married yesterday. And, I mean, we've barely talked, but we were going to have a marriage summit today and—"

"We can have it over the phone," she said, tilting her head to the side and grinning at him like everything was fine, like she wasn't leaving for LA on a whim the day after their wedding. What the hell was going on with her?

"Over the phone?" He searched her eyes, dread joining panic because she looked happier and more excited than she'd looked in two days. "Maybe I could go with you."

"Pres," she said, blinking at him like a deer caught in headlights, "that's crazy. Your job is here. I'm not standing between you and your career."

"Fuck my career," he said, trying to ignore the painful tightening in his chest. "You're leaving for LA for the next few months without even talking to me about it. Elise, come on. What's going on with you?"

Her mouth dropped open in surprise, then tightened into a thin line. "I wish you would try to understand."

"I *am* trying to understand, but ten minutes ago I was about to make love to you in our bed, looking forward to spending the rest of my life with you, and now you're leaving to go to LA, possibly for several months. I mean, I'm happy to wait—"

"You're definitely *not* happy."

"Okay, fine. You're right. I'm not happy about this. Sorry. I thought . . . I thought today was the first day of my marriage, and instead it's—"

Her eyes were stark when she interrupted him. "Are you trying to get me to stay?"

"You're my *wife*," he said slowly, because he didn't seem to be getting through to her, and frustration was joining panic and dread for a fairly awful trifecta. "We're married. I want you to *want* to stay."

She bit her bottom lip, looking away from him. When she raised her eyes, they were sad, and it went against every natural instinct that Preston had to make her sad, but watching her walk away from him without putting up a fight was unthinkable.

"Pres, I was *always* honest with you about my career," she said defensively. "You know how important it is—"

"Yeah. But I also know that yesterday you promised to love, honor, and cherish me for the rest of your life."

She wiggled off his lap, standing in front of him with her hands on her hips. "I do! I will! I'm not going to Timbuktu! Just LA. Just for a little while. It's not forever. Please stop blowing it out of proportion."

He stared at her like he didn't know her, and part of him—a large part—felt like maybe he didn't.

When she started speaking again, her voice was calmer and gentler, but he could tell it was forced, too. "Listen, we'll talk on the phone, and maybe you can, I don't know, come and see me in a week or two? For a weekend?" She walked over to the closet, and when she turned around, there were several dresses hanging over her forearm. "And when it's over, I'll come back."

I'll come back.

Three words. Three words that told him there was no room for conversation anymore. Her mind was made up. She was leaving. No. She was already gone.

"When?" he asked softly, his heart aching. "When exactly will you come back?"

"When filming's over."

"How long will that be, Elise?"

"My guess is three months."

His eyes widened, and it felt like she'd sucker-punched him in the throat. "Three *months*? We haven't been apart for more than a night since you moved in. We got *married* yesterday. We're . . . we're starting our life. Here. In New York. Together."

He would have winced at the sound of his voice—the tone a man in the 1950s would have used to boss around "the little woman"—but he was too upset with the entire situation to critique his behavior.

She answered him crisply, unsmiling. "We'll just have to start it when I get back."

He skewered her with his eyes. "And what happens if they offer you another role after this one? Then what?"

She looked away from him. "We'll deal with that when it happens."

Not if, he noted. *When.*

"Elise, we never discussed LA as a possibility. I'm not licensed to practice law in California. I have a job here. A career here."

"I know that!" she yelled.

Elise placed the dresses in the duffel bag and stared down at her floor, clasping her fingers together and taking a deep breath. Preston reached forward, snagging the pinkie of her left hand and pulling her over to him. She stood between his legs, and he adjusted their fingers, lacing his fingers through hers.

"I can't pass this up," she murmured, her voice breaking as she stared down at their fingers.

He felt a vulnerable spot and pushed his advantage. "Of course you can. What about *Our Town* at the Barrymore? You were so excited for that tryout next week. You were going to be *amazing* in that."

"I haven't even auditioned yet."

She started to draw her hand away, but he tightened his grip, pulling her between his legs and wrapping his arms around her waist.

"So, audition for it, sweetheart," he said gently. "Get the part and stay here with me. Don't go."

She lifted her head, her eyes wide and disbelieving. "*What?*"

"Stay here with me, sweetheart. *Please* don't go."

Her whole body stiffened and recoiled, and he loosened his arms as she took a step back, searching his face like she couldn't believe what he'd just said.

"That's what my mother said to me the day I boarded a bus to New York. '*Stay here with me, Liebling. Don't go.*' I can't believe you just said that. I can't believe you would . . . I can't . . ." She blinked her eyes frantically, sucking in a huge gasp of air and turning away from him. When she whipped back to face him, her cheeks were red. "You would stand in the way of my dreams? You would put yourself between me and everything I ever wanted? Everything I've worked for?"

"Elise—"

"What if the shoe was on the other foot? What if you *hadn't* hurt your rotator cuff? What if you were willing and able to go to the Olympics and someone had stood in *your* way?"

He leaned back on the bed, his eyes narrowing. "Is the theoretical someone in this scenario you?"

She shrugged. "It doesn't matter."

"It *does* matter," he said, his voice low and tight. "It matters if we're talking about *you*, because you're not just anyone, you're my *wife*."

"Okay, fine. Me. What if I stood in your way and asked you not to go?"

He felt—*felt*—his heart breaking. "Do you seriously not know the answer to that question?"

She stared back at him, her jaw tight, her eyes welling with tears.

"Elise, I would *do* anything for you. I would *give up* anything for you. I would *be* anything for you. Would I have given up the Olympics for you? Hell, yes. No question. Sweetheart, there's *nothing* I wouldn't give up for you if you asked me to."

She took a deep, ragged breath, wiping the tears off her cheeks with the backs of her hands.

"Now. But what about then?"

He shook his head. "I wouldn't have let anything come between me and the woman I love."

"You're so sure."

"It's the truth."

She shook her head as more tears trailed down her cheeks. "It's easy to say because the choice was taken away from you."

"*Easy?* You think it was *easy* for me to train for almost a decade and be sidelined at the last minute? It was a lot of things, but it wasn't *easy*."

"That's not what I'm saying." She shook her head with frustration. "I know it wrecked you *at the time*. That's my point. It wrecked you to miss out on your dream then, just like it would wreck me now. Can't you see that? Preston, what you sensed yesterday? The 'distance' you mentioned? It's because we're in two different places. Your dream, your Plan A, is dead. You already moved on to Plan B. But *my* dream, *my* Plan A, is still very much alive."

"As far as I knew, your Plan A never included Hollywood. You were already living your Plan A by auditioning for leading Broadway roles."

Elise took a deep breath and sighed, her face sad and frustrated.

"What do you want from me?" she asked softly, her voice cool.

"You want me to say it? Fine." He narrowed his eyes, his tone frank and clear. "I want you to say no to Hollywood. I want you to stay in New York. I want you to take one of the amazing roles Donny's going to find for you, and I will support you in every possible way until our apartment is covered in Tony awards. I want you to stay here and be an amazing actress and also be my wife." He paused, his voice dropping to a tender whisper as he searched her eyes. "Sweetheart, I am begging you not to go."

She lifted her chin, though her eyes glistened with tears. "I have to."

Then she picked up an outfit she'd placed on the bed, walked into the bathroom, and closed the door behind her.

Preston stared at the bathroom door in a state of semi-shock, frozen in place. After a few seconds, he finally exhaled the breath he'd been holding and placed his hand over his heart. It was like she'd reached into his chest with a fist made of nails and squeezed, because he could swear his heart was bleeding out inside his body.

He knew she was ambitious.

He knew that she had given up a lot for her career.

He'd known—from almost the first moment he met her—that her dream of becoming a successful actress was the most important thing in her life.

But somewhere along the way . . . perhaps when she moved in, or when she told him she loved him, or when she married him, or when she gave herself to him last night over and over again . . . he'd tricked himself into believing that what they had was at least as important as her career, if not more so.

He was wrong.

He was so very wrong, and he should have known, but he'd fallen so hard and so fast, he'd deluded himself that she could be ambitious but still prioritize their relationship. That she could love him just as much as he loved her. That he could be just as important to her as she was to him. And it hurt to realize he wasn't. Oh God, it hurt so bad.

Closing his eyes, he forced himself to take a deep breath, dropping his hand from his chest. And suddenly it was as though he could feel an icy wall going up around his heart— around his bleeding, stupid, vulnerable heart that had rushed headlong into love—and he welcomed it. At this moment, when he understood his lack of worth to Elise, he almost would have welcomed its death, but he settled for its torpor instead and welcomed the growing numbness that surrounded it.

She came out of the bathroom in jeans and a black T-shirt, her hair in a ponytail and her eyes red-rimmed but determined. Pausing in the doorway, she flicked her glance to Preston, then looked away quickly as she headed for the bed, zipping up the duffel bag and hefting it onto her shoulder.

He almost reached for it—to help her, to carry it downstairs and pack it into the trunk of the car and stand there like a fucking chump waving good-bye as the love of his life drove away in a car headed to LA. But his almost-glacial heart held him back.

Forget it. Fuck it. She could carry her own goddamned bag.

"I'll miss you," she said softly, swiping at a tear sliding down her cheek.

His face felt like stone as he looked up at her.

"I'm sorry, Preston."

He stared back at her in silence.

"I have to do this. Please understand."

He couldn't speak. One small part of his heart remained warm, holding out hope, trying to fend off the approaching frost. If he spoke, he'd scream at her, or beg her to stay, or cry like a fucking baby. None of those outcomes was acceptable. He straightened his spine and said nothing.

She walked over to him and kissed his cheek, her lips soft and warm. He closed his eyes as the last of his heart froze over, then cracked in two. When he opened his eyes, she was looking at him, and he knew the expression: she was seeking his approval, his permission, his reassurance, his love.

And he couldn't give her any of it. He kept his eyes expressionless.

"I'll call you when I get there," she said, her voice breaking. "We'll figure it out, okay? I promise."

I don't believe you.

She turned at the bedroom door and looked back at him. "Pres . . . please."

I love you, Mrs. Winslow . . .

How was it possible he'd said those words to her less than an hour ago? They circled in his head, taunting him, torturing him, making him feel stupid and vulnerable and grieved beyond words, beyond bearing.

It was too painful to hold her eyes anymore, so he dropped them, staring down at his lap in misery. When he looked up again, she was gone.

The ink on their marriage certificate wasn't even dry . . . and his wife was gone.

Part II

Chapter 12

Present Day

Preston Winslow didn't date.

. . . a fact that didn't stop his little sister, Jessica Winslow, from making Preston's dating life one of her top priorities. The more he stonewalled her? The more she rose to the challenge. And as her wedding loomed—yes, *loomed*, thought Preston, ignoring the automatic bitterness that accompanied the word "wedding" in his head—closer, she was more and more one-track minded.

"But Pres," whined Jessica, "you can't come stag to my engagement party. It's just weird!"

"Then I guess I'll just be your weird big brother."

"Nope," she said, putting her hands on her hips and following him from his bedroom, where he'd just dropped off his bags for the weekend. He walked down the second-floor gallery of Westerly, their family's estate, with Jess on his heels. "Sorry, but I got you a date."

Preston stopped at the top of the stairs and whipped around to face her. "Are you nuts?"

Jessica stepped back but raised her chin bravely. "No, I'm not. Brooks is flying home tonight with Skye, Cameron is bringing Margaret Story, and Christopher's bringing Connie Atwell."

"And who, pray tell, am I supposed to be bringing?"

Jessica cleared her throat, having the decency to look sheepish as she murmured, "Be—At—."

Preston cupped his hand around his ear, skewering her with a glare. "Sorry, didn't catch that name."

She took another step back from him and said clearly, "Beth Atwell."

Beth. Beth Atwell, Connie's cousin, whom he'd been dating the night he first saw . . . saw . . . he swallowed the lump in his throat, pushing all thoughts of *her* out of his mind.

"Well then you can just call Beth Atwell and cancel."

"I can't do that," said Jessica, following him down the stairs. "She's staying the weekend with Connie, and it would be rude for Connie to come and not to invite Beth."

"Not my problem," said Preston, sidestepping a caterer who was crossing Westerly's front hallway with a large tray of gleaming champagne glasses.

Jessica got held up momentarily behind two enormous flower arrangements but caught up with Preston in the west parlor, which housed a large billiard table and doubled as a TV room. She jerked her head toward the pool cues racked on the wall.

"I'll play you. If you lose, you be nice to Beth tomorrow night."

Preston narrowed his eyes at Jessica. She didn't need to cheat, but she often did. "No cheating."

"Got it," she said, pulling a cue from the wall and rubbing the tip in blue chalk.

"I mean it . . . if I catch you cheating, you forfeit and you can't bother me about my dating life for a full year."

Jessica stuck the pool cue under her arm so that she could use her incredibly annoying air quotes as she asked, "Dating life?"

Preston rolled his eyes at her and pulled the triangle off the wall so he could rack the balls.

"For me to ignore your"—air quotes again—"*dating life*, you'd need to actually have one."

"God, you're annoying," said Preston, fishing the cue ball out from a tray under the table. "I don't know how Alex stands you."

"He loves me," said Jess, aiming for the yellow ball at the front of the neat triangle and splitting two stripes into the back corner pockets with a sassy grin. "That's how."

Thirty minutes later, Preston had a date to Jessica's engagement party, although he could have sworn she palmed a ball into the side pocket while he bent down to tie his Top-Siders. Oh well. It was his own fault for letting his guard down for even a moment. He should know better than to trust a woman . . . even his own sister.

"Beth's getting to Connie's tonight. Why don't you give her a ring and tell her how much you're looking forward to renewing your acquaintance?"

"Why don't you butt out? I said I'd be nice, and I'll be nice, but I'm not interested in her."

"You're not interested in anyone," said Jessica softly, sitting next to her older brother on a brown leather couch. "How come?"

Preston looked askance at her, trying hard to look bored and annoyed, even though this particular conversation always got his heart pumping uncomfortably. "Why do you care, Jess? You and Alex will live happily ever after. You got Brooks saddled with Skye, God help him. Cam's been following Margaret around like a puppy dog for weeks. How about leaving me alone?"

"I can't live happily ever after if you're *un*happy ever after," she said, leaning her head on his shoulder. Her coal-black hair was back in a ponytail, but it tickled his cheek. It had been a long time since a woman's hair had brushed against his cheek. Since . . . since . . .

"I'm not unhappy," he murmured. "I'm busy."

"You're a good lawyer, Pres." She paused. "Everyone knows that. But you're lonesome."

"I'm not—"

"Yeah, you are," she said. "You . . . you changed."

"What are you talking about?"

"It's obvious, Pres." Jessica took a deep breath and sighed. "Something happened to you. Before you came back to Philly."

Preston's whole body tensed at her words. Brooks was his only sibling who knew about—well, who knew what had happened. Had he told Jessica? Were all of his younger siblings talking about him and feeling sorry for him behind his back? Damn it. He'd be furious if Brooks had blabbed about Preston's personal business. He had no interest in discussing it.

"I don't know what you mean," he said. "Lean up. I'm getting a drink."

Jessica increased the pressure of her head on his shoulder, trapping her brother, and Preston huffed in annoyance.

"I know it hurt when you couldn't be in the Olympics. I know that being a lawyer was your second choice, not your first. But you seemed okay with it when you went to Columbia. Better than okay. Happy. And you were dating Beth for a while there. I remember because you two took me out for dinner when I visited you in New York. And then, suddenly, out of nowhere, you quit your job in New York, sold your apartment, and came back to Westerly. You were drinking too much—"

"Jess, what are you *talking* about? You weren't even here. You were in London!"

"Cam told me."

"Cam has a big fucking mouth."

"Yep," she agreed, picking up where she left off. "You drank too much, and you were living here for a while doing nothing, and then—"

"And then I got my shit together and went to work for Clifton, Jackson, and Webb. End of story."

"Well," she said, and he could almost feel her holding back the air quotes. "If *getting your shit together* meant that Brooks pulled strings to get you a job, and you—"

He pulled away from Jessica sharply, standing and watching as she fell over onto the couch.

"You know what, Jess? I don't need this crap from my little—"

"Gah! You're such a *jerk* now! Such an unhappy, argumentative, *jerk*! No wonder you win all your cases. Who would want to go more than two rounds with you?"

"And yet again, I have to wonder why the hell Alex English is shackling his life to yours!"

"Like you would know *the first thing* about shackling *your* life to *anyone's*!" she bellowed, jumping to her feet in front of him.

He felt his whole face flinch as he stared down at her.

A sudden and humiliating lump rose up to the top of his throat, and Preston blinked his eyes, trying to swallow over it, but it hurt. It ached. It made his lungs burn and his heart throb. Clenching his jaw, he stared down at Jessica in misery.

He knew the first thing.

He *only* knew the first thing.

The rest was taken away from him before he could learn any more.

"Oh. Oh, Pres . . ." she whispered, her eyes flooding with tears as she reached out to touch his arm, realizing that she'd inadvertently pushed him too far.

He wanted to tell her to get lost, to beat it, to leave him alone, but that goddamned lump in his throat wasn't allowing him to form words, so he blinked again, then turned away from her. Striding across the room to the wet bar in the corner, he opened the fridge and took out a Heineken. Popping open the cap, he took a long swig before turning around.

"Don't follow me," he said.

Then he turned and headed out the door.

It was hot outside compared to the artificial coolness inside Westerly, and the bottle Preston was holding immediately started to sweat as it adjusted from a cold refrigerator to the eighty-eight degree evening.

Why had he come home a day early? Because tomorrow was a dark day for Preston, and he didn't want to spend tonight or tomorrow alone. But a smarter man would have known that an engagement party for his couple-crazy little sister was the worst possible place to be. He should have just showed up at the party tomorrow night. Breezed in. Kissed Jessica and his mother hello. Shaken Alex's hand. And left. Instead, he'd come home early to escape the heat of the city and the bleakness of his memories only to be harassed and harangued by Jess.

For just a second, he felt bad. She clearly knew nothing about his ill-fated marriage to Elise, or she never would have said such a hurtful thing. He was relieved that Brooks hadn't spilled the beans after all, and glad he hadn't acted on his suspicions.

Brooks had never gotten the chance to meet Elise in person, but several weeks ago, Brooks had picked up Preston at his apartment for a night out on the town. While Preston was in the shower, Brooks had rooted around his desk for an envelope and inadvertently come across the divorce papers that Preston still hadn't sent to his wife. When Preston returned to the living room, showered and ready to head out to dinner, Brooks had looked up from the desk where the papers were laid out in front of him.

"A divorce? Divorce papers?" His face was shocked, his eyes sorry. "Pres, you *married* her?"

"Jesus, Brooks! Snoop much?"

Preston had whipped the packet off the desk, neatened it quickly, and held it against his chest. Brooks remained seated at Preston's desk, tenting his fingers under his chin.

"You married her," Brooks repeated softly.

Preston had closed his eyes against the onslaught of pain that almost always accompanied his thoughts of Elise, then taken a seat on the leather love seat across from Brooks.

"It was a mistake."

"You were in love with her."

Preston shrugged.

"That wasn't a question. I remember."

Brooks paused so long that Preston eventually raised his eyes to his big brother. "It didn't work out."

"Clearly," said Brooks, flicking his eyes toward the papers Preston still held against his heart. "What happened?"

Preston didn't want to talk about it. Truly, he didn't. But suddenly he heard his voice recalling the night Donny Durran knocked on her dressing room door. He told Brooks about walking her home, their picnic the next day, and seeing her face on the steps of the library when he was sure he wouldn't see her again.

He smiled sadly as he recalled her moving in, told Brooks about the keys and about her unusual background. His eyes watered when he recalled his impromptu proposal, and he wiped the tears away when he told Brooks about her leaving for LA.

"And then what?" asked Brooks.

"That was it," said Preston, finally standing up. It was dark now, and they'd missed their dinner reservation. "I don't feel like going out. I'll order some Chinese. What do you want?"

"Pres," said Brooks in the voice he reserved for telling Chris and Jess what to do—his "dad" voice—"what happened?"

Images of his disastrous trip to LA circled in his head, making his breath hitch and his eyes burn. How to sum up the worst three days of his life?

She didn't want me there . . .

She didn't want to be married . . .

She wasn't in love with me anymore . . .

Or how about the ensuing two years when he hadn't been able to forget his wife . . . or cheat on her, for that matter. So many times, he'd gone home with a gorgeous woman after getting plastered at a party or fundraiser, but when it came time to kiss her, to touch her, to make love to her, Elise's face would flash through his mind, and he wouldn't be able to follow through. Along with his general misery and close call with alcoholism, his fucking celibacy could be laid at her doorstep too.

He took a deep breath, blinking away the memories. He came very close to making himself a scotch on the rocks, but he'd sworn off hard alcohol since getting his life back in order.

"Okay. You don't have to tell me," said Brooks. "But I guess that's why you went off the deep end for a while? Quit your job? Moved back to Philly? Tried to pickle your liver?"

Preston nodded. But the truth was that he hadn't quit his job. He'd resigned after fucking up a major case. The partners had covered his mistake and managed to appease the client with a large, quiet settlement that Preston had paid out from his personal account. But everywhere he went reminded him of what he'd lost. He couldn't work. He couldn't bear to stay in New York without her. He'd put his apartment up for sale, thrown her stuff in a dumpster, and moved back to Philly without a second glance.

"Why didn't you talk to me about it? Why didn't you come to me?"

"And say what? I got married and it didn't work out? My wife left and didn't come back?"

I'm dying inside because I'm hoping every day for a call . . . a text . . . an e-mail . . . anything. My heart is breaking because it wants her and needs her and she's gone.

"So . . . when are you sending her the divorce papers?"

"I don't know."

The memory faded as Preston walked farther and farther away from the house and Jessica's irritating interrogation.

As the sun set over Westerly, the air cooled, but the mosquitoes were coming out, and Preston wished he had some bug spray. But fuck it. He wasn't going back to the house just to get some.

As for Brooks' question? Weeks later, Preston still hadn't answered it. The papers were still sitting in the bottom drawer of his desk where Brooks had found them. He looked at them once or twice a week and had even addressed a yellow envelope care of Donny in New York, but he couldn't bring himself to send them yet. Why? He didn't know, and he truly didn't care to think about it.

He took another sip of beer and kept walking back to a secret garden, beyond the bridle path, in the rear corner of

Westerly that had a hidden hammock. It was a great place to be alone . . .

. . . unless your little sister totally ignored your warning and decided to follow you outside.

"You don't have to call Beth," said Jess, climbing next to him on the hammock and handing him a can of bug spray.

He sprayed himself quickly, then pillowed his elbow under her head as they swung back and forth. "I'm sorry I said that stupid comment about Alex shackling himself to you. He's the luckiest bastard in the world, Jess."

"I know," she said in an overconfident, singsong voice that made Preston chuckle softly.

They rocked back and forth in silence as the woods chirped and hooted around them, and the sun slowly set until they were alone together in the twilight. How many times had Preston and Jess rocked together in this very spot? A thousand, he'd wager. It was their favorite spot to catch up.

"I'll be nice to Beth," he said softly. "A deal's a deal."

And it was time to sign the divorce papers and send them to Donny. It was time to get back out there and start dating again. It was time to take back the heart that Elise had trampled. It was time to find someone else who might want it.

It didn't matter that tomorrow was the second wedding anniversary of his failed marriage.

In a strange way, maybe it was almost perfect.

It was time to start living again.

Chapter 13

"Folks, we're about to begin our descent into the greater Philadelphia area. Local time here is ten 'till nine, and we should be at the gate, oh, just a little after the hour. Please take a moment to lift and lock your tray tables, move your seats to their full and upright position, and buckle up. We know you have choices when it comes to air travel, and we thank you for choosing United. Have a great weekend here in Philly, the city of brotherly love!"

Elise Klassan looked out the first-class window. It was dark on the ground, but the city of Philadelphia sparkled like it had been painted with a fluorescent-orange highlighter. She wished she could appreciate the beauty of it, but her stomach clenched a little tighter with every inch the plane descended.

It was her first time back on the east coast in almost exactly two years. It was her first time ever in Philadelphia. Swallowing over the enormous lump in her throat, she wondered what the next few days would hold and prayed, with all her might, that she was doing the right thing.

Almost two weeks ago, her west-coast agent, Gene Miller, had requested a meeting with Elise to pitch a new part in an upcoming movie. She thought it would be another period piece or maybe even a guest spot as "the rambunctious

American" on *Downton Abbey* or *Selfridge's*, but it wasn't. Not at all. Not even close.

"Elise!" said Gene, standing from his desk to welcome her into his office with a hug. "My shining star."

She doubted she'd ever get used to all of the disingenuous hugging and air kissing and hand-holding in Hollywood. It didn't come naturally to her, and deep down it made her terribly uncomfortable, even after two years.

"Hello, Gene," she said, pulling away from him to push her sunglasses to the top of her head and smooth her designer linen sheath.

He gestured to a white leather couch, and she took a seat, accepting a bottle of Evian as he crossed his legs toward her.

"You look well," he said. "All recovered from *Grapes*?"

"I guess," she said. "It was a tough shoot."

"No one ever claimed that Steinbeck was cheery . . . but it's a career-maker, Elise. You know that."

A *career-maker*.

According to Gene, they'd *all* been career-makers.

After working with Gene on *The Awakening*, she'd segued right into filming a biopic of Consuelo Vanderbilt and followed it up with a supporting role in Woody Allen's *I Loathe You, Tijuana*. She'd planned to take a few weeks off then, but she'd been offered the role of Rose of Sharon Joad in a remake of *The Grapes of Wrath*. Unable to turn down the part, despite her exhaustion and increasing depression, Elise had accepted it and spent the ensuing six months in a simulated dust bowl on a Hollywood sound stage.

"A career-maker," she repeated tonelessly.

"What's the matter, princess? You seem down."

She *was* down. After four projects and twenty-four months in LA, she was so very lonely and so terribly tired.

"I think I need to take a break," she said softly, knowing that Gene would be upset by her reticence to take another part right away. She didn't want to upset Gene—he'd been very good to her. But unsupported and alone in the vast plastic pressure cooker of LA, her almighty ambition was running on fumes, and she just didn't have the energy to jump back into another project.

"A break? No, no, no, Elise! The iron's hot! Red hot! White hot! We have to keep striking, darling!"

She dropped his eyes, feeling an ever-present weariness surround her like a shroud. "Gene, I've given it a lot of thought, and I really think—"

"Darling, you're just starting to break through. Now is *not* the time to slow down! I'm your agent. I have your very best interests at heart, and I have an amazing part for you." He leaned forward, patting her thigh consolingly. "And it's not another depressing shoot, darling, I promise. In fact, it's farce! It's fun! Scout's honor."

Like Gene Miller had ever been a Boy Scout.

She eyed him warily. She had money and security now, and the reviews of *The Awakening* had been fantastic, but Elise had never been more unhappy. She missed the stage . . . she missed a live audience . . . she missed New York . . . and she desperately missed—

"Elise? Darling, you're so spacey today!"

"Gene," she said. "The reality is, I miss the east. I want to go—"

"Well, then . . . you're going to *love* this part! Hear me out?"

Her shoulders slumped in defeat as she twisted open the cap on her water bottle. "Go ahead."

"Drumroll please!" he said, his eyes sparkling as he did jazz hands in the air between them, "*The Philadelphia Story!*"

At the very mention of Philadelphia, she gasped, sucking a gulp of water into her lungs and launching into a full-blown coughing fit.

"Oh, honey!" said Gene, reaching over to thump her on the back and yank away the offending bottle of water.

Philadelphia.

She took a deep breath and wiped away the tears in her eyes.

Philadelphia.

"Are you okay, love?" asked Gene, fussing over her.

"I'm fine," Elise sputtered, clearing her throat.

"Fine? You're coughing up a lung, poor princess."

"*The Philadelphia Story*?" she asked weakly after taking two more deep breaths.

"Actually, they're calling it *The Philly Story*! It's a remake!" He nodded, his eyes sparkling and animated. "And you'd be playing Tracy! The star, darling! The star!"

Elise knew the original movie starring Katherine Hepburn and the musical remake, *High Society*, starring Grace Kelley. She'd loved both when she watched them in a "Reboots and Remakes" class at Tisch, and the idea of acting in lighter fare did appeal to her.

"And the best part since you're missing the east? It's being filmed on location in Philadelphia! Isn't that divine?"

In Philadelphia.

Preston's face flashed before her eyes, and she held back a whimper of longing.

"Divine," she murmured.

The door to Gene's office opened, and his assistant, Melinda, peeked her bespectacled face through the crack. "Mr. Miller, you asked to be alerted when Miss Rousseau arrived?"

"Ah, yes!" Gene winked at Elise. "The plot thickens," he said dramatically, rubbing his hands together with glee. "I'm going to say hello to Miss Rousseau for a moment, and then—as long as it's okay with you, darling—I'd like to introduce you to each other. She's local legal for this project in Philly, and I understand she was just given an assistant producer credit for a Very. Important. Reason."

"Yes, of course," said Elise, grateful for a few minutes alone.

As the door closed, she took a deep breath, settling back into the couch and giving her misery full reign.

Originally, Elise had thought that Hollywood would be a legitimate escape from the panicked, trapped feeling she'd had the moment she said "I do" to Preston, but it wasn't. Being apart from Preston had only magnified their love affair: forced her to review his persistent, patient courtship, his wholehearted devotion, his thoughtfulness, his tenderness, his love. Missing him so terribly kept the best memories of him on constant repeat, and by the time she'd been in LA for two weeks, she was starting to recognize the terrible mistake she'd made: it hadn't been in marrying him; it had been in leaving him before she'd given them both a chance to adjust to their whirlwind nuptials.

Except by then she'd signed the contract for *The Awakening*. She was on-set filming for twelve hours a day and trying to figure out her way around LA the rest of the time. For better or worse, she'd made her decision, and it was too late to change it: too late to go back to New York, too late to be Preston's wife, too late to choose her heart over her career. She'd told him as much when he'd visited her.

You're not happy here. I can tell. Come home, Elise. Come home with me.

You're *making me unhappy*, she'd responded frantically, *by putting this pressure on me! I can't be your wife. Don't you see that? I don't choose you. I choose acting. This is my home. This is my life, and you're not a part of it.*

So what was I? he'd asked tightly. *What were we?*

Lovely, she'd answered, watching his face flinch with pain, then harden in anger.

The moment the taxi whooshed away, she'd cried her eyes out, but the reality was that she'd already chosen her destiny, and it didn't include a New York-based husband who wanted her living with him back east.

In those dark days after he left LA, she expected divorce papers to arrive in her mailbox every day. After shooting, she'd come home to her rented bungalow and open her mailbox with trembling fingers. And every day that she didn't find a manila envelope with his return address felt like a reprieve and gave her hope. False hope, probably, but hope nonetheless.

Maybe he wouldn't stop loving her.

Maybe he loved her enough to hold on.

Maybe someday they would find each other again.

But then she would remember his face as he stepped into the taxi. His shattered face. His cold, green eyes. She saw hate in those eyes—or something close to it—and the memory made her want to die because his love had been the purest and best thing her life had ever known.

Days turned into weeks, turned into months, turned into a year, and losing Preston—something that Elise had willfully engineered—became the biggest regret, the biggest heartbreak of her life. But the more time that stretched between them without contact or correspondence of any kind, the more impossible it felt to address it, let alone fix it.

The night she wrapped up filming on *The Grapes of Wrath* and returned to her dark, quiet home without the distraction of an early call the next morning, she'd stared at the ceiling of her bedroom, the question circling in her head as she longed for her husband's arms around her:

You haven't seen or heard from him in almost two years. And sure, you've finally realized what you lost, but there's no chance he will ever forgive you for walking out on your marriage . . . so what now? Elise had no answer for that question, so that's where her internal dialogue had ended.

Since it was impossible for her to entertain thoughts of a future with him, her thoughts of Preston were confined to the past. With a perspective that came with time, Elise had been able to look at their courtship and marriage objectively over the past two years, and she'd come to fully understand her raw urge to run to LA when the opportunity was offered.

Two years ago, she simply hadn't been ready for marriage. She'd loved dating Preston, being his girlfriend, even living with him. And she'd been in love with him for certain, but she hadn't been ready to prioritize her marriage to him over her career. Her Broadway career had barely taken off. She'd invested years of her life—and all but severed ties with her family—in order to be a star, and it was finally on the verge of happening. She didn't need to be distracted by a hot, loving, thoughtful lawyer who wanted to give her the world. She'd feared him getting in the way of her ambition, or in any way interfering with her career. She'd almost resented the power of his love for her, and hers for him, because it was a weakness that could eventually jeopardize everything she'd worked so hard for.

What had confused things terribly in her head was that she had been more than ready to lose her virginity to Preston at the time . . . something her Mennonite conscience wouldn't countenance without a formal commitment between them. Most girls would have gone ahead and had sex with him as the next logical part of their relationship, but she wasn't able to do that. So when he'd proposed so romantically, she'd reviewed her feelings—*deeply in love, check*—and her ever-increasing desire for him—*scorching, check*—and jumped into matrimony without a sober review of her readiness to be someone's wife.

It made her profoundly sad to think about all of this, to realize that despite their deep love for each other, their timing had been, once again, epically shitty. Preston had wanted their marriage vows to suddenly mean that they had morphed overnight into this happily bound unit . . . whereas Elise was too independent and ambitious to let anyone, even her husband, get in the way of her dreams.

Two years ago, Elise Klassan wasn't ready to be Elise Winslow, and rushing into marriage had been a mistake.

Two years later, with the gift of time and perspective, what she wanted most in the world was another chance with Preston Winslow.

At some point, she'd realized that her career, which she'd always assumed would be enough, *wasn't* enough. Knowing Preston, living with Preston, coming home to Preston, being loved by Preston had ruined her for Hollywood, had ruined her for Broadway . . . had ruined her for anything that didn't include him. It wasn't that she didn't have talent, she did. She had work and accolade and praise, too. But she didn't have happiness. Her happiness, with her heart, remained with him.

Coming home to a dark bungalow after a successful shoot felt empty when she remembered the way he'd wait up for her after every show. Celebrating small victories on her own was so depressing, she had stopped celebrating them. Even praise for her work didn't matter to her anymore; there was no one to share it with her. No one to read to or sit with on long cab rides. No one waiting outside the sound stage to take her out to dinner or wrap his arms around her when she'd had a bad day. Without his support and gentle kisses, hard body and deep well of love for her, her success had become all but meaningless. It had been a hard two years of self-discovery and self-recrimination, and what she had realized, beyond any shadow of doubt, was that giving up Preston had been the biggest mistake of her life.

She was finally ready to be Elise Winslow . . .

. . . two years too late.

When Elise was so lonesome for Preston she thought it would break her, she would hike up into the Hollywood hills, find a quiet spot, and meditate. Most often, she'd close her eyes and think of her mother back on the farm in Lowville, imagining the advice her mother would give her if they had the sort of wise, loving, mother-daughter relationship that included long conversations about matters of the heart. Sometimes it comforted her. Sometimes it made her feel worse. But it always helped her sort out her feelings.

Sitting on the white leather couch in Gene Miller's office, Elise closed her eyes, focusing on her mother's face, and whispered words dropped from her lips:

"I still love him, Mama. I miss him awful. And I ruined things between us. Me. I h-hurt him. I pushed him away, Mama. It makes me ache inside to think about what I said to him when he came all the way out here to see me." Bile rose in her throat, and she winced as her eyes filled with tears. "I don't know how to get him back. I don't know how to say I'm sorry after all this time. I don't want to give up my career, but I would, Mama. Now I would. I hate it out here. I m-miss the stage and New York and I miss P-Preston more than anything because I was really happy with him, Mama. Really, really happy. I've made a mess of my whole life . . . and I just—I j-just don't know what to do."

Picturing her mother's weathered face, she saw her mother's eyes soften for just a moment before turning to gray steel. Her no-nonsense voice echoed in Elise's head:

Stop your crying. This isn't a stage, and as usual, you're making your life so much more difficult than it needs to be, Liebling.

You say you're sorry. You ask for forgiveness.
You talk to him. You hope he listens.
You offer honesty. You hope for trust.
You offer love. You hope that it's returned.
You understand that making room for someone you love isn't giving up something, it's getting something far better in return; it's the very core and basis of marriage. You each give up a little of yourselves to make way for something new, to make way for love, to make it work.

Say you're sorry.
Ask for forgiveness.
Talk.
Be honest.
Love.
Make room.
Make it work.

Opening her eyes, she was almost surprised to find herself in Gene's office, because a profound peace had settled upon her as she'd meditated. Peace. And hope.

Gene was literally handing her the opportunity to reconnect with Preston on a silver platter. She'd go to Philadelphia to work, yes, but she'd make time to look for Preston, find him, talk to him . . . and maybe—just maybe—she'd figure out a way to get him back. After all . . . legally, at least, they still belonged to each other.

Elise looked up just as the office door opened again, and Gene walked back in, followed by a stunning, dark-haired woman, whom Elise guessed to be about her age.

Elise stood up, taking the other woman's proffered hand.

"Jax Rousseau, meet Elise Klassan. Elise, this is Jax," said Gene.

"It's nice to meet you."

"You too," said Jax, with a smile that doubled her considerable beauty. "I loved you in *The Awakening*. Hey! Let's take a selfie!"

Surprised but charmed by Jax Rousseau's exuberant request, Elise nodded. "Sure."

Cheek to cheek, Elise smiled for Jax's camera and watched the brunette load the picture onto Facebook before they sat down side by side on the couch. Gene pulled up a chair across from them.

"So, Elise . . . like I said, Jax is one of the assistant producers on the project, and she's also our legal contact in Philly." He turned to Jax. "Want to fill her in on the rest of the details, precious?"

"I'd love it!" said Jax, flashing her million-megawatt smile and turning her whole body to face Elise. "*High Society* is my favorite movie of all time, so obvi I love *The Philadelphia Story* . . . when I bought the rights to remake a modern version and sold them to Warner, it was under the condition that all shooting would take place onsite at my family's estate in Pennsylvania. You know, my little way of memorializing my childhood home."

"Wow," said Elise, realizing that despite this woman's apparent youth, she was a mover and shaker. "I love it . . . but the rest of your family doesn't mind? Filming on location can be . . . intrusive."

Jax shrugged. "We don't actually live there anymore. My oldest brother recently relocated to New York. My twin sister and I have a condo in Philly. My other brother lives with his fiancé, but they're getting married at Chateau Nouvelle this winter, which is why we need to start filming right away. I promised Étienne and Kate we'd be finished by October at the latest."

"Chateau Nouvelle?"

"The name of the estate," explained Jax. "They all have names in Haverford."

Elise had been smiling in a friendly, encouraging sort of way, but at the mention of Haverford, she felt her breath hitch and her face fall. Her voice cracked as she repeated, "Ha-Haverford?"

Preston's hometown.

Jax nodded. "You know it?"

"No," she whispered, looking down at her lap and trying unsuccessfully to compose herself.

She *should have* known Haverford. She should have known Haverford very well, but she'd left before she'd given Pres the chance to introduce her to his brothers and family home in Haverford.

"Here's the scoop . . . well, wait. First, can you be ready to go east in two weeks?" asked Jax, breaking into her thoughts.

"She can and she . . . *will*?" asked Gene, raising his eyebrows and giving Elise a cajoling smile.

"Two weeks?" asked Elise weakly.

Only two weeks to figure out how to win back the love of my life after two years apart.

"Yes! Let me explain why . . . the daughter of our neighbors is getting married in September, but they're having this massive Main Line-style engagement party on July thirtieth. I mean, this is some serious *Great Gatsby*-style shit—er, uh, stuff. Anyway, I thought you could attend as my guest, Elise. It'll be *perfect* for research! And then you can stay at Chateau Nouvelle until filming begins . . . you know, become familiar with the house and neighborhood so you can really embody Tracy when we start filming on August tenth!"

"It's a great idea, of course, and I'd love the chance to settle into my surroundings, but won't your friends mind my barging in on their family celebration?"

"The Winslows?" asked Jax, shaking her head. "No way. We've lived next door to them for decades. Friends forever. They won't mind a bit."

Elise. Stopped. Breathing.

The Winslows.

Good God, it couldn't be a coincidence. Her hand fluttered up to her chest and covered her heart, which was racing like crazy.

"The Winslows."

Jax nodded. "Yes! Maybe you've heard of Brooks Winslow? The Olympian?"

Brooks Winslow. Preston's brother. She'd heard of him, all right.

Elise could barely breathe now, and she stared back at Jax in shock. *You're an actress,* bellowed a voice in her head. *Act!*

She wasn't sure how she managed it, but she offered Jax a confident, beaming smile. "The Olympian. Of course."

"And he has a gaggle of *gorgeous* brothers."

Yes, he does, thought Elise, sitting up a little straighter. *And one of them, technically, belongs to me.*

"And as far as I know? They're still single," said Jax, winking at Elise. "I swear you'll have a blast, and it'll be the perfect opportunity to do research!"

And get reacquainted with my husband, she thought, shock giving way to excitement.

Elise had kept that smile frozen on her face as Gene and Jax had finalized the details, but her mind raced with questions and possibilities and ignored warnings, her heart thundering with hope, hope, blessed hope.

A week later, she'd signed the contract attaching her to *The Philly Story,* packed up her bungalow, broken her lease, and shipped all of her belongings to a storage facility outside of Philadelphia. Returning to LA wasn't part of the plan.

She only had one plan and reviewed it in her head as she looked out the window, as the plane taxied to the waiting gate at the Philadelphia International Airport:

Say you're sorry.
Ask for forgiveness.
Talk.
Be honest.
Love.
Make room.
Make it work.

Eight steps. Eight steps that she would follow no matter what. Eight steps that would filet open her heart for Preston to take or turn away. Eight steps that would either restore her marriage or end in divorce.

Eight steps that suddenly held the balance of her entire life's happiness.

Chapter 14

Say You're Sorry

When the Winslows hosted large parties, Westerly was often called "the palace" by visiting friends and neighbors—possibly because Olivia Winslow was British, but more likely because no expense was spared and no detail overlooked. Every celebration was fit for royalty.

The light music of glasses clinking together was just a tone above the five-piece string ensemble that played Broadway tunes only loud enough to be heard, not overtake conversation. Tuxedo-clad waiters passed hot hors d'oeuvres, and waitresses in black cocktail dresses offered bite-sized desserts on gleaming silver trays to the three hundred or so guests in attendance.

At the entrance to Westerly's grand ballroom, Alex and Jessica received their guests, flanked on one side by Preston's mother, Olivia, and Brooks, and on the other side by Tom and Eleanora English, Alex's parents. Preston didn't envy them the long hour they'd stood there with perma-smiles frozen to their faces as they graciously shook hands with people. Briefly remembering his own impromptu engagement made his heart tighten and clutch—not that he'd wanted an event as lavish as tonight, but he'd never even gotten the chance to introduce his fiancée to his family.

Preston clenched his jaw, sharply ending his train of thought before it went any further, turning away from his little sister and back to the conversation between Christopher and the Atwell cousins. He had warmly greeted Beth and Constance the moment they walked into the ballroom this evening, and Beth had stayed close to Preston ever since. He wasn't unhappy to see her, and he didn't mind acting as her escort.

Frankly, Beth looked great. Her light-blonde hair had been cut since the last time he saw her, and the short style complimented her gamine face. He'd always gotten along with Beth—she wasn't especially fascinating to him, and his attraction to her wasn't off the charts, but she was amusing and she had a good heart. If Preston was actually in the market for a girlfriend right now, Beth would be a decent choice. It wouldn't be a high-maintenance relationship; he'd only see her on weekends, since she still lived in New York and he was based in Philly. It was certainly something to consider. Hell, he could ask her to stay over tonight, and they could slide seamlessly back to the place they'd been before . . . before—

"Pres? Help me out here! What do *you* think?"

Preston started, turning his glance to Christopher. "Sorry. I was miles away. What do I think about what?"

"So distracted tonight," said Beth, taking his arm as she looked up at him with a playful grin.

"How could I not be . . . distracted?" he asked, letting his eyes slip suggestively down the neckline of her dress and linger before returning. The least he could do was make an effort, right?

Beth's cheeks flushed. "Tease."

"Pres," said Connie, her voice annoyed, her eyes narrowed and shrewd, "Christopher needs to think bigger, don't you think? City Controller is nothing. It's a glorified bookkeeper. Chris has more ambition than that!"

"Ambition isn't everything," said Preston tightly. *It certainly doesn't always bring you happiness.*

"Here, here, Pres," said Chris, clinking his beer bottle against his older brother's. "And being the Chief Fiscal Watchdog of Philly hardly makes me a slouch, Con."

Connie Atwell pouted. "But you could be so much mooooore." Suddenly her expression soured drastically. "Oh, God. Weston English. Kill me now."

Preston looked up to see two of Alex's brothers, Fitz and Weston English, approaching the bar beside their small group, and Preston nodded to them in greeting. Bypassing the bar, the brothers headed for Preston and Christopher to say hello.

"Congratulations," said Preston, smiling at his old friends. "Alex is a very lucky guy."

Fitz chuckled. "No argument here."

"Where's your lovely wife tonight?" asked Christopher, shaking Fitz's hand.

"She and Molly just headed back to Haverford Park to check on Caroline. I'm sure she's absolutely fine with Susannah Edwards, but Daisy's a new mom. She worries."

"Well," said Connie, skewering her ex-boyfriend, Weston, with a glare, "luckily she has a *milkmaid* with her if she runs into any maternal troubles."

Connie was referring to Weston's current girlfriend, Molly, who had grown up on a farm in Ohio . . . and had solidly ousted Connie from her place in Weston's heart.

"Connie, you surprise me!" said Weston smoothly. "I wouldn't have thought the word 'maternal' was in your vocabulary."

Connie's eyes widened in fury, but she wrinkled her nose, glancing at her cousin conspiratorially. "She grew up on a *farm*. Can you imagine?"

Preston couldn't help the way his mind zipped back to the first time he ever walked Elise home. *We grew cows on forty acres . . .*

"*I* can imagine," he heard himself saying, cutting his eyes to Connie and letting her know that ridiculing Weston's girlfriend any further wouldn't be tolerated in his family's home. "There's nothing wrong with honest work."

Connie shrugged, an irritated pout back on her pretty face as she grabbed her cousin's hand. "Let's go freshen up, Beth."

"Oh, I . . ." Beth looked up at Preston, her eyes soft and apologetic.

"It's okay," he said, gently extracting her arm from his and watching as Connie pulled her away.

"Well thanks, Wes," said Christopher, taking a few steps over to the bar and ordering a double scotch. "Connie's all pissed off now, which means I'm probably not getting any tonight. Thanks. Really."

"You're not missing out on anything special," said Weston under his breath, and Fitz turned back to the Winslows and quickly changed the subject. "So! Have I been hearing rumors about you running for City Controller, Chris?"

Christopher nodded. "Though Connie thinks I should aim higher."

"Higher than the most important elected position in the whole city?" asked Weston acidly. "Stop listening to her!"

Preston suppressed a chuckle as his phone buzzed in his pocket. Palming it, he looked down at a new message from Brooks: *I need to talk to you!*

Looking over the heads of his mother's guests to the entrance where Brooks stood with Jess and Alex, he saw his brother shaking hands with two women—a blonde and a brunette—both of whom had their backs to Preston. From the rear, they both looked incredibly intriguing—one in a very, very short, tight, black cocktail dress, and the other in a thigh-length, very tight, blue-and-white dress swirled with flowers. He couldn't see their faces, obviously, but there was still lots to admire from this vantage point.

His phone buzzed again, and he glanced down to see the single word: *Now!*

Was this another plot of Jessica's to set him up with yet another eligible Philadelphia bachelorette? Or two? And had she somehow roped Brooks into helping her?

What's the rush? he typed, looking up again to see that the two women were now shaking hands with the Englishes. Preston watched as Eleanora English's face broke out into a surprised smile before shaking the hand of the blonde woman and leaning forward to engage her in animated conversation.

Suddenly the brunette turned around, and Preston realized it was Jax Rousseau, his next-door neighbor from adjacent Chateau Nouvelle. He had recently heard that Jax had joined a competing firm in entertainment law, though he hadn't had a chance to congratulate her yet . . . or tease her a little bit about stealing her clients.

"I'll be back," he said to Chris, putting his phone back in his pocket and making his way across the ballroom to say hello to Jax. As long as he was over there, he could find out what was going on with Brooks, too.

As he moved closer and closer, he caught Jax's eye, and she grinned at him, waving hello. But then suddenly, her companion turned around, and Preston froze in his tracks as all the air was sucked out of Westerly's ballroom. He blinked twice, wondering for just a moment if he was hallucinating. He wasn't.

The hot blonde in the tight dress was Elise Klassan.
His wife had just walked into Westerly.

"Remember those gorgeous brothers I mentioned?" asked
Jax, nudging Elise in the hip as she turned away from Eleanora English. "Brace yourself. Here comes one now."

And that was how Elise Klassan came face-to-face with
her husband, on the evening of their second anniversary,
after two miserable years apart.

He was still stunningly handsome, his hair as thick and
dark as she remembered, with that rogue curl still kissing
his forehead. Tall and broad, he looked like heaven in a suit,
and her fingers twitched, remembering how it felt to push
his suit jacket down his muscular arms and listen to it pool
on the floor. Gathering her courage, she raised her gaze to
his face, locking her blue eyes on his green.

"Pres," she whispered softly, breathlessly, working to keep
her face from crumpling or launching herself into his arms.

He stared back at her in shock, unspeaking, unmoving,
his face stony and unwelcoming.

"Wait a second! Do you two know each other?" asked Jax.

"We've met," said Preston.

Elise scanned his face—his beautiful face—that was so
cold and distant.

"In New York," she added.

"Oh! When you were on Broadway?" asked Jax, wrangling
two champagne flutes off a passing tray and handing one
to Elise.

Preston's eyes widened, then narrowed with disapproval
as she touched the glass to her lips and let the bubbles
tumble down her throat. In the movie *I Hate You, Tijuana*,
Elise's character had had an insatiable love of champagne,

and although Elise had never drunk more than a few sips, she had to admit it *was* delicious.

"Off-*Off*-Broadway," said Preston derisively.

Elise lowered the glass, her cheeks flushing as she remembered the humiliation of playing Matilda to half-full houses . . . and how Preston had come to see her not once, but twice.

"I bet she was still amazeballs," said Jax, leaning forward to touch her cheek to Preston's and ask about his law firm, which gave Elise a moment to recover as she studied him.

He looked so angry, so remote, nothing like the warm, open man she'd fallen in love with two years ago. It hurt her heart to realize that she'd done this to him—stolen the sparkle from his eyes and the warmth from his voice.

". . . film it *here*, so of course I thought tonight would be an *epic* opportunity to see the Main Line in action, and your mother didn't mind at all. She's always been the *sweetest*. Oh! Cort Ambler is here? Be a *doll* and chat with Elise for a moment, would you?"

Jax sailed away on a cloud of Dior Poison, leaving Preston and Elise facing one another in a veritable sea of awkward.

What the hell was she thinking, showing up here without an invitation? My God, how inconsiderate, how foolish. Her fingers trembled, she could barely breathe, and she had a sudden urge to thrust her glass at him, race across the ballroom to the nearest exit, and escape from this person who clearly despised her.

But first she had something to say to him, and she wasn't leaving until she said it.

"Pres," she started, barely able to keep her voice from breaking. "It was a mistake to come here, but I just wanted to say that I'm—"

"Leaving? What a surprise. That's your MO, isn't it?"

"No, I—"

Preston grabbed her wrist. "You're a guest of my mother's. And you've already caught the attention of almost everyone in the room. If you leave now, you'll cause a scene."

"Please let go." She let her chin drop to her chest. "I'm going to cry."

"No, you're not," he said in a cold, deeply irritated voice. "You're a much better actress than that, and we both know it."

She winced, but his words—said with such quiet disgust—were exactly what she needed to blink back her tears and raise her chin. "I'm *not* acting."

He dropped her wrist. "It's so hard to tell."

What had she expected? Understanding? Forgiveness? That he'd take one glimpse at her face, tell her he still loved her, and beg her never to leave him again? He'd already done that. Twice. And both times she'd walked—no, *run*—away.

Feeling utterly miserable, she took a deep breath and pursed her gloss-covered lips. "You look well, Pres."

"Thanks," he said, his face barely civil. "You look . . ." He raked his eyes down her bare neck to the swell of her breasts, lower still to the curve of her hips, then back up again. "*Lovely*."

Lovely.

The ridiculous word she'd used to describe their marriage before he left her in LA.

It hurt her just as much now as it must have hurt him then.

"Thank you," she whispered, refusing to break down in the middle of his mother's ballroom.

"I didn't mean it as a compliment."

"I know."

He flinched, tightening his jaw as he searched her eyes. "Why are you here, Elise? Why the hell would you walk into my sister's engagement party without—"

"Without?"

Preston looked around quickly, then reached for her wrist again, moving her hand to his elbow. "We're attracting attention. Come with me."

She tried not to think about the warm muscle encased in his dark-blue suit sleeve. She remembered what it felt like to be held by that arm, to feel it around her shoulders at the end of a long day, the hot weight of it slung across her bare breasts as she fell asleep beside him.

"Why the *hell* are you here?" he leaned down to whisper, guiding her toward a French door that presumably led outside.

"I'm shooting a movie next door, and Jax is producing it. She thought . . . I mean, she thought that coming tonight would be good research . . ." She let her voice trail off. It sounded so contrived and made her feel foolish and thoughtless.

Preston held the door for her, and Elise preceded him outside onto a quiet patio bathed in lavender twilight.

"Did you know whose engagement party this was?" he demanded.

"Yes."

"Then I don't understand."

Say you're sorry.

"I'm sorry," she blurted out.

His face, so fiercely angry, softened for just a moment before turning to stone again. He jerked his chin toward Chateau Nouvelle. "I'll tell Jax you weren't feeling well."

She gulped, scanning his face. "You're kicking me out?"

"This is *my* home," he said, locking his eyes with hers and throwing back the words she'd said to him in LA. "*My* life. And you're not a part of it."

"I'm still your wife," she answered softly, shocked by the words, wondering where in the world they came from.

His eyes narrowed and he scoffed. "That's a joke, right?"

"Pres . . ."

"That's a *joke*," he said more forcefully, taking a step toward her.

She stood her ground, refusing to be intimidated by him, tilting back her head to look up into his face.

Say it again.

"I'm sorry."

"Well, you can fix that by leaving. Now."

"No," she said. "I'm not just sorry for being here tonight. I'm sorry for hurting you. I'm sorry for leaving you. I'm sorry for . . . everything."

His breathing was so rapid and shallow, his chest almost touched hers every time he inhaled, but as she choked out the word "everything," she heard it hitch. She heard it pause just for a moment.

"Preston," she whispered, stepping closer to him. "I'm so desperately sorry."

His eyes were wild, dark, and furious as he stared down at her, and for one nail-biting moment she imagined he was deciding between kissing her or slapping her . . . and she honestly couldn't decide which one she'd welcome more. She longed for the first, but felt she deserved the second. In the end, he did neither. He stepped back from her, clenching his fists by his sides and flexing his jaw before looking up at her again.

"I don't need your sympathy."

"It's not sympathy, it's remorse."

He winced, his eyes softening again, the tension slipping from the thin line of his lips as he gazed down at her. Suddenly he blinked, as if rousing himself from a trance.

"I have divorce papers," he informed her, crossing his arms over his chest. "Can you come by my office on Monday and sign them?"

Her initial instinct was to say no. *No, I will not come and sign divorce papers, because there is no part of me that wants a divorce. I still love you. I know I messed up terribly, but I want another chance to be your wife.* But she knew that if she refused him, he would withdraw his invitation. And if she was going to ask for his forgiveness, she desperately needed the opportunity to see him alone.

"What time?"

His lips parted in surprise and his face fell. For just a moment, he searched her eyes before dropping them. When he looked up a moment later, his glare was as flinty as sharpened steel. "Ten."

"I'll be there."

"I work at—"

"Clifton, Jackson, and Webb."

"Y-Yes. That's right."

The door to the ballroom opened suddenly, and a petite, blonde woman in an elegant, very expensive cocktail dress stepped onto the patio. "Pres!"

He turned to the woman, stepping toward her and holding out his hand.

"Beth."

His voice was warm, and it sounded so much like the Preston she'd pushed away two years ago, it made her breath catch.

"I've finally found you." The woman laced her fingers through Preston's easily, and Elise could barely contain the acid-like flare of jealousy that made her want to scratch the woman's eyes out. "Wow! I recognize you! You're Elise Klassan. You were in that movie . . ."

"*The Awakening*," offered Preston, raising Beth's hand to his lips and kissing it slowly as he kept his eyes locked with his wife's.

"Yes, of course! That was it. You were marvelous!"

Elise slid her eyes from Preston's to the pretty blonde, forcing a smile. "Thank you."

"You didn't tell me you knew a famous movie star, Pres!" said Beth, beaming at him as he lowered their hands.

Preston's eyes didn't flinch from Elise's as he answered.

"That's because I don't . . ." He paused, staring at her intensely. ". . . *know* her."

Beth gestured to the ballroom, offering Elise a kind smile. "Won't you join us inside? I think Olivia's about to make a toast."

"No, I . . ." started Elise, but her voice failed her.

She was bereft. She was stupid and ridiculous and way too late. He hadn't waited for her. Not that she'd given him any reason to, but seeing him with someone else hurt like hell. Worse than hell. Like nothing she'd ever felt before. He had moved on with this woman, this interloper, this Beth, who, *damn it,* seemed genuinely nice. Elise's eyes burned as her heart plummeted.

"Miss Klassan isn't well. She was just leaving," he said, his voice oddly gentle after so much vitriol. "Weren't you?"

"Yes," she said, thanking God for every acting lesson that was helping her get through the rest of this scene.

"What a shame," said Beth. "Another time, then."

"Good night, Miss Klassan," said Preston softly, turning his back to her and ushering his girlfriend back into the ballroom.

Chapter 15

Ask for Forgiveness

Preston barely heard a word his mother or Brooks said, only clapping when the rest of the guests had already broken into applause, his brain buzzing to the point of aching and his heart beating so loudly it throbbed in his ears.

Once his brother had finished speaking, he leaned down and whispered in Beth's ear, "I'll be right back."

Hoping she would assume that he was using the restroom, he strolled out of the ballroom as casually as possible, accepting handshakes and congratulations on behalf of his family and exiting through a side door that led down a corridor to the back staircase. He quickly climbed until he'd reached the second-floor landing, striding down the gallery to his father's study, which his mother had kept preserved as a place for all of the Winslow children to find communion with their father after his passing. He slammed the door shut behind him and stood in the dark, empty room that still smelled comfortingly of cigar smoke even after eighteen years.

Clenching his fists together, he bellowed a sound somewhere between a roar and a sob, his chest heaving with the ragged force of his breathing. Finally taking a deep breath through his nose, he held it for a long moment before releasing it slowly and crossing the room to the bar where his father had always kept good scotch on hand. Preston picked up the crystal decanter, holding the bottle up to the moonlight that flooded through the massive windows behind his father's desk. The amber liquid sloshed around in the cut glass, the angles catching the light from Chateau Nouvelle next door.

Setting the bottle down unopened, Preston stepped behind the desk, sitting down on the window seat that looked out over Westerly's lawns and gardens to the Rousseau mansion . . . where his wife was presently in residence.

His *wife*.

His breath caught as he stared at the house in the distance, wondering what she was doing. She'd been on the verge of tears when he left her on the patio. He could see them in her eyes and hear them in her voice. They had almost softened his heart at the last moment . . . made him forget how she'd callously rejected him when he'd visited her in LA. Even now, his heart lurched with compassion and regret at the very idea of upsetting her.

Old and inconvenient feelings, he thought, turning away from windows.

She was every bit as beautiful today as she'd been two years ago—not as fresh-faced and far more sophisticated, he thought with a sad smile, but she was still Elise, and his masochistic heart had throbbed with love for her as they'd stood together on the moonlit patio. Over the past two years, he'd desperately wished for someone to unseat her as the loveliest woman he'd ever seen, but now that he'd seen her again, he knew it was impossible. He couldn't imagine being as attracted to another woman alive as he was to his wife. At one point, before Beth had interrupted them, he'd actually considered yanking Elise into his arms and kissing her wildly, madly, punishingly . . . for every torturous night without her, for every moment that he'd missed her, for every beat of his treacherous heart, wishing it didn't still belong to her.

Huffing at himself with disgust, he shifted his gaze back to his father's darkened study, remembering how quickly she'd agreed to sign the divorce papers tomorrow. She hadn't even hesitated, only asking him for a time and confirming where he worked. Huh. She'd known where he worked. Did that mean she kept tabs on him? His stupid heart leaped with pathetic hope, and Preston crushed it as quickly as possible. *Of course she knows where you work.* Asking *her* for a divorce was probably just beating her to the punch. She wanted her freedom. That was more than clear.

Pulling out his father's desk chair, he couldn't help thinking back to the last time he'd seen her in person (which excluded the six or seven or fourteen times he'd watched *The Awakening* drunk before banning himself from further showings).

After Elise left New York, she'd called him a couple of times, leaving him weepy voice mails even though he refused to answer her calls or call her back. At first, he'd been incredibly hurt by the way she'd left New York, abandoning their brand-new marriage. But as days turned into weeks, he'd had ample time to think about his whirlwind proposal, their forty-eight-hour engagement, and the fact that she'd not only gotten married, but lost her virginity in the space of an afternoon.

He could tell—both on their wedding day and on the morning after—that she had worries. She'd expressed some of them to him, but more than that, even, he'd sensed it. Her suggestion that they have a "marriage summit" to discuss their careers and futures had clued him into the fact that she was concerned about how their lives and careers would mesh. He knew how hard she'd worked to be where she was, and he truly celebrated her success; he'd never have willingly gotten in the way of it. The problem was that she'd been spooked . . . and she'd rushed off to LA, he believed, because it offered her a plausible escape from dealing with the challenges of blending their lives.

But what bothered him the most over those terrible, lonely two weeks was the fact that he couldn't remember one time that she'd told him she loved him after the wedding and before she left. He'd been so distracted by their engagement, taking the bar, their wedding, and finally sleeping together that at the time, he hadn't really acknowledged how much distance she'd put between them . . . or how much it indicated, proportionally, that she was freaking out.

So much that she hadn't even been able to give them a chance.

Angry with himself for not putting their emotional intimacy first, Preston had booked a ticket to LA, opting to surprise her with a visit and hoping to have a chance to really talk to her, reassure her, and get things back on track between them. He'd arrived on Saturday around lunchtime and taken a cab to her house, only to find it locked and dark. After three hours, he'd finally given in and texted her: *Here in LA. Can't wait to see you.*

The text had gone unanswered for three more hours when his phone finally buzzed at a nearby café with the message: *You're here? Why didn't you tell me? Still at rehearsal for three more hours. See you at nine?*

He'd been disappointed to have to wait even longer, but had returned to her house around eight o'clock, sitting on her front porch with her favorite herbal tea and hoping she might be earlier. She wasn't. It was almost eleven when she finally showed up in a cab.

But Elise's smile—her larger-than-life, beaming smile and glistening eyes—had suddenly made it all worthwhile. She'd hurtled herself into his arms, and he'd held her and kissed her, running his hands through her darkened hair as he inhaled the sweet smell of his wife.

"I missed you!" she said, drawing back to look at him.

He couldn't help but notice the dark circles under her eyes and the fact that she appeared to be considerably leaner than she'd been two weeks ago.

"I hated the way we left things," he said, searching her eyes for a sign that she did too.

Her expression had clouded for a moment, her smile faltering. She drew away from him, fishing her keys out of her pocket, then facing him again. "How long are you here?"

"My flight leaves tomorrow afternoon."

She dropped his eyes. "My call is at six a.m."

"Elise, we have to talk," he said.

"We have seven hours," she'd murmured, her eyes swimming with tears when she raised them to look at him.

"Call in sick tomorrow. You get sick days, don't you?"

"Not an option," she'd said softly, but firmly.

Her refusal frustrated Preston mightily. They'd had a scorching fight the day after their wedding that was completely unresolved, hadn't seen each other in two weeks, he'd flown all the way out here, waited around for eleven hours to see her, and she needed to go back to work in seven hours?

Putting his frustration aside, however, he looked at her more closely: exhausted and emotional, her bottom lip trembled as she shrugged her thin shoulders with regret and . . . and what? Defeat. She looked like she was giving up on something, and since it wasn't her career, it must be . . .

Them.

Desperately, he tried to buy time. "How about you sleep a little, and then we'll . . . we'll . . . talk."

"Okay," she'd murmured, and he'd put his arm around her shoulder as they walked inside her house.

Even now, sitting at his father's desk almost two years later, he could remember the feeling of despair, of frustration, of disappointment that had infused him as he'd walked into her house. It was as sharp today as it had been then. It hurt just as much. He'd felt her slipping away in New York, but by the time he'd gotten to LA, she was almost gone . . . and unfortunately, it had just made him try to hold on tighter.

And after he'd left LA? She'd never called him or written to take back the ugly words she'd used to push him away. Until tonight.

How many times had she said "I'm sorry" tonight? He counted at least three, plus she'd corrected his impression of sympathy as remorse. What was she sorry about? He considered her words: For hurting him. For leaving him. For everything.

Did she still love him? Could she possibly be here in an attempt to reconcile? His palm moved on its own to cover his aching, yearning heart, which was still desperately in love with her. He hated how much he still wanted her, how much he hoped that her work was only secondary to their reconciliation.

"Stop it. You know her better than that," he whispered bitterly into the darkness.

He did. Unfortunately, he did.

He knew her too well to let himself believe even for a moment that she was here for him. She wasn't here to reconcile with him. She was here to work, first and foremost, and secondly—it appeared from the haste with which she'd accepted his invitation to sign the divorce papers on

Monday—for her freedom. He could see her motivations as clear as day. She wasn't here *for* him. She was here to *say good-bye* to him once and for all.

Glancing at his watch, he realized he'd been in his father's office for almost half an hour, and surely Beth would be looking for him. Though he had no interest in spending the night with her anymore, he wasn't interested in hurting her feelings either.

He stood from his father's desk and crossed the quiet office.

Elise is here for work and a divorce, not for you.

Preston vowed to be cold as ice as he watched her walk away for the final time.

And God help me, this time I will let her go.

Being kicked out of Westerly on Saturday night had been unexpected.

Though Elise *had* expected Preston to be surprised and yes, angry with her, she hadn't expected the level of vitriol she'd received. Looks aside, he seemed like a totally different person from the playful, charming, patiently persistent man she'd fallen in love with in New York. Not to mention, with perfect *Beth* on his arm, it certainly seemed too late for a ninth-hour reconciliation.

After telling Jax that she wasn't feeling well, Elise had spent most of Sunday in her room, crying about what Preston was probably doing with *Beth* and hating herself for waiting so long to ask him for another chance. She thought hard to remember if she'd seen an engagement ring on Beth's hand, but she couldn't recall. Two things were for certain: first, with the papers all drawn up and ready to go, Preston was certainly eager to get a divorce, and second,

Beth appeared more than happy to take Elise's place as the next Mrs. Winslow.

She narrowed her eyes, whipping the covers off her body, and reminded herself that until they signed those papers she was *still* Preston's wife, regardless of *Beth*.

Crossing the guest room purposefully, she flung open the closet doors and pulled out a new dress that she'd bought to impress Preston. Likely something *Beth* would choose, it was a tailored, coral-colored Escada power suit with a peplum skirt that looked both elegant and trendy while still managing to be flirty. Checking the time, she had over an hour to do her hair and makeup and choose a pair of matching shoes and—

Holding the suit in front of her body and staring at herself in the mirror, she was distracted by the sight of her favorite jeans slung over the back of a chair behind her. She'd worn them around her room yesterday, and they looked worn-in and comfortable. In fact, they were the same ones she'd worn all the time when she lived in New York, when she'd fallen in love with Preston and he'd fallen in love with her.

She considered the suit for another moment before hanging it back up.

Tugging on the jeans, she plucked a sky-blue T-shirt from her bureau and pulled it over her head. While the rest of her figure had slimmed down, her breasts had remained stubbornly voluptuous, and the words "Keep Calm and Carry On" stretched across her chest, the little white crown a beacon at the valley of her breasts. She pulled her hair into a ponytail, securing it at the nape of her neck with a simple tortoiseshell barrette, and eschewed her usual makeup for a little mascara and a swipe of strawberry Chap Stick.

Looking in the mirror again, she almost didn't recognize herself. She looked awfully young and worried, but she also looked like her *real* self after playacting at "Hollywood Elise" for two years. She wasn't wearing sunglasses or designer clothes or a shopping bag full of Sephora on her face. She didn't look sophisticated or polished. In fact, she looked like a farm girl who had decided to stop playing dress-up . . . and to her immense surprise, it felt so good and so familiar to be casual again, she couldn't helping smiling at herself. In a strange way, it was a little bit like coming home.

"Hmm," she breathed softly. Since when was being a farm girl okay with her? Since when was it something she didn't feel the need to hide or conceal?

Her mother's voice, so frequently her companion of late, intoned, *Maybe since you stopped being so scared of everything.*

It was true.

She'd been so scared of leaving home and so scared to stay.

She'd been scared to move to New York City on her own and scared to pass up an opportunity to go to Tisch.

She'd been scared to turn down mediocre parts, and scared to stop waitressing, and scared to get her own apartment, and scared to date Preston, and scared to marry him.

And where had all of that fear landed her?

On a career path she couldn't stand, living in a city she hated, way too far away from the man she loved. She'd let fear rule her life for years. She'd let fear wreak havoc on her dreams. In a shocking turn of events, fear had turned out to be stronger than ambition.

But not anymore.

Taking a deep breath, she lifted her chin and remembered Preston's face that afternoon when he walked down the steps of the New York Public Library to find her waiting for him. That look of surprise. Of happiness and relief and . . . brand new love. He'd loved her so desperately even then. Had she any right to hope that she still had a place in his heart?

"Believe that you do," she said softly. "Keep believing that you do until he tells you that you don't. And even then . . . even then, Elise, hold on."

She swallowed over the lump in her throat, grabbed her purse and the keys to her rental car, and headed downstairs, praying she'd missed Jax. The last thing she wanted to do was drag her producer into her personal life or answer awkward questions about how she knew Preston.

As luck would have it, there were pastries on the kitchen counter and a note from Jax saying that she hoped Elise was feeling better, she was leaving for LA for the next three days, and she'd be back on Thursday. Elise was to make herself at home, ask the housekeeper for anything she needed, and call Jax with any concerns. Grabbing a cup of tea and a croissant for the road, Elise headed to her car.

As she drove into Philadelphia, Elise acknowledged that Preston had every right to be angry with her . . . and hurt . . . and cautious. She'd like to think that if she'd been less overwhelmed and more well-rested on that fateful LA morning, that she'd never have said such cruel things to Preston, but the reality was that after telling her that he understood and respected her fears, he'd all but demanded that she return to New York when *The Awakening* was over.

You're not happy here. I can tell. Come home, Elise. Come home with me.

He'd played into all of her fears, and in retaliation, she'd struck out at him, hurting him deeply, placing the sort of distance between them that she'd regretted almost immediately.

Clenching her eyes shut for a moment at a stoplight, she shifted her thoughts away from LA to the conversation that had preceded it two weeks earlier. Though many parts of that conversation had haunted her, there was one part that had circled in her head more than any others, keeping her up late at night, needling her, and making her second-guess her decision to move out to LA.

Preston had said:

As far as I knew, your Plan A never included Hollywood. You were already living your Plan A.

Reflecting on these words had helped Elise learn something significant about herself in the two years they'd been apart.

He was right.

She'd already been living her Plan A in New York. She was on her way to becoming a famous Broadway actress, which was the future she'd been working toward all her life. A career on the stage, with the energy of the audience feeding her performance and the lesser fame that accompanied a Broadway career allowing her to have a somewhat-normal personal life. Plan B—Hollywood—had *never* been her dream, though it *had* offered her an escape from the pressures of her marriage under the guise of drive and ambition.

Once upon a time they'd both had a Plan A . . . but Preston's had been ripped away, and Elise had done everything possible to kill her own.

Two years later, no longer blinded by enterprise, she knew what she'd had and grieved what she'd lost. She wasn't afraid of anything anymore but living the rest of her life without her husband.

She wanted her Plan A back.

She wanted Broadway.

She wanted New York.

But most of all she wanted Preston.

It was time to ask his forgiveness.

Preston arrived at the office at eight o'clock as usual, but wasn't able to get anything done. He kept glancing up at the clock, willing it to move faster, then slower, then faster. It was nine thirty now, and his hands were sweating as he fidgeted with two paper clips on his desk, unfolding them and then trying to shape them back into their original form. There were still thirty minutes until she arrived, but he'd already taken out the divorce papers, then put them away and taken them out again. Looking at them for just a moment, he swept them off the desk and shoved them into the top middle drawer just as someone knocked on his office door.

"Come in."

Preston's secretary, Nicole, opened the door and peeked in.

"A Mrs. Winslow is here to see you."

Preston frowned. "My mother?"

Nicole shook her head and opened the door a little wider to show Elise standing behind her.

Surprised, he sucked in a breath, rising to his feet.

In a shirt that matched the color of her eyes, with her hair in the same ponytail she'd always worn when he fell in love with her in New York, she was so beautiful and so familiar, it hurt his heart to look at her.

"Mrs. Winslow," he said softly, working hard to recover from the shock of the title she'd given his secretary. "Uh, yes. It's fine, Nicole. It's an old joke between me and Miss Klassan."

Nicole stepped aside, and Elise walked into his office, standing across from his desk as the door closed behind her, leaving them alone.

"What the hell was that?" he asked her, trying desperately not to drop his eyes to her too-tight T-shirt.

"The truth," she said, meeting his eyes.

"What *truth*? Being someone's wife is more than just saying a few meaningless words in front of a judge."

She flinched, then nodded. "Fair enough."

He sort of hated it that she didn't argue with him, but then he reminded himself bitterly, *Elise didn't stay and argue. When she was uncomfortable, she ran. A little more rudeness and she'd be halfway back to Chateau Nouvelle.*

"You're early."

"Is that okay?"

He huffed, the sound belligerent even in his own ears. "I was in the middle of—"

"I'll wait," she said. She searched his eyes for a moment, gesturing to one of the two chairs in front of his desk. "May I sit down?"

"I guess you're very eager to get to the business at hand."

She didn't respond to this comment, merely looked at him inquisitively, her hand on the back of the guest chair, still waiting for permission to sit.

Setting aside his surprise that she still hadn't run away, it occurred to him to *push* her away—to open his desk, hand her the papers, tell her to sign them and send them back to him via courier when she was done. But he couldn't help himself. Damn his weak, foolish heart to hell and back, he wanted this moment alone with her. Especially since it was likely the last he'd ever have.

He shrugged. "Whatever."

She pulled out the chair and sat down, the light, floral scent she still wore hitting his nostrils at the same time he fell back into his own chair. He loved her. Dear God, how he loved her. And how he despised himself for it.

"You were in the middle of something?" she asked, offering him a small, polite smile.

He swallowed past the lump in his throat, keeping his face impassive. "It can wait."

Elise placed her hands on his desk, one on top of the other, staring at them for a moment before lifting her eyes, and Preston realized that she was wearing the engagement ring he'd given her so long ago. They'd never actually exchanged wedding rings; he'd meant to buy them with her after their "marriage summit," but he'd never gotten the chance.

"I should ask for that back."

She didn't flinch and she didn't run. She just looked back at him with those deep, blue eyes. "It's been a long time since I've worn it."

"Why now?" *Just to torture me?*

She searched his face, then said softly, "I need to ask for your forgiveness."

Her multiple apologies on Saturday night had clued him into the fact that she was seeking peace with him. Or rather—in a leaner approach—he didn't sense that she was interested in making things worse between them. He'd been nasty to her several times before throwing her out of the party, and she'd taken it all without retaliating or running. And he might be wrong, but he sensed again, this morning, that she wouldn't rise to the bait no matter what he said to her or how much he pushed her. Her mission appeared to be peace between them, though he had no idea why. They didn't need to be on good terms to dissolve their marriage. Honestly, all things equal, he'd just as soon hold on to his bitterness. It was a protection of sorts. It kept him cold, and that made things easier for him.

"Is this a Mennonite thing?" he asked.

"How do you mean?"

"Pacifism and forgiveness?"

"I don't recall you knowing very much about Mennonites."

"I learned a little," he confessed.

After quitting his job in New York and whiling away his days feeling sorry for himself at Westerly as he polished off most the liquor in the mansion, he'd trolled the Internet for news about Elise or *The Awakening*. When there was none to be found, he'd read myriad blogs about life as a Broadway hopeful and about the Mennonite religion and way of life. It was all in an effort to understand her better, to try to understand why she'd pushed him away.

She raised her eyebrows in surprise but said, "I was raised in a culture of forgiveness, yes, so that mentality is certainly part of who I am. But this isn't just about my need for forgiveness. It's about you and me."

"There is no 'you and me.'"

Her bottom lip wobbled for the first time since entering his office. "Which is part of the reason I'd like your forgiveness."

"Why?" he asked.

"Why do I want your forgiveness?" she asked. "Because I left you. Because I didn't give our marriage a chance. Because I told you that you weren't a part of my life when you visited me. Because I let you believe I didn't care for you."

Did you? Did you care for me?

The words perched precariously on the tip of his tongue, but he forbade himself to ask, to sink to that level of humiliation—begging her for crumbs that were blown away years ago.

Suddenly he felt angry. He didn't want to hear her apologies or grant her some late-game forgiveness so she could walk away with a clear conscience while he tried to put the pieces of his broken heart back together. It was flaying him open just to be in the same room with her because the seminal fact remained: she was here to sign divorce papers.

Just get it over with.

"It doesn't matter anymore." He opened his drawer and pulled out the stack of papers, laying it on the desk between them, then placing a pen on top of them. "You don't need to say you're sorry, Elise. You don't need my forgiveness. You don't owe me anything."

She flicked her glance to the papers, then back to his face. "What I said to you in LA wasn't true. You asked what we were. And the truth is that we *were* lovely, Pres, but we were so much more than that. We were in love, but we were premature. We happened too fast, too soon. *We* frightened me."

"If you had stayed, we could have figured it out together."

"I don't think so," she said, her voice so melancholy it tugged at his heart. "At the time, I felt panicked. I felt lost. I ran toward something safe rather than staying somewhere that scared me."

He knew this was the truth. He'd known it on their wedding day. He'd known it the morning after. An epic night of sex had obscured it but not eliminated it. But she'd still left. She'd still placed her fears and career over him, above their marriage.

"Did you love me?" he demanded, the words just as surprising to him as they appeared to be to her.

"Completely," she said, her voice thready with emotion. "But it wasn't just about love. It was about our lives, my career, your career. I didn't know how to weave the two together. I didn't know how to share my life with someone, how to give up the control I'd fought for. And Pres, when you came out to see me in LA, I was still *exactly* where I'd been when I left you in New York. *Still* confused. *Still* frightened by us. *Still* running."

He flinched when she mentioned LA and felt his face harden. "Do you *remember* what you said to me?"

"I'm so sorr—"

"Do. You. *Remember*?"

She spoke slowly, tears streaming down her face as she recited the same words she'd said then, owning them all over again but with regret instead of anger this time. "You're making me un-unhappy. I can't be your wife. I don't ch-choose you. This is my life, and you're not a part of it."

She finished in a whisper, and Preston realized he'd been holding his breath as he listened, waiting for something—anything—to soften the pain of hearing them again, but the only thing he had ever wanted was her, and the papers between them proved she didn't want him.

Finally he dropped her eyes. He couldn't bear it. He couldn't stand to rehash the most painful days of his life in the name of granting her peace and forgiveness.

"Sign them," he whispered, pushing the papers toward her.

"Forgive me," she begged him, her voice strangled.

He looked up at her, at her beloved face slick with tears. "I can't."

She stared at him for a long time, her eyes soft and sad, beseeching him, then dropping to her lap.

"I understand," she murmured.

"You need to go," he said. "Please, Elise, just . . . go."

Without another word, she stood up, walked to his office door, opened it, walked through it, and closed it behind her.

Chapter 16

Talk

Just because you ask for forgiveness doesn't mean you're going to get it.

She heard her mother's voice in her head as clear as day: short on comfort and long on common sense. And really, it wasn't that Elise had *expected* him to forgive her, but she'd certainly hoped, and she couldn't deny it hurt her that he wasn't able to.

It had been three days since she went to see Preston at his office. Three days wondering if she'd hear from him again or if he'd send her the divorce papers via courier and be done with it. Well, he could try that, but she still wouldn't sign them. He was rude and belligerent to her on two separate occasions, kicking her out of his home the first time and out of his office the second. And yes, there was *Beth*, and yes, Elise's hopes of them getting back together were dwindling, but right now, for this moment, he still belonged to *her*. He was still *her* husband, and until they had a chance to talk—*really talk*—she wasn't signing anything, and too bad if he didn't like it.

Curled up on a love seat in the front parlor of Chateau Nouvelle, Elise dropped her glance back down to the script on her lap. She had seven more days to learn the lines, but her heart wasn't into the part of Tracy Samantha Lord, divorcée and second-time bride. A divorcée was just about the toughest role she could imagine for herself right now, and she sipped her late-afternoon tea with annoyance before setting it back down and looking at the scene she'd been reading. Giving up on it, she flipped to the back of the screenplay instead, reading the lines she'd already solidly memorized: the scene where Tracy and her ex-husband, Dexter, get back together.

"What am I going to do? I'll be the laughingstock of Haverford!" she said aloud, then read to herself:

DEXTER: Tell them the wedding's been canceled. Tell them it'll be rescheduled sometime soon. Very soon.

Elise gasped. "I can't. I . . . I *can't*. It's a lie. I'm not marrying George."

DEXTER: Don't you trust me?

"I do, Dex, but . . ."

DEXTER: Say "I do" again, Sam.

"I do," she murmured, her voice thick with wonder and gradual understanding.

THEY KISS.

DEXTER (shrugs): I will if you will.

"I will." She sighed, tears jumping into her eyes.

The ringing of the doorbell startled Elise, and she was so into the scene, it took her a moment to return to reality. Listening for Marie's footsteps from the kitchen, Elise waited for the Rousseau's housekeeper to answer the door, but all she heard was silence . . . and the doorbell rang again. Perhaps Marie had stepped out.

Placing her script on the couch, Elise headed for the door and opened it, gasping in surprise to find Preston Winslow standing on the Rousseau's front steps.

"Hi," she said, her face breaking into a beaming smile.

"Hi," he replied, his face annoyed.

She couldn't help letting her eyes roam over him—over his crisp, blue-and-white-striped shirt, silver cufflinks, and gray suit pants. Slowly she let her eyes travel back up his abs, his chest, his neck, finally landing and lingering on his lips for a long moment.

"It's good to see you," she finally said, raising her eyes to his. The heat she found there was unmistakable; he'd watched her slowly peruse his body and apparently wasn't entirely immune to her attention.

"You forgot to sign these," he said, thrusting a manila folder at her.

"Ah," she hummed as her smile faded. She turned and walked back into the house . . . hopefully leaving him no choice but to follow her. "Close the door, please. They keep it air-conditioned."

She heard the door close and click shut behind her and smiled to herself, heading back into the front parlor and resuming her spot on the love seat.

He stood in the doorway of the room looking uncomfortable. "Can we *not* draw this out any longer, please?"

She looked up at him with wide eyes, an idea taking shape in her head. "Oh, I *am* sorry, but you caught *me* in the middle of something this time." She waggled her script at him. "Learning my lines."

"Take a break."

"Can't," she said with a sweet smile, then looked back down at her script serenely as her heart pounded a mile a minute. "Have to learn them."

"So what am I supposed to do? Wait here for you to finish?"

"If you like," she said lightly. "Or I suppose you could help me run them . . . if you wanted me to hurry up."

"I don't have time for games, Elise."

"Do you have somewhere else you need to be?"

Thoughts of *Beth* swirled around in her head, and it took all of her strength not to ask about the woman who'd been handling her husband with way too much familiarity for Elise's comfort.

"Yeah. I have plans."

"Now?"

"In an hour."

She shrugged, feeling relieved (that he had an hour) and upset (that he was probably going out with *Beth*) at the same time. Refusing to let either emotion show, she turned the page of her script and quipped, "Then I guess I have about fifty-five minutes, huh?"

He huffed in annoyance, placing the file on a table by the room entrance and walking over to her. "Fine. I'll run your goddamn lines with you."

"Great," she said, standing and handing him the script. "You're Dexter. I'm Tracy."

"What is this?"

"*The Philly Story*. It's based on *The—*"

"*Philadelphia Story*," he finished, a very slight grin turning up his lips. "Dexter and Tracy. Sure. I love that movie."

"Me too," she said, smoothing out her pink T-shirt over her black cotton shorts.

"Where do you want to start?" he asked.

Her cheeks flushed with anticipation. "Top of the page."

He glanced down at the script. "Fine. Go."

Tracy Lord. Tracy Lord. Tracy Lord.

She stepped toward him.

"What am I going to do? Oh, God, I'll be the laughing-stock of Haverford!"

Preston looked up at her.

"Tell them the wedding's been canceled. Tell them it'll be rescheduled sometime soon. Very soon."

"I can't," she said, worrying her hands together. "I . . . I *can't*. It's a lie. I'm not marrying George."

"Don't you trust me?" he asked her, his green eyes searing as they captured hers.

She took another step closer to him. "I do, Dex, but . . ."

Preston searched her eyes desperately.

"Say 'I do' again, Sam," he whispered.

"I do," she murmured.

Preston's eyes dropped to the script, then lifted quickly. She heard his sharp intake of breath as he read the direction to kiss her, then felt the heat of his eyes linger on her lips before he raised his gaze. Suddenly he flinched, thrusting the script at her. "I can't do this."

She stared at him, unmoving, daring him to kiss her or smack her or grab her or anything—*anything*—to let her know that he still felt something for her, that there was still a chance for them. His eyes were distraught as they searched hers, furious then tender, confused, and uncertain, and she stayed rooted where she was, refusing to take the script back.

"Damn it, Elise!" he yelled, letting go of the script and turning on his heel.

As the book fell to her feet, she heard the front door open and slam shut. She didn't think. For the first time in the history of their relationship, *she* ran after *him*.

"Wait! Stop, Pres! Wait!"

He heard her calling after him, which only made him walk faster. He sped across the gravel driveway, over the green grass, closer and closer to the little white gate that separated Chateau Nouvelle from Westerly.

"Don't run away!"

"Yeah, sorry!" he yelled over his shoulder. "That's *your* move!"

Reaching the gate, he threw it open and strode through without bothering to relatch it.

"Talk to me!" she demanded from behind him.

He looked back at her red face, her hair escaping its bun, her little hands clasped into tight fists at her sides, her pink T-shirt and simple black short-shorts. And damn it, she looked just as gorgeous as ever.

"About *what*, Elise?" he asked, turning back around to stride through Westerly's gardens on his way back to the house. "What the hell do we have to talk about?"

"Us!"

He turned to face her and found her standing about ten feet behind him with her hands outstretched and fingers splayed open. Stalking back toward her, he felt a bit of satisfaction as she backed up three paces, looking at him with wide eyes.

"What *us*?" he spat. "There IS. NO. *US!*"

"There could be!"

"What the *fuck* are you talking about?"

She made a sound—a frustrated sound like a sob or a whimper—as she put her hands on her hips and searched his face with bright-blue, fiery eyes.

"First I need to know . . . are you an 'us' with *Beth*?"

"*What?*"

He was having trouble keeping up with whatever the hell was going on here. *You and me . . . us . . . there could be . . . Beth . . .* What was she saying? What was she trying to say? And what the hell did Beth have to do with it?

"*Beth*! Perfect *Beth* from Saturday! Are you an 'us' with her?"

"An 'us?'"

"Are you *with* her?"

"Why do you give a shit?" he yelled, looking down at her face, unable to ignore the intense heaving of her breasts under her T-shirt. His eyes slid from her chest to her face, which was even redder than before. "What the *fuck* do you want from me, Elise?"

She swallowed, wincing. "Are you with *Beth*?"

"No!" he roared.

Her eyes closed and she sighed. "Oh." She dropped her chin to her chest as her shoulders slumped with . . . what? Relief? She was *relieved* that he wasn't with Beth? Why would she . . . ? What was—

"Thank God," she whispered.

When she opened her eyes, he was still staring down at her, and he searched her gaze, finding it tender and soft, relieved beyond measure.

"Elise . . ." he said, feeling vulnerable and confused and immensely stupid for caring, but he couldn't help asking, "What did you mean by . . . *there could be*?"

Her eyes flooded with tears, and she opened her mouth to say something, but the words seemed to get stuck. Her tongue darted out to lick her lips, and it drew his eyes like a beacon, tightening his body with need and making him take one step closer to her, completely closing the distance between them. She inhaled raggedly, and her chest pushed into his, her breasts crushed against him as they'd been so many times before. He swam in her glassy eyes, searching them wildly, loving her, hating her, desperately hopeful for something he couldn't bear to even put his finger on.

His breath caught as she reached up, placing her palms on his cheeks, her thumb gently stroking his stubbled skin as she pulled him down to her and—

A loud guitar riff broke into the moment, making them both jump. She gasped, smiling up at him nervously.

"My phone," she said.

The Elise he knew would drop her hands now and reach for the phone, because nothing—certainly not Preston—was as important as her next big role.

"Aren't you going to get it?" he asked, remaining completely still as she held his face.

"No."

"Why not?"

She didn't answer.

The guitar riff played loudly twice more, and they waited it out, staring at each other intently. Finally it was quiet.

"Where were we?" he asked.

"There *could* be," she reminded him.

"How?" he asked.

She gulped softly. "Well, I—"

The guitar riff broke into the intimacy of their conversation again, and Preston stepped away from her, leaving her hands suspended in midair.

"As much as I want to know where this is going, you either need to turn off your phone or answer it."

Clicking her tongue, she reached into her back pocket and pulled it out, glancing at the screen. Her face, which was annoyed and dismissive, changed instantly. Her lips slackened. Her eyebrows furrowed. The guitar riff sounded again.

She looked up at Preston. "It's a 315 number."

"Is that LA?"

"No. Upstate New York," she said.

Where her family lived . . . "Answer it, Elise."

She nodded, swiping her finger across the phone. "Hello?"

At first her face was quizzical, then her eyes darted back and forth, blinking as though in disbelief, and she gasped. And then, as he watched, her face totally collapsed. It crumpled in agony, just as it had the first night he'd ever seen her playing Matilda, only this time, she wasn't acting.

"*What? What do you mean?*"

Her eyes, which had already been watery during their intense exchange, spilled forth, rivulets of tears falling down her cheeks.

"When?" she whispered, her voice breaking into a sob.

She placed her hand against her forehead, shielding her eyes, and turned away from Preston, her shoulders shrinking inward and shaking.

"No . . ." she keened. "*Oh, nooo.*"

Her breathing was jerky and ragged, and she made terrible, high-pitched little noises as she nodded her head slowly.

Finally she whispered, "*Ja, Datt.*"

Her arm dropped to her side, the phone slipping from her fingers and falling onto the grass.

"Elise?"

She turned around slowly, swaying slightly, her face a mask of despair.

"Pres," she sobbed.

Worry knotted his gut as he searched her eyes. Something terrible had happened. He knew it in his bones, and it made him feel sick with grief for her.

"What, sweetheart? What is it?"

"Pres," she said again, her shoulders shuddering from the force of her sobs.

He opened his arms and she fell into them.

Elise's mother had died of a stroke.

She had passed away early in the morning and was rushed to a nearby hospital only to be declared dead upon arrival. Elise's sisters had seen to her arrangements before their father had called his youngest daughter to inform her that visitation would take place on Thursday and Friday and the funeral would be on Saturday.

With Preston's arms around her, Elise cried her heart out, weeping over the loss of a woman who'd never understood her, who'd always been disappointed in her, who'd never accepted Elise's chosen path. The recent fantasy-confidant version of her mother aside, Sarah Klassan been a hard-working, no-nonsense woman who had raised Elise, fed her, clothed her, and held her hand when she was ill. Their relationship had been fractured and fractious, but she'd still been Elise's mother, and her loss—especially without forgiveness, peace, and understanding between them—hurt badly.

"Please tell me what's happened," said Preston, his strong arms like iron around her, holding her up, keeping her from drowning in her sorrow.

She sniffled against his shoulder, trying to catch her breath. "My-My . . ." She whimpered softly before continuing. "My mother d-died this m-morning."

Once the words were said, a fresh deluge of tears spilled from her eyes, drenching Preston's shirt. His arms tightened around her.

"I'm so sorry."

"It was a-a s-stroke," she managed, trying to take a deep breath and failing.

"Breathe, sweetheart," he coached her, rubbing her back gently.

"She's d-dead, Pres. My m-mother. She's go-o-o-ne."

"I know. I'm so, so sorry."

She whimpered again, closing her burning eyes and finally managing to take a breath that filled her diaphragm. Taking another, she held it for a moment, breathing in the smell of Preston's starched cotton shirt and familiar after-shave. Suddenly she realized how profoundly inappropriate it was for her to be crying all over him.

"I'm sorry." Stepping away, she wiped her eyes with the back of her hand, blinking up at him. "I have to go."

He leaned down and picked up her phone, wiping it on his pants before handing it to her, his eyes soft and concerned. "Okay."

Her gaze drifted to the wet splotch on his shirt. "Sorry for that."

"I don't mind."

She nodded, then shook her head back and forth as more tears sprang into her eyes. Her mother had been so disapproving of her career, her move to New York, Tisch, Broadway. *Stay here with me, Liebling. Don't go.*

"Elise."

Preston's voice broke into her thoughts, and she realized she was still standing on his lawn, weeping soundlessly, clutching her phone to her chest, atrophied in the midst of her grief. She looked up at him. *My mother is dead. My mother is gone. Help. Please, help.*

"Where are you going?" he asked.

"Home," she said. "L-Lowville."

He took a deep breath, releasing it on an "ahhh" sound as he nodded, his face somehow managing to be determined and uncertain at the same time. "I'm going with you."

"What?"

"I'll drive you."

Her face crumpled again, and she shook her head back and forth, staring at her bare feet on the grass. "N-no. You d-don't—"

He pulled her back into his arms, and she sagged against him, so grateful for his strength and kindness and the way she didn't feel alone for the first time in two years.

"Yes, I do. For now, you're still my wife and—"

"Pres," she sobbed.

He sighed deeply. "I can't let you go alone."

Surrendering to everything good that was her husband's arms around her, she rested her cheek on his shoulder, taking the comfort he offered. She thanked God that she wouldn't be alone over the next three terrible days and promised every angel in heaven, including the very newest named Sarah, that if she was given another chance with him, she would never, ever run away from him again.

Chapter 17

Be Honest

Preston had walked Elise back to Chateau Nouvelle, his arm around her trembling shoulders, and left her at the front door, instructing her to pack a bag.

"I'll be back in twenty minutes," he said. "And we'll go."

"B-But . . . your plans."

"I'll cancel them."

"I'm sorry."

"It was just dinner with Jess. She'll understand." He'd reached for Elise's face, forcing her to meet his eyes. "Listen to me. I know you're in shock, but I need you to walk upstairs and pack a bag. I'm going to go next door and do the same."

"We won't get there until after midnight."

"That's fine. You'll be there with your father and sisters in the morning."

She had started crying again, head bent, shoulders shaking, and Preston had pulled her into his arms again, clenching his jaw, wishing that he could absorb her grief, eliminate it, take it away. It didn't matter what had happened between them. He loved her. He couldn't bear to see her in this much pain.

Pressing his lips to her hair, he spoke softly. "Walk upstairs. Pack a bag. I'll be waiting."

Then he'd slowly lowered his arms and stepped away from her.

"Why are you doing this?" she asked.

Because I love you. It's as simple as that.

"We'll talk on the drive," he said, turning around and heading down the steps to walk back to Westerly.

Thankfully, Preston always kept a couple of suits, some jeans, and a few T-shirts in his room at Westerly, and unsure of the dress code at a Mennonite funeral, he packed a little of everything. Heading back downstairs to his car, he'd called Jessica.

"Pres, I'm running late. Can we make it 6:30?"

"I have to cancel, Jess."

"What? Come on! I'm already on the way to Westerly!"

"Sorry, it's . . ." How in the world could he explain this? *My wife of two years just walked back into my life, her mother died this morning, and I'm heading to upstate New York to attend the funeral with her.* Umm . . . no.

"It's what? More important than dinner with your only sister?"

"'Fraid so, Jess."

Jessica's tone changed when she asked, "Pres, what is it? What's happened?"

Preston threw his garment bag and suitcase into the trunk of his car and opened his door, swinging his body into the comfortable leather seat.

"How about I tell you when I get back?"

"Get *back*? Where are you *going*?"

And suddenly the words fell from his lips in a rush. "My wife of two years just walked back into my life, her mother died this morning, and I'm heading to upstate New York to attend the funeral with her."

He heard his sister's shocked gasp as he pulled out of Westerly's driveway and headed up the road half a mile to Chateau Nouvelle.

"Your—your—wi—"

"Talk to Brooks. He'll explain."

"Preston Downing Winslow, don't you *dare* hang up this—"

He pressed end, silenced the ringer, and placed his phone in the center console of the car as he pulled up in front of the Rousseau's mansion. Elise sat on the bottom step, her face tear-splotched and bleak, a rolling suitcase standing at attention beside her.

What were the words again?

Be able to forgive, do not hold grudges, and live each day that you may share it together—as from this day forward you shall be each other's home, comfort, and refuge, your marriage strengthened by your love and respect for each other.

Two years ago last Saturday, he'd promised to be her comfort and refuge, and until those divorce papers were signed, he intended to honor his promise.

They rode in silence for a while before Preston asked Elise if she wanted to listen to some music.

"I mostly have classical, but I have a little country," he said. "And jazz. I have some soft rock, too, or—"

"'Für Elise,'" she said softly. "Do you have that?"

"Sure."

He nodded, fumbling with his iPhone for a moment before the familiar classical music surrounded them.

Her eyes burned with shed and unshed tears, her heart throbbed with a strange mix of regret and gratitude, and her head ached, trying to understand everything that was happening in her life . . . and failing. Her mother was dead. Her estranged husband was driving her to her mother's funeral. It was almost too much for her to comprehend, so instead of trying, she closed her eyes and leaned her head back, remembering the morning, so long ago, when she'd woken up to find Preston in the kitchen listening to "Für Elise," and he'd asked her to move in with him. A lifetime ago. When they were happy. When he'd loved her.

"Elise," he said softly from beside her. "I forgive you."

She took a deep breath and opened her eyes, twisting her neck to look at him.

"You asked for my forgiveness."

She nodded, reaching up to brush a falling tear from her cheek.

"You have it."

"Thank you," she whispered, placing her hand on the bolster between them.

He covered it, closing his fingers around her hand and stroking the back with his thumb. "Tell me about your mom."

She took a deep, ragged breath through her nose, then released it slowly, willing herself to stop crying.

"She was . . . plain. Not totally, but close. She wore simple clothes. Jeans, mostly, or long skirts with long-sleeved cotton shirts. Always long-sleeved for modesty." She paused for a moment, picturing her mother, and a fresh stream of tears poured from her eyes. Unable to stop them, she just let them fall. "She smelled like soap . . . and hay. Sometimes like bread. Always like milk. Like fresh air at the start of the day before she started working. She liked hymns. Her favorites were 'Blest Be the Tie That Binds' and 'Come, Thou Font of Every Blessing.'"

Turning her face away from Preston, she looked out the window at the trees that blurred into a watercolor of green through the haze of her tears, and heard her mother's strong alto voice in her head: *O to grace how great a debtor daily I'm constrained to be! Let thy goodness, like a fetter, bind my wandering heart to thee. Prone to wander, Lord, I feel it, prone to leave the God I love; here's my heart, O take and seal it, seal it for thy courts above.*

Her mother had been unable to bind her wandering heart. *Stay here with me, Liebling. Don't go.* Elise had left and she hadn't looked back. She'd lived her whole life running away.

"I'm sorry," she said out loud. "I'm so sorry I ran away from you."

Preston's fingers tightened around hers, and she realized that her quiet apology to her mother applied just as well to him.

"I know why you left," he said softly. "I knew then. I knew that you were in over your head. I just . . . I just loved you too much to let you go."

"Pres," she sobbed. "It wasn't your fault."

"It wasn't yours either," he said. "You were scared."

"I just wasn't ready," she said, turning her head back to look at him.

He nodded, squeezing her hand again before withdrawing his fingers and swiping them under his nose. "I know."

"I thought I was. That morning when you asked me? I said yes because it was so romantic and I loved you so much, Pres. It wasn't until after the wedding that I realized how much we hadn't discussed or shared . . . I didn't know your family, and you didn't know mine. We hadn't talked about children or the future or Philadelphia or our career plans or what we expected from each other or what we wanted. I should have had more faith in us, but . . ."

"You panicked."

"I did." She sighed, reaching down for her water bottle. "I ran."

"You're good at running."

"I was," she said, taking a long sip.

"Was?"

"I'm not running anymore," she said, placing the water bottle back on the floor.

He jerked his head to look at her quickly, his eyes searching and uncertain, before turning back to the road.

"Tell me more about your mother."

Elise took a deep breath, not as ragged this time. "She baked and cooked everything by hand. She tended a garden behind our house and always wore a floppy-brimmed hat while she worked to shield her face from the sun. In the spring and summer, she dried our clothes on a line outside, and when it was really hot, she took us to a swimming hole beyond the fields, in the cool woods. She worked the farm with my father. She drank tea every evening after dinner. She called me 'Liebling' and still used some of the Pennsylvania Dutch expressions of her parents. She attended church on Sundays and led the alto section of worship." Elise smiled, tears welling. "She loved singing. I think she was happiest singing. Sometimes she'd share the gift of a solo with our congregation."

"Like you," said Preston.

"Not at all like me!"

"Like you," he repeated evenly. "Performing."

"It *wasn't* a performance. It was worship."

"It was self-expression," he said. "It was joy in singing. It was leading a whole section of worship or singing solo because she was talented and comfortable. It wasn't on a stage, and it was for an audience of one, but surely you see the similarities."

Elise furrowed her eyebrows, thinking about this. Was it possible that she and her mother had had more in common than she'd long thought? Sarah had sung to God, and Elise acted for millions, but yes, they both found pleasure in performing.

"What else?" asked Preston.

"She . . . she believed in discipline. In hard work and commitment. She didn't make excuses. She woke up every morning at five and attacked the day. Cooking, cleaning, milking, making pies for the fellowship group, mending clothes, knitting little caps for the babies at the hospital, helping my father on the farm. She took such joy in her work."

"Like you," said Preston again.

"No," said Elise, turning to him. "No, not at all like me. She worked on our farm. She worked for our food and our clothes and for ministry—"

"Discipline, no excuses, commitment . . . joy in her work? You don't hear yourself in that description? You don't see that you could just as easily be talking about yourself?"

"I . . ." She started crying again, sobbing with regret and for her blindness and for the possibility that she'd actually been emulating the woman she'd been so desperately trying to escape. "Pres, am I like her?"

"I never knew her," he said. "But it sounds like it . . . to me."

"But I never wanted that: the farm life, the small community, the—"

"It doesn't matter," he said. "We can't escape our past. We can't run away from it. It's in our blood. It's in our bones. You made a lot of different choices, Elise, but it was unavoidable that you'd create your own version of some of hers. Your mother was happiest performing, happiest working. So are you. You just took it somewhere else."

"Stop the car," she said.

He jerked his head to look at her in confusion.

"We're on the highway. I can't just—"

"Pull over," she demanded, because she had promised herself honesty, and she hadn't been honest yet.

He slowed down gradually, finally rolling onto the shoulder, stopping the car, and turning to look at her.

"I'm sorry for hurting you," she said.

"I've accepted your apology."

"Forgive me."

"I do."

"You understand why I left you?"

"Yes."

"Then this is the truth you need to know: I'm *not* happiest performing and working. Not anymore."

He searched her face, his brows furrowed, trying to understand.

"Preston, I was *happiest* with you."

He gasped softly, the muscles of his jaw clenching as he stared back at her in the dim light of the car.

Be honest. Be honest. Be honest.

"I loved you when I married you. I loved you when I left you in New York. I loved you when I pushed you away in LA. I loved you every moment I spent apart from you. And I love you now. Right this minute, in this car, on the side of the highway, I love you."

His eyes widened, shocked and distraught. His lips parted, and his hands curled into fists around the steering wheel. She gulped softly, reaching deep for courage, and continued.

"I'm not asking you for anything. I don't expect anything. But the truth is that I'm still in love with you," she said, "and I need you to know that."

Preston wanted to believe her.

With every cell in his body, he was desperate to believe her.

He'd dreamed of these words more times than he could count. They'd tortured him, giving him false hope, and imprisoning his heart in a cell of useless longing.

But her mother had just died.

And her history with her mother was fraught and unresolved.

As much as he wanted to believe her, he couldn't. Not right now. Not here. Not while her grief was a jagged, open wound and her high emotions could lead her to say things she would regret tomorrow.

"Okay," he said, managing to give her a small, reassuring smile. "Okay."

"You heard me?"

He nodded. "I did. Thank you for telling me."

The color in her cheeks deepened, and she dropped his eyes, looking down at her hands clenched in her lap. "Okay."

Part of him wanted to open his arms and draw her into them. Hold her, kiss her, tell her that he loved her too, that he'd never stopped and never would, that she was the girl of his dreams come to life, and no matter what had happened after, the day he married her was still the happiest day of his life. But he'd lived in daily, unceasing pain since he'd lost her, and he wasn't sure he'd survive it a second time.

"I think we should get going," he said. "We can . . . I mean, we'll have lots of time to talk. Over the next few days."

"Yeah," she murmured, looking away from him, angling her body toward the window.

He didn't know if she was hurt or embarrassed. Maybe disappointed. Maybe a mixture of all three. And he didn't want that. He didn't want to add to her pain right now.

"Hey, Elise."

As she turned to him, he saw that her eyes were guarded and uncertain.

"Remember on the steps of the library?"

She nodded, a small smile lifting the edges of her mouth for the first time in hours.

"Our timing was never good, was it?" he asked gently.

She shook her head. "It was always shit."

He smiled back at her, letting the tenderness he felt for her soften his eyes. "I promise we'll figure it out. Okay?"

The strain on her face eased, and she nodded again. "Okay."

She turned back to the window, and he started driving again, but there was a tension thick between them now that hadn't accompanied them before, and with "Für Elise" long finished, the car was dark and quiet as they left Pennsylvania behind and crossed into New York state.

I'm not asking you for anything. I don't expect anything. But the truth is that I'm still in love with you, and I need you to know that.

The words circled in Preston's head as he drove on through the darkening night, the red-and-white lights of cars ahead of him and behind him streaking the highway.

I was happiest with you . . . I'm still in love with you.

His heart clenched with a hope that he'd barely dared to dream of, and he felt a growing lightness in his soul for the first time in years. Was it possible that their epically bad luck with timing had been the ultimate saboteur and not their feelings for each other? Was it possible that their feelings had been pure and true, only obscured by life's demands and expectations and pressures? God, he hoped so.

And yet . . . he wasn't actually sure where they could go from here. Resume a marriage that had never started? Start a marriage that had barely been born? How? She was a Hollywood actress. He was a Philadelphia lawyer. And if memory served, neither was very good at compromise.

Don't let go of your heart yet, his head warned, remembering the dark days of drunken rages at Westerly as he wallowed in self-pity, suffering over her rejection and desperately missing his wife. *You can't leap before looking this time. You must be smarter and more careful.*

Preston was fairly certain that Elise was asleep, so it startled him when she said, "I made a terrible mess of things. My mother would be so disappointed in me."

Without a thought, he lifted his hand and held it out to her, his heart fisting with gratitude when she clasped it, lacing her fingers through his and resting both on her thigh.

"The thing is," he said gently, "it's never too late to make the right choices."

"Do you mean that?" she asked, her voice breathy and tired.

"I do."

She lifted their joined hands to her lips and pressed a long, soft kiss to the back of his hand before resettling them on her lap.

"I love you," she whispered, leaning her head against the window and closing her eyes.

I love you too, he thought. *But love was never our problem.*

Chapter 18

Love

"Elise . . . Elise, wake up. We're here. Elise . . ."

It was Preston's voice, which meant she was dreaming, because she hadn't seen her strong, beautiful, tender husband since she'd pulled his heart out of his chest on a chilly Los Angeles morning and ripped it in half.

"Sweetheart," he intoned, low and close to her ear, "wake up."

Keeping her eyes tightly closed, she turned her face toward his voice, and the bristles of his beard skimmed her cheek.

"Oh, Pres," she sobbed softly. "I need you so much."

"I'm here," he said, his lips moving against her cheek. "I'm right here. Come on. Let's get you inside."

It took effort to open her aching eyes, but when she did, Preston was standing beside her, leaning into the passenger side of the car, and relief flooded her body, making her sag against the car seat. He was here. He wasn't a dream.

He leaned over her body and unlatched her seat belt, offering her his hand.

"Come on. I got us a room. You need some sleep, sweetheart."

She looked up at him, disoriented, her eyes focusing on his face lit up by the interior light of the car. Suddenly it hit her like a punch to the throat.

"My mother."

He nodded, taking her hands and pulling her from the seat.

Taking a shaky breath, she settled her feet on a gravel driveway and looked around. "Where are we?"

"The Blowin' Wind Motor Lodge."

"I don't know it," she said, glancing around at the unfamiliar, one-story, roadside motel.

"We're just outside of Lowville," he said. "Your bag's in the room. Come on."

Putting his arm around her waist, he helped her toward the door that creaked as he opened it. She stepped inside, taking in the wood paneling and shabby, olive-green carpet. There were two beds covered with navy-blue, flowered bedspreads and a TV from the 1980s on a scratched bureau. An air conditioner under a window that looked out at the parking lot hummed noisily, and a fluorescent brightness in the far corner of the room indicated the bathroom. A north-country motel room. She'd know one anywhere.

Releasing her waist, Preston closed and locked the door behind her, and then hoisted her suitcase on top of the bureau.

"Do you want the left or right?"

"What?" she asked, still half asleep.

"Do you want the bed closest to the door or closest to the bathroom?"

"Bathroom, I guess," she said, taking a few steps into the room and sitting on the edge of her bed.

Wringing her hands in her lap, she wondered what time it was. How much time did she have before she had to see her father and sisters, all of whom disapproved of her life, all of whom knew that she'd had no closure with her mother?

Suddenly Preston squatted down before her, his palms comforting on her knees, his tired, green eyes looking up into hers.

"Do you want to change?"

She shook her head.

"Use the bathroom?"

Her lip quivered with sadness, and she blinked back a fresh onslaught of tears as she shook her head again.

"*Elise*," he whispered. "*Please* tell me what I can do to help you."

There was only one thing she wanted. Only one thing she needed.

"Hold me."

His face looked sad, but he nodded.

Standing up, he killed the overhead light by yanking on a pull cord and closed the bathroom door until it was only open a crack. Elise leaned back onto the bed, scooching up until her head found a bedspread-covered pillow. As Preston's knee depressed the bed to her left, she rolled toward him, pressing her body against his chest as his arms came around her.

Closing her eyes, she leaned her weary forehead against his strong chest, surrounded by the comforting, beloved smell of him, and cried herself to sleep.

Eventually he felt her sobs and shudders subside until she settled into a deep and even sleep, curled into him, her fists unfurling under her chin and her breasts pushing against his chest with every breath she took.

I love this woman, he thought. *I love her more than anything.*

And yet, whispered his heart, *you did nothing to hold on to her.*

I did! he thought indignantly. *I asked her to stay. I visited her.*

You pressured her, said the whisper. *You threatened her future. You made her choose. She chose safety. She chose her dream, but you forced her hand.*

What else could I have done? he demanded.

You could have joined her. You could have been patient with her. You could have understood that the woman you married loved her career, and making her choose between it and you was a losing battle.

She should have chosen me, he thought. *She should have loved me enough to choose me.*

Maybe you should have loved her enough not to make her choose.

Preston took a deep breath, nuzzling her hair and drawing her as close as possible. For so long he'd laid the blame at Elise's feet, his anger and self-pity fueling his grudge against her. But now he tried to look at it from a different angle.

Had he forced her to choose? Had he married a woman deeply devoted to her career only to try to wedge himself between her and her dreams on the very first day of their marriage?

What if he had celebrated her opportunity in LA and planned to visit her every other weekend during that first movie? What if he had offered to relocate to LA to be closer to her? He could have taken the California bar eventually. For so long he'd thought that he was the one ready for marriage and she was the one who got spooked and ran. But in his own way, Preston hadn't been ready either . . . because he hadn't been ready to compromise or bend or respect the very drive in her that had so attracted him in the first place.

More words from his wedding ceremony circled in his head:

Preston and Elise, as the two of you come into this marriage uniting you as husband and wife, and as you this day affirm your faith and love for one another, I would ask that you always remember to cherish each other as special and unique individuals.

She *was* special and unique. She was a Mennonite farm girl who'd gotten a scholarship to a prestigious Manhattan drama school, who'd made it to Broadway on her own merit and then to Hollywood. And instead of supporting her dreams and encouraging her to spread her wings, his first order of business as her husband had been to try to clip them.

No wonder she'd run.

No wonder she'd been spooked.

He'd become the very thing she'd most feared—someone who didn't respect her ambition. Someone who threatened her dreams.

What kind of love is that? he asked himself.

She whimpered in her sleep, and Preston felt a hot tear slip from the corner of his eye and slide onto the pillow.

"I can do better," he whispered, pressing his lips to her head again. "I promise, sweetheart. I can do better."

She sighed, flattening her hands against his chest, and Preston closed his eyes, his arms tight around his wife as he drifted off to sleep.

Elise woke up alone on Thursday morning, still fully dressed in her pink T-shirt and black shorts, her comforter wrapped around her body as steam wafted out of the motel bathroom. She knew where she was and who she was with, and had woken up with the heaviness of grief as her companion. Today was the first of two "Visiting" days when members of their church community would be stopping by her parents' farm in a steady stream with food, to give comfort and company, pray together, and remember Sarah Klassan with her family.

It would be a long two days, ending with her mother's funeral on Saturday morning led by the elders of her parents' church.

She needed to shower after Preston and get dressed. She'd brought two dark-colored maxi dresses and a black cardigan sweater. Her family's community didn't wear traditional Mennonite clothes, but modesty—for both men and women—was still expected.

As she sat up, the bathroom door opened, and Preston appeared in the doorway, a towel wrapped around his waist, and despite the fact that her heart was heavy, she'd have to be catatonic not to note that Preston's pectoral and abdominal muscles hadn't lost a shred of definition in their two years apart. If anything, he appeared even harder-bodied than before. She suppressed a whimper as almost-forgotten muscles deep inside her body clenched.

"Good morning," she said, finally lifting her eyes to his face.

A small smile played on the edges of his lips. "How are you?"

"Sad. Tired." She cocked her head to the side and managed a very small grin for him. "Grateful for you."

"I don't know what to wear," he said.

"Jeans. And a nice shirt. Dark pants and a nice shirt on Saturday. We're not fancy."

"*We're* not fancy," he said, raising an eyebrow.

"What?"

"When I first met you, you would have said, '*They're* not fancy.' You wouldn't have included yourself."

He was right. "That's true. But this is a part of me whether I like it or not."

"Of course it is," he said.

"And so is New York."

"Yep."

"And Hollywood."

He nodded at her.

"And you."

"Yes," he said, "I am."

"Is it okay if I call you my husband over the next few days? They won't understand if I show up with a man who isn't—"

"Of course you can call me your husband." He crossed from the bathroom doorway to the foot of her bed, sitting gingerly on the edge and holding her eyes. "That's who I am."

Her eyes swam with tears, and she dropped her head, hunching her shoulders as her chin rested on her chest. His words were such nourishment to her starving heart, such a balm to her aching soul.

Reaching for her hand, he wound his fingers between hers and tugged a little, pulling her to him and enfolding her in his arms. She rested her cheek on his bare shoulder and closed her eyes, inhaling his smell—soap and warm water and clean man. Her lips rested close to the pulse in his throat, and she imagined leaning forward to kiss it, pressing her lips against his life force and lingering there.

"I love you," she whispered instead. "Thank you for being here with me."

"There's nowhere else I want to be."

His arms tightened for a moment before he slid them slowly down her back and pulled away. He stood up and turned away, and Elise watched him bend over his suitcase, wondering if he would ever be able to return the words . . . if there was still room in his heart to love her. She hoped so.

An hour later, she and Preston pulled up in front of her family home, the Klassan farm, where several pickup trucks were parked, and people were already gathered on the front porch. Not having been home during the two years she'd been in Los Angeles, Elise had no idea what to expect. Certainly she didn't deserve a warm or effusive greeting, which is why—when her father leapt up from his rocking chair and jumped down the porch steps to embrace her—she lost control of the hard-won composure she'd finally found while showering and dressing.

"Elise," he said, cradling her face in his rough, weather-beaten hands. "Elise, *mein Liebling*. You've come home."

As he clutched her to his chest, Elise broke down in tears yet again, letting go of Preston's hand and embracing her father—the prodigal daughter who had finally returned. She wept for their estrangement, which had been tense but never bitter. She wept for her mother's loss and for her father's strong, tan arms holding her. She wept because he welcomed her and loved her, and for so long she had pushed those she loved away, uncertain of how to live the life she wanted and include the people she loved. She wept because she was finally starting to figure it out . . . and it was too late for her mother, and she only prayed it wasn't too late for Preston.

"And who's this?" asked her father, finally noting the man behind her who looked wildly out of place in his designer jeans and crisp, yellow dress shirt.

"*Datt*," she said, releasing her father and reaching for Preston's hand. "This is Preston Winslow. My husband."

Hans Klassan stared at Preston with hard eyes.

"You married our Elise?"

"I did, sir."

"Officially?"

"Yes, sir."

"In a church?"

"No, sir. It was a civic ceremony."

"When?"

"Two years ago last Saturday, sir."

Her father flinched, cutting his eyes to Elise, and she bit her lip to keep herself from crying more. He was hurt that she hadn't told them, hadn't included them, hadn't given her mother a chance to know her husband. And her regret—already profound—increased.

"Preston?"

"Yes, sir."

"Where are you from, Preston?"

"Pennsylvania, sir."

"Ah! We know many faithful in Pennsylvania."

"I'm not Mennonite, sir."

"No? No. You don't look simple."

"I'm Lutheran."

"Lutheran. Humph."

Elise's oldest sister, Abby, who'd been watching this unusual introduction, stepped off the porch and tapped her father on the shoulder. "The Lutherans and Mennonites have reconciled, *Datt*."

Elise watched as her father—somewhat cautiously—held out his hand and offered Preston a firm handshake.

"Take Elise to your Lutheran Church with you. She is too long away from *Gott*."

"I'll do my best for her, sir," said Preston, reaching for Elise's hand and lacing their fingers together.

Stepping forward onto the porch, Elise introduced him to her sisters and their husbands, and the many neighbors and church members visiting.

The rest of the day was full of stories about her mother, tearful prayers, and finding room in the farmhouse refrigerator for the dozens of casseroles that arrived in a never-ending stream. Like Elise, her sisters drifted seamlessly between tears and laughter, remembering the many sayings of their mother, swapping stories and reminding each other of almost-forgotten laugh-out-loud moments.

As the sun started to set, Elise helped her sisters, Caitlyn and Lillian, straighten up the kitchen, giggling as Caitlyn swatted Lillian on the butt while she swept the floor.

"Elise," called Abby from the doorway.

She turned to look at her sister.

"Come with me."

Elise placed her dish towel on the counter and followed Abby through the living room and up the stairs to their mother's room. It had been years since Elise had entered her mother's room, and her eyes burned as she inhaled deeply, smelling her mother, picturing her here, even hearing her hum one of her favorite hymns as she got ready for church on a Sunday morning.

Abby sat down on the bed and patted the simple, handmade bedspread. "Sit with me."

Sitting beside her sister, Elise wondered what was going on.

Reaching under their mother's pillow, Abby pulled out a binder and placed it gently in her younger sister's lap.

Elise searched her sister's face, but finding no answers, she opened the three-ring binder, surprised to find a *New York Times* clipping about her very first show at Tisch carefully glued to a plain piece of white paper. Flipping the page, she found another clipping and another with a picture of Elise as Cordelia in *King Lear*. She found a Playbill from *Ethan Frome* and a small article from *USA Today* about *The Awakening*. Her vision was blurred from tears, so she closed the binder carefully as she looked up at Abby.

"She was so proud of you," said her sister, placing one hand on top of the binder and swiping away tears with another. "She just didn't know how . . ."

"She followed my whole career. She knew everything I was doing. She . . . she . . ."

"She loved you," said Abby, smiling through tears. "Her littlest. Her *Liebling*."

"Oh, Abby," wailed Elise, reaching for her sister and clasping her as tightly as she could. "I didn't know. I didn't know. I didn't know . . ."

They held each other for a long time, crying on each other's shoulders, united in grief, surrounded by the love of a mother who couldn't share her approval in life, but had left behind the evidence that would assure her *Liebling* peace when she was gone.

Chapter 19

As Preston drove Elise back to the motel, he sensed a difference in her, and he suspected it had something to do with the simple black binder on her lap. But she would share it with him when she was ready. He was finished pushing and pressuring her. One thing he had learned about his wife . . . when he pushed, she ran. When he gave her space, she'd come and find him. He just wished he'd learned that lesson two years ago.

"I liked your family," he said. "They weren't what I expected."

She turned to him, a tired but contented smile playing on her face. "What did you expect?"

"I think I expected them to be more . . . I don't know. Disapproving. Strict and cold."

"That's because of how I talked about them," she said softly. "I led you to believe that."

He didn't argue with her, and she knew she was right.

"I was so desperate to break away. I was so frightened of anything or anyone standing in my way. I went about it badly," she said, and Preston saw clearly that what she was describing had happened twice in her life: once with her family and again with him. "My mother kept this binder, Pres. It's clippings about the shows I was in at Tisch, and off-off-Broadway. *Ethan Frome* and the movies I shot in Hollywood. She was following my career the whole time. Abby said she was proud of me."

Preston turned into the motel parking lot and cut the engine. "Of course she was."

"But I truly *thought* she was disapproving, strict, and cold. Why couldn't she have *told* me she was proud of me? Why couldn't she have supported me?"

"I don't know," said Preston. "I didn't know her."

"It would have meant the world to me." She paused, smoothing her hands over the plain, black binder cover. "And yet, I'm so grateful to know it now. I never believed I'd find closure, Pres. I thought I'd grieve her forever, and you know? I will, but at least I know she loved me. At least I know she was proud of me. At least I know she was watching."

"I'm glad for that," he said, reaching out to cup her cheek.

"You made today bearable," she said, leaning into his hand. "Thank you for being here with me."

She was so beautiful, her eyes wide and open as they stared back at him with a world-weariness and maturity that seemed so much deeper than the girl he'd met in an off-off-Broadway dressing room two years ago. She had changed a lot, and though it frightened him to hope, he couldn't help the words that tumbled from his mouth as he stared at her.

"I don't want a divorce."

"Neither do I," she said, shaking her head, her smile suddenly brilliant. "I never did."

"Really?"

"Really. I came back east to reconcile with you, Pres. I never wanted to let you go. I just needed time."

She sniffled, and he swiped at an escaping tear with his thumb. He tried to hold on to his smile, but it faded as he furrowed his brows together. "But I still don't know how to be married to you. I don't know how to make us work."

"If I tell you that we'll figure it out this time, will you believe me?"

"I want to," he said.

"Anything's possible," she said, "where there's love."

"There's love here," he said, holding her eyes, feeling the risk of saying more and silencing the declaration that threatened to break free.

She smiled at him, covering his hand with hers. "Come lie down with me?"

He nodded, letting his hand linger on her face for an extra moment before dropping it, leaving the car, and following her into the motel room.

As he closed the door behind them, Elise turned to look at him. "Can I ask you something?"

He nodded as he unbuttoned his cuffs, rolling up his sleeves and removing his watch.

"I won't blame you, and I won't judge you. I just need to know . . ."

"Anything," he said, placing the watch on the table by the door and slipping out of his shoes. He was tired, and holding her as they fell asleep sounded like the perfect way to end a long day.

She swallowed, dropping his eyes, her chest heaving as her breathing became faster and more shallow. His first instinct was to reach for her, but it was more important to give her the space she needed to stay and move, to speak and be silent, to live at her own pace, not at his.

When she lifted her eyes, they were clear but cautious, and still he waited, patient, though increasingly anxious.

"How many . . ." She paused, taking a deep breath before beginning again. "How many women have you been with since you were with me?"

His eyes widened for a moment before his shoulders relaxed, and with a smile that held all the love in his heart, he answered, "None."

She gasped. "None?"

"None," he confirmed. He leaned his neck to the side, smiling at her tenderly. "I'm married."

"M-Me too," she said as tears slicked down her face. "I haven't been with anyone but you."

He took a step toward her. "I missed you."

"I missed you so much, it felt like dying," she said, taking a step toward him.

"Like thirst and hunger," he said, reaching for her. "All the time."

"Like frost. Like ice. Like there was no warmth on the earth," she said, stepping into his arms.

"Like eternal winter," he agreed, pulling her tightly against him.

"Like happiness was a fairy tale. Like joy was a myth. Like love . . ."

". . . was impossible," he finished.

Elise leaned her head back, her eyes dark and wide in the dim light of the motel room. "You're here with me."

"I'm here with my wife."

He'd dreamed of this moment so many times, and yet nothing he'd fantasized could compare with Elise's upturned face telling him that she didn't want a divorce and never had. She still wanted him, still needed him, still loved him.

Skimming his hands up her arms, their breath mingled hot and sweet between them, and Preston cradled her neck between his palms, her throbbing pulse under his thumb. He took his time leaning down, his lips moving closer and closer to hers until they touched the sweet softness that he'd missed so desperately, and he sealed his mouth over hers.

What started soft and gentle, however, turned fierce immediately. Elise's hands, which had been flattened against his chest, skated up and wound around his neck, pulling him down to her, and Preston's hands slid higher, into her hair. Plunging his tongue into her mouth, he swallowed her deep moan, dropping his hands to her waist and turning so he could push her against the motel room door. Her fingers untwined from his neck, gliding down his shoulders and unbuttoning his shirt, which he shrugged off his shoulders. He took her hands and raised them over her head, holding her wrists against the door with one hand as Elise arched into him, pressing against his straining erection, whimpering for more. Sucking her tongue into his mouth, he reached down for the hem of her camisole, pushing it up over her head and over the tips of her fingers until it dropped to the floor.

Sliding his hands down to her ass, he lifted her up and into his arms, her back still against the door, her ankles locking around his waist. He stepped back toward the bed, savoring the feeling of her wrapped around him, moaning, whimpering, kissing him like she'd never get enough of him. And he'd never, ever get enough of her: of the way she tasted, of the way she felt in his arms, pressed against his body, the thin, sheer fabric of her bra the only thing keeping her bare chest from colliding with his. Lowering them both to the bed, he fell on top of her, bracing his weight on his elbows as she leaned her head back into the pillow and plunged her hands into his hair to pull him back down to her.

He trailed his lips along her jawline, gliding down the soft, warm skin of her throat, then slid to her ear lobe, which he bit gently, eliciting a hotter-than-fuck "ahh" sound from his wife, who arched off the bed and razed his scalp with her fingernails, demanding his lips again.

He kissed her as he'd dreamed for two long years apart from her, his body hardening to the point of pain as it always had, wanting her, remembering how they fit together, how it felt to be inside of her, and how they'd moved as one. He wanted her. Fuck, he wanted her so bad.

And yet . . .

He drew back, panting, resting his forehead against hers as he tried to catch his breath. She leaned up, trying to catch his lips with hers, trying to kiss him again.

"Elise . . . wait, sweetheart. Wait . . ."

One of her hands fell from his hair, and she bent her arm over her head, the pose decadent and so sexy, he could almost convince himself to take what she was definitely offering and deal with the consequences tomorrow.

Except . . .

"Pres . . ." she moaned, pushing her breasts against his chest as she looked up at him with dark eyes and glistening lips.

"Oh, God," he muttered, shaking his head. "I've never wanted anything as much as I want you right now, Elise, but the timing . . ."

She sighed—a huffing, frustrated sound—and nodded, panting as she unlocked her ankles and slid her legs down the back of his. ". . . is shit."

He rolled off of her to lie beside her, placing his hands over his chest and staring up at the ceiling. Her side pressed into his, hot and damp, despite the air-conditioned room. He leaned up on his elbow, looking down at her.

"I can't lose you again."

She reached up and caressed his cheek. "You won't."

"It almost destroyed me," he said, clenching his jaw as he held her eyes. "I barely made it out alive, Elise."

Tears sprang into her eyes, and her thumb gently rubbed the stubble along his jaw. "I didn't know."

"It was bad. I missed you. I loved you. I'd been rejected by you," he said, scoffing a little in self-deprecation. It sounded so pathetic when it was laid out like that.

"I'm so sorry," she said softly, starting to draw her hand away.

He reached for it, pressing it back against his cheek, then turned his neck slightly until his lips were pressed to her palm. Sighing against her skin, he said, "We jumped into it last time, hoping everything would work itself out. We need to do it right this time."

She nodded in agreement.

"How about we get some sleep? We can talk more after this weekend, okay?"

"Okay," she said, leaning forward to kiss his lips softly before flipping onto her side.

Preston bent his knees and pulled her against him, her back to his front, his nose in her hair, his lips pressed to the back of her neck, her barely covered breasts spilling over his arm.

"I love you, Preston," she whispered, on the verge of sleep. "I'll never hurt you like that . . . not ever again."

Tell her you love her. I love you, too. I love you, too. I love you . . .

Instead of answering her, he held her tighter . . . and prayed that he could find the strength to trust her with his whole heart once again.

One of Sarah Klassan's favorite expressions had been, "Love is a verb."

And even if Preston was unable or unwilling to return Elise's "I love you" verbally, the next day, he managed to return it in countless, heart-clenching, hope-giving ways. Standing beside her, he helped her greet the many visitors who arrived in an endless stream on Friday, taking casseroles to the refrigerator and freezer, helping old Mr. Sanders to the men's room, and jump-starting Mrs. Schneider's ancient Chevy truck when it wouldn't turn over. He was everywhere at once—beside her, behind her, before her—in her head, in her heart, as organic as her own self, as necessary as air to breathe, and she knew why LA had felt so terribly wrong: because after having Preston *in* her life, her life was empty with him *out* of it.

In the late afternoon, when there was a lull in the number of visitors, Abby found them on the back porch swing together rocking slowly, Elise tucked into the nook of Preston's arm. She encouraged them to get away for a bit and take a walk.

"*Datt* is napping, *Liebling*. Why don't you and Preston take a walk? You've been sitting on this porch all afternoon. Get some fresh air. Show your husband the farm."

Abby had a quiet calm, and the tender way she mothered her two small children and shared not-quite-covert, intimate gazes with her husband, Ethan, made Elise long for what her sister had. She seemed satisfied and settled, yet still vital, stepping into the shoes of matriarch with a gentleness that Elise and her sisters needed.

Taking Preston's hand, she led them away from the tidy farmhouse toward the barn, bypassing it for a rolling green field just beyond where two dozen black-and-white cows stood grazing. Resting their forearms on a white split-rail fence, Preston and Elise gazed out over the meadow together.

"They're Holsteins," she said.

"Is that a baby?" he asked, pointing to a smaller one.

She nodded. "About three months old."

"They're so calm."

"They're happy here."

"I can see why. It's very beautiful. Fresh air, green grass, plenty to eat, safe place to sleep . . . what more could a cow want?"

Indeed. There was something paradisiacal about her parents' farm now that she had escaped it. The colors were vibrant, the lifestyle simple, the food honest and delicious, the people plain but happy . . . so much less complicated than her own life had become.

You're making your life so much more difficult than it needs to be, Liebling.

She had, hadn't she? Instead of appreciating Preston when she had him, she'd taken him for granted and almost lost him. Same with her family. She felt the sharp blessing of second chances and breathed deeply, grateful for her husband beside her, grateful for the warm and loving welcome she'd received from her family, and even for this place she'd worked so desperately to escape.

"I want to come back up here more often. I want our children to—" she gasped, wincing. "Oh, I didn't . . . I mean . . . oh."

Her face burned, and she clenched her eyes shut, wishing the ground would swallow her whole. They'd barely decided to stay together, and she was already talking about kids? She cringed inside, wishing he'd say something . . . or just be quiet. Yeah, that would be better. Maybe they could forget she'd said anything.

His voice was low and happy when he broke the silence between them. "I'd want our children to know where their mother grew up . . . to know their aunts and uncles, their grandfather and cousins. The swing on the porch, that baby Holstein. I'd want them to know all of it." As Preston spoke, he stepped behind her, wrapping his arms around her waist, and her whole body relaxed against him. His voice was soft in her ear, barely an audible rumble but thick with emotion. "I wasn't even sure if you wanted kids."

"Of course I do." She turned around in his arms, leaning her back against the fence, looking up at his face. "I want yours."

His lips tilted up, and his eyes—which looked back at her with such intense and deep love—softened as they searched hers. "You do?"

"Yes." She shrugged, smiling back at him, wondering why he was so surprised.

"But . . ." His smile faded, though his grip around her waist tightened. "How will that work? Would we raise our kids in LA? With you off on movie shoots? Far from your family and mine? Spending holidays without my brothers or your sisters? That's just not how I imagined having a family, Elise."

She stiffened. "I never said that's how I envisioned it, either."

"Well then . . . how?"

"I don't know. I haven't . . . I mean, we'd have to talk about it. Figure it out."

"When exactly?" he asked, dropping his arms and taking a step back from her. "When will we figure it out?"

She had a fleeting feeling of panic, but when she examined it, she realized it wasn't because she felt pressured by Preston, but because she feared hurting him or losing him. She stepped toward him, leaning into their discussion, and said, "When we get home."

"Home? And where exactly is that? Philly? New York? LA? Hell, we don't even know where we're going to live . . . or if we're even going to live together."

Refusing to let herself be drawn into an argument when they hadn't even had a chance to discuss things logically, she placed her hand on his arm, curling her fingers gently around his sun-warmed skin. "When we get back to Philly, we'll discuss it. All of it."

He searched her face, then sighed loudly, a huffing noise of frustration and angst, and it flipped her heart to know that she was causing him any more pain.

"Preston . . ."

"What?" he snapped, his troubled green eyes vulnerable as they held hers.

"I am committed to this. To you. I *promise* you that we'll figure it out."

"How?" he asked again, his eyes increasingly bleak despite her reassurances.

And suddenly she had an idea. A good idea. An idea that was aborted long ago and saved for today.

"We'll have a marriage summit," she said, grinning up at him.

Her words surprised him; she could tell because he couldn't keep his lips from twitching, and his free hand reached up to cover her fingers resting on his arm.

"A marriage summit?"

"Mm-hm," she said. "When we get back to Philly, we'll sit down for hours and talk about all of it: kids, where we want to live, our careers, our families, what's important, what we can bend on, what we can't. We'll stay up all night until the morning . . . until we know how we want this marriage to look. And then we'll make it happen."

"We will?"

"Mm-hm," she said, pressing against him, relaxing as his arms circled around her. "We're goal-oriented people. We're good at making plans and doing whatever we need to do to make our dreams come true. You're my dream."

"And you're mine," he murmured, his voice full of warmth and wonder. "You're very certain we'll make it work."

"There's love here," she reminded him, tilting her head back as he lowered his lips to hers.

Chapter 20

Make Room

The service at Elise's Mennonite church on Saturday morning was quiet and respectful, with the congregation carefully reciting Sarah Klassan's favorite hymns and solemnly remembering Elise's mother as a pillar of their community. Her burial service was similarly simple, and the meal afterward at the Klassan Farm only included Hans Klassan, his daughters, and their husbands. It was a somber lunch, but afterward—as the women washed the dishes and tidied up the house—Preston felt a palpable release of tension as he hung out with the men on the front porch in the afternoon sun. They swapped stories and laughed more than they had in days, talking about their plans for farming the end of the summer and teasing each other good-naturedly. To Preston, it seemed as though the last of the funeral rites had been observed and life was resuming.

Sure enough, when Elise finally exited her father's house, she found his eyes with a tender smile, then started saying her good-byes. Wednesday was her first day of filming, and Preston had already missed two days of work without much notice, she explained. It was time for them to return to Pennsylvania, and after tearful hugs and promises to come and visit again soon, they left the farm and packed up their dingy, little motel room. As they refolded clothes and zipped their suitcases, they agreed that Elise would come home with him, and tomorrow, Sunday, they'd have their marriage summit and figure out "what happens next."

After reaching over to kiss Preston in the car and tell him once again how grateful she was for his company this weekend, Elise had curled up in her seat and promptly fallen asleep. And knowing what a long, emotional few days it had been for her, Preston was relieved to see her relaxed and recharging. Plus, it gave him some much-needed time to think.

By the time they'd returned to their motel room last night, it was very late, and they'd been too tired to do anything but crawl into bed and hold each other until morning. And he wasn't necessarily complaining, because Preston would never get tired of falling asleep beside Elise or waking up with his wife warm and soft in his arms, but the reality was that Preston wanted more. Much more.

He wanted a stable, long-term plan that included a permanent home on the east coast and holidays that alternated between her family and his—the kind of life into which they could add children one day. Since she'd mentioned having children, it seemed like all he could think about. And why not? Brooks was having his first child with his fiancée, Skye, in March, and with Jessica and Alex getting married so soon, they could easily be next. Preston wanted his children to grow up with theirs . . . and with Abby's little ones, too. He wanted family. He wanted normalcy. And he wanted it with his wife.

He looked over at her angelic face in slumber and grimaced. As much as he wanted to believe her words about staying married, making a plan for their lives together, and—God, *please*—even having kids one day, he was still worried that being at the farm, with the sorrow of her mother's passing so sharp and fresh, may have impacted her judgment. He feared that when she returned to Philadelphia and immersed herself back into her Hollywood lifestyle, those precious words would suddenly become less valid, less true—emotional promises made at an emotional time. And he didn't know how he would bear it if she slowly started pulling away again.

Taking a deep breath, he kept his eyes on the road, hoping that by the time they reached Haverford, he'd figure out a way for them to move forward while still leaving the worst parts of the past behind.

"Sweetheart," he was saying. "Sweetheart, wake up. We're home. We're here."

Elise stretched in her seat, her eyes rebelling against having to open. The car was dark and warm, and Preston was right beside her. She could have slept for hours more. As her lids fluttered open, she turned her head to look at Preston and smiled.

"Hi," she murmured.

"Hi," he said, smiling back at her, reaching for her hand.

"Are we at your place?" she asked, finally turning her neck to look out the windshield. She blinked in confusion. They weren't in downtown Philadelphia. They were parked in front of Chateau Nouvelle. "This isn't . . ."

"It's Chateau Nouvelle," he said, reaching out to caress her cheek. "I need to talk to you. Let's get out and walk for a few minutes, okay?"

He dropped his hand and opened his car door, closing it quickly behind him. She glanced up at the rearview mirror as he took her suitcase out of the trunk, and her heart plummeted as he wheeled it to the front walkway.

What was going on? They'd decided to go to his apartment in the city and have their marriage summit tomorrow. What were they doing in Haverford? Why had he brought her back here, and what did he want to talk about?

She dragged her hands through her hair, her stomach buzzing and flipping uncomfortably as she wiggled her feet into her shoes. Had he rethought their tentative plan to stay married? Did he decide that he couldn't trust her enough to give her another chance? Maybe it wasn't worth the risk of another broken heart. Her own heart started to race painfully at the thought of losing him, and she noticed that her hand was shaking as she opened her car door and stepped outside on wobbly legs that had less to do with waking abruptly from her nap and more to do with fear.

Preston walked around to her side of the car and took her hand.

"I can hear you overthinking," he said softly, pulling her along beside him. "Stop. We're just going to talk."

"About what?" she asked, lacing her fingers through his, amazed that even though her worries were about him, his touch calmed her.

Preston sighed as they walked through Chateau Nouvelle's dark gardens, which had had a lot of film and production equipment added to the landscape since they left a few days ago.

"I'll be honest, Elise. I'm concerned that your mother's passing and the emotions you must be feeling may have clouded your judgment over the last few days. I'm concerned that you may have made some promises you didn't intend to make, and I think it would be unwise for me to hold you to them witho—"

"No! Hold me to them! Please hold me to them. Pres, I meant every word. I came back for *you*. I don't want Hollywood, I want you. I didn't make these decisions this weekend. I made them weeks and weeks ago. Months ago. A year ago! I just didn't know how to say what I wanted to say. I didn't want to just barge in on your life, and I was sure you hated me and—"

"You didn't let me finish," he said gently, pausing in their walk to face her. He ran his free hand through her hair, cupping the nape of her neck so that she was forced to look up at him.

He was beautiful in the moonlight, his face soft and tender, his hair jet black like onyx, his green eyes dark and deep, and Elise's heart clenched and wept at the thought of ever losing him again.

"I think it would be unwise for me to hold you to them without giving you a few days to be sure," he finished. "Because if we decide to stay married and move in together and keep moving forward? I'm going to give you my heart all over again, and it'll be yours to take or break. And if you break it again, Elise, it will destroy me. I'm willing to take the risk, but I've got to hedge my bets a little. I need you to be sure you want marriage this time."

"How much time?" she murmured, tears springing into her eyes as she imagined his pain over the past two years, and—if she was honest—dreading the thought of falling asleep without his arms around her tonight.

"A week." He laughed ruefully, tilting his head to the side, his fingers gently massaging the back of her neck. "I'm not sure I can stand more than that."

She took a step closer to him. "I love you, Pres. I love you so much. I don't need a week. My feelings aren't going to change in a week."

He searched her eyes, wetting his lips like he was tempted by her offer, but then he sighed, dropping one of her hands. "Please go along with this. For me."

She sighed. "Okay."

"What time should I pick you up on Friday?"

"I insisted we wrap at six every day."

"You did?"

She nodded. "It's in my contract. I was planning to bother you every night until you agreed to stay married to me."

He grinned at her. "Then I'll pick you up on Friday at six, and we'll have our marriage summit then. I mean, if you still want to."

"Of course I'll still want to." They started walking again, this time back toward the front entrance of Chateau Nouvelle, and Elise tightened her grip on Preston's hand. "I'll miss you. One week is going to feel like twenty."

"For me, too," he said as they rounded the house. "But I had hours to think about it, and I think I need it. I need to know that you had time to think it over."

"I understand," she said, her voice catching. How she hated the thought of him leaving her. How she dreaded the moment he drove away. And getting into bed tonight all alone? More tears burned her eyes at the thought.

But twice now, he'd referred to their time apart over the last two years—how much it had hurt him—and she understood that giving him this time would reassure him as to her intentions. She knew she didn't need it, but what hurt a little was that he did. The least she could do was give it to him.

"Elise," he said softly as their feet crunched onto the driveway gravel.

"Hmmm?"

He stopped walking, and she faced him, looking up at his face, which was fraught, like he was in pain. He shook his head, then seized her eyes again, holding them, searching them.

"You have to know . . . I need to tell you . . . I . . . I love you. I'm *completely* in love with you, even more today than I was two years ago. I'd do anything to make you happy, to be with you, to belong to you, to know that you belonged to me."

"I *do* belong to you," she insisted, her heart thundering with gratitude and awe for his words.

He loved her.

He still loved her.

Though she had already suspected it was true, hearing the words in her ears was so welcome, so heartbreaking, she couldn't help the tears that slipped from her weary eyes.

He leaned down and kissed her, pressing his lips gently against hers, plucking and nipping, first her top lip, then her bottom. His arms came around her waist, and he pulled her against his body, his tongue seeking hers and finding it, sliding slowly, then more urgently against hers. She moaned into his mouth, winding her arms around his neck, her fingers playing with the soft, black hair on his nape as goose bumps lit out across her skin.

This man was her husband.

Hers.

And he loved her.

He groaned softly, releasing her lips and gathering her close as he leaned his forehead against hers. "I'm a masochist for even *suggesting* we wait a week."

She was inclined to agree with him, but didn't. This is what he needed, and she needed to support him. "No, Pres. It's smart. When you see me on Friday, you'll know I'm yours forever. You'll know that I choose you, and hopefully you'll be able to start trusting me again."

He sighed, a frustrated huff that almost made her smile.

Leaning away from him, she buried her fingers in his hair, pushing it off his forehead and grinning up at him. "Now go. And remember how much I love you."

He released her slowly, his eyes dark and burning as he nodded, got into his car, and drove away.

The next morning, Preston woke up at Westerly, having decided the night before not to drive back into Philly at midnight, and although his first instinct was to race over to Chateau Nouvelle and check on Elise, he knew that their plan was sound. She'd be learning lines and blocking scenes on Monday and Tuesday. Then filming on Wednesday, Thursday, and Friday, and hopefully that would be enough of her "real life" for her to evaluate what it would look like with Preston in it. Lord knows that more than a week apart felt impossible.

Rolling onto his side, he opened his eyes and started. Jessica was standing beside his bed with her hands on her hips and a very, very disapproving look on her usually pretty face.

"You're *married*? You're *married*? I just . . . I mean, I can't even . . . *YOU'RE MARRIED?*"

He couldn't help it—he did the worst possible thing when his little sister was on a rampage: he smiled at her.

But instead of beating him senseless with his own pillow, she surprised him by widening her eyes and smiling back. Her body relaxed, and she sat down on his bed, in the curve of his body with her back to him, looking at his face over her shoulder.

"I haven't seen that smile in a long, long time," she said thoughtfully.

"I haven't felt much like smiling."

"And now you do."

He nodded. "And now I do."

"You've been married to a movie star for two years, and none of us even knew? How could you keep that secret, Pres? Why?"

He sat up, pulling the sheet to his waist as Jessica shifted to face him.

"We loved each other, but we weren't ready," he said. "We rushed into it, and it was kind of a . . . disaster."

Well, not all of it, he reminded himself, thinking of their wedding night. His body hummed with the hope that she'd be in his bed again this Friday.

"Elise Klassan is your *wife*," said Jessica, obviously impressed. "I don't even know what to say."

"Say . . . don't let her get away this time," said Brooks from the doorway of Preston's room, making his way to the bed and plopping down beside Jessica. "Because you have looked like shit for two years, my brother, and you finally look human again."

"Thanks, Brooks. And good morning to you, too."

"I'm serious. I know you got your life back on track, but you still weren't happy. Suddenly you look a lot better."

"You do," agreed Jessica. "Is Elise why you moved home from New York? Why you were drinking so much?"

Preston took a deep breath and nodded. "Even though we weren't ready, it hurt a lot when she walked away."

"I'd feel like dying if Alex walked away," said Jessica.

"Or Skye," agreed Brooks.

"Then you understand how I felt," said Preston. "I was lost without her. Even though the timing was all wrong, she was my wife, and I . . . I loved her. I still love her. I'll always love her. It hurt like hell to be apart."

"Does she know all of this?" asked Jessica with a twinkle in her eyes.

Damn, but his little sister loved meddling. Thank God he'd already talked to Elise about everything or he could imagine Jess marching over to Chateau Nouvelle right this minute.

"Yes, she does," said Preston firmly. "I don't need any help."

"Well, I can't wait to tell everyone that my sister-in-law is a famous actress."

"Not yet," said Preston, his eyes full of warning. "We're still working things out. I mean it, Jess. Mum's the word for now."

Jessica nodded solemnly.

"Not to be nosy—" started Brooks.

"Why stop now?" deadpanned Preston.

Brooks gave his little brother a look and continued, "What are you doing here . . . *alone*?"

"We're giving it a week."

"Ugh!" exclaimed Jessica. "What?"

"A week!" Brooks winced. "Why?"

Preston laughed softly at the appalled looks on his siblings faces. Not that he needed to know, and granted, it was sort of a gross thought, but he suspected that they burned as hot for their mates as he did for Elise. And yes, he had to admit that a week felt like hell when holding her was heaven on earth, but . . .

"Because we're doing things right this time," he said softly, looking first at Jessica and then at Brooks, who nodded in understanding. "Because this time is forever."

Chapter 21

Make It Work

Precisely at six o'clock p.m. on Friday night, Preston pulled up in front of Chateau Nouvelle to pick her up, and Elise bounded down the stairs, leaping into his arms as he exited the car. Never, ever had a week felt so long.

He caught her easily, and she cupped his cheeks, covering his face with kisses as she locked her ankles around his waist, held close by his strong hands under her backside. She wouldn't let him speak, wouldn't let him do anything but hold her until she'd had her fill of kisses, until she felt like they'd made up for a little bit of the deprivation they'd both suffered during these long, lonely days apart.

"I missed you," she gasped, taking his bottom lip between her teeth and arching into him when he groaned, his fingers tightening.

"Me too," he panted, sealing his mouth over hers and thrusting his tongue forward. She circled it with her own, arching her breasts against him, feeling the tight, taut points push against the hard wall of muscle that was his chest.

"Oh my God, you two! Get a room!"

They broke apart from each other, with glistening lips and dazed, happy eyes, turning in tandem to see Jax standing in the doorway of the mansion, shaking her head.

"There's still crew wrapping things up out back. And who knows? There could be paparazzi in the bushes!"

As Preston gently lowered Elise to the ground, she noted the manila envelope in her hostess's hand. Elise's eyes widened, cutting to Jax's face as Preston's arms tightened around her.

"I take it you don't need these papers anymore?" Jax asked, waggling the envelope and raising her eyebrows. "I found them in the parlor after you left for the funeral . . . I peeked inside, but I didn't think it was any of my business."

"You were right," said Preston sharply. "It's not."

Jax held out the envelope, rolling her eyes at the neighbor she'd known all her life. "Calm your tits, Winslow. Here you go."

"You didn't . . . tell anyone, did you?" asked Elise.

"Like I said," said Jax, turning back to the house, "it's none of my business. But can I give you two a little advice? If you're going to keep doing *that*, you might want to figure out how to tell the rest of the world that you've been married for two years. It's going to get out, and it's better to get ahead of these things." Before closing the door, she faced them once more. "And whenever you're ready, I'd *love* to hear the whole story."

Preston turned back to Elise once Jax was gone. "Don't worry. I've known Jax Rousseau forever. She won't say anything."

"Okay," said Elise, feeling relieved.

"So, about tonight . . . you've had a week to think things over . . ."

She stared at him in disbelief. "You're uncertain about my intentions? After that greeting?"

He shrugged, grinning at her. "Just want to hear you say it, sweetheart."

"Marriage summit. You and me. Tonight."

"And then?" he asked in a gravelly voice, and she could feel his erection through his pants, hard and pulsing, pushing against her belly.

"And then I was thinking we should consummate our marriage . . . all over again."

His eyes widened. "Are you sure you're my wife? You're much bolder than she was."

"Any complaints?"

"None."

"She wasn't ready," said Elise with a saucy grin. "But *I* am."

"Thank God."

He kissed her again, more slowly this time, caressing her tongue with his and loving her lips with gentle nips and tugs. Her legs were jelly when he finally drew away, and she suspected her eyes were just as dark and hungry as his when he opened her door and helped her into the car.

Preston had originally decided to order Chinese food and serve it to her at his apartment as an homage to their New York days, but frankly, he wasn't sure they'd be able to keep their hands off of each other long enough to have an actual conversation, so he decided to park at his apartment building but take her to a small, local French bistro instead. First they'd talk. Then—he smiled to himself, trying to ignore the raging hard-on he'd had since she'd leapt into his arms—they'd reconsummate.

Parking his car in his usual spot, he turned to her. "There's a place up the street that reminds me of Bistro Chèvrefeuille. I thought we could have dinner there."

She turned to him, and for the first time, he noticed her outfit. It was a strapless, flowered romper with short shorts that made her legs look ten miles long. Her shoulders and neck were bare, and he suspected the entire contraption was held up with the hem of ruched elastic just over her breasts, which meant that one little tug would bare her to him. His body tightened with need, and his heart throbbed with anticipation.

"I sort of thought we would have dinner at your apartment," she said softly, licking her lips.

He bit back a groan, adjusting himself in his seat. "If we step foot into my apartment, that provocative little outfit you're wearing is hitting my floor in a New York second, sweetheart."

"And that's a bad thing?" she asked in a low voice laced with need. Her skin was flushed, and her breasts heaved against the floral fabric.

Damn, but this was a rare torture.

"No," he said, using every last reserve of strength and knowing if she pushed any harder, he'd fold like a beach chair and haul her up to his apartment like a caveman. "But we need to talk first."

She took a deep breath and unsnapped her seat belt, giving him a much less sultry grin. "You're right. And besides, I've barely eaten today."

"You need food, wife. I promise you'll need your strength for later," he said, lifting her hand to his lips and kissing it.

He helped her out of the car, took her hand again, and led her out of the garage, onto the bustling sidewalk of his tony Rittenhouse Square neighborhood. The café was very close, and after showing them to a quiet table in the back, the maître d', who looked at Elise twice but couldn't quite place her, handed them menus and left them alone.

She scanned the menu quickly, then folded it and placed it on the table beside her napkin, looking at him intently.

"I want to get started," she said, stretching her hand across the table.

"No small talk? No 'how was your week?'" he teased, lacing his fingers through hers.

She shook her head. "No. We've waited two years to have this conversation. I officially call the marriage summit to order . . . now."

He nodded, squeezing her hand, excitement and anticipation warring for precedence in his head. Bearing in mind her greeting and flirtation, however, he felt safe letting excitement take the lead.

"What do you want, Elise?" he asked, holding her eyes as she stared back at him.

"I want to stay married to you. I want to be your wife. I love you. I belong with you."

Relief coursed through his veins, warm and hopeful, and he released the breath he'd been holding.

"What do *you* want?" she asked.

Using the same words, he replied, "I want to stay married to you. I want to be your husband. I love you. I belong with you." He paused. "I belong *to* you. I have from the very first moment I saw you in that godawful play. I fell hook, line, and sinker when stupid Cyril turned you down and you collapsed on stage. I couldn't stop thinking about you that night, and I haven't stopped since."

She blinked back tears, smiling at him with tenderness and love. "For me, it was when you bought me that bouquet of flowers the first night you walked me home. It felt like a fairy tale to get an audition for *Ethan Frome* and meet you on the same night. I had to pinch myself later to make sure it hadn't been a dream."

"I fell for you all over again when you walked into my sister's engagement party saying you were sorry for everything that had happened between us. My God, it hurt to watch you walk away."

"You *made* me go!" she exclaimed.

"I was a cad," he said sheepishly. "But you shocked the hell out of me showing up like that."

"I know," she said, stroking his skin under her thumb. "I'm sorry."

"I'm not."

She sighed, squirming a little in her seat, the heat from her eyes scorching the air between them. He was dying to be alone with her.

"When you told me that you'd drive me to upstate New York four days later, I couldn't believe it. You were still so angry with me, but that's when I knew you still cared."

They were clasping both hands across the table now, and when the waiter returned, they didn't pull away. Placing their orders quickly—main courses only, no drinks, no appetizers, go away, please—they turned back to one another.

"What about the rest?" asked Preston. "What about us? Now?"

"I didn't like LA," she confessed. "It felt so foreign and strange. I didn't fit in; I didn't drink or go clubbing. I missed walking everywhere. I missed you." She took a deep breath. "And I missed the audience. I always loved performing in front of a live audience, and a movie set is nothing like an audience. There's no clapping, no laughing, no gasps or feedback or . . . energy. Just me, acting in a vacuum, going home alone every night." She sniffled. "I hated it, Pres. I traded you, someone I loved, for something I ended up hating."

"Maybe you had to try it," he said gently.

She shrugged. "Maybe. But you know what I've been thinking about this week?"

"Tell me, sweetheart."

"You had a Plan A—the Olympics—and it didn't happen. So you went to Plan B and became a lawyer. Your dream was shattered, and you had to choose a new one. But me? I *had* Plan A. I had Broadway in the palm of my hand, but I panicked about us and let my ambition take over my life, and I suddenly woke up living this awful Plan B that I never wanted. I traded the right plan for the wrong one. But it's not too late to go back . . . to find work on Broadway, where I was happy, where I really felt that I belonged. And stay here . . . with you."

"Are you sure that's what you want? Are you ready to give up Hollywood? And to be clear, I'm not asking you to do that. We're just talking."

"I'm sure," she said. "I didn't tell you this, but I broke my lease when I came out here two weeks ago. I had all of my belongings shipped to a storage facility outside of Philly. I have no open projects in California. When *The Philly Story* is over, I'm free to do what I like."

Preston's heart leaped with gladness because he wasn't expecting this. She had told him that she had returned east for him, but her actions spoke loudly, backing up her words, and he felt relieved and increasingly more hopeful for their future.

"So what do I want?" she summarized, adjusting their hands and stroking his thumb with hers. "I want you. You first. From now on, *always* you first, Pres."

Her blue eyes were luminous and open, her lips saying words he'd dreamed of for so long, it almost seemed impossible that they'd finally come true. Overcome with emotion and unable to speak, he took a deep breath and nodded at her to continue.

"As long as it fits in with *our* life, I'd like to go back to Broadway. Donny's ready to set up some auditions as soon as I say the word, and though I'd prefer to live in New York, I could make Philly work. I looked into the train schedules, and it's not bad. I could commute."

Her generosity overwhelmed him, and he squeezed her hands again, trying to let her know how much this meant to him.

She smiled—a sweet, shy grin—and continued in a softer voice. "I definitely want children. I wouldn't mind raising them in New York, if that was okay with you. More than anything, I want to be close to your family and mine. When I'm not working, I'd like to spend weekends with our families. I want for our children to grow up with their cousins. For me, that would be ideal."

He had tried not to talk while she was speaking but couldn't help himself now, his joy bubbling up from a marvelous place deep inside that had always belonged to her. "How many do you want?"

"Two or three," she answered, her cheeks flushing pink. She shrugged, one creamy shoulder almost kissing the lobe of her ear.

"When?" he asked. "I mean . . . now?"

"If it happened now, that would be okay with me. But ideally, I'd like to wait a year or two. I'd like to take a few roles first to reestablish myself in New York so that if I took some time off to be with the baby, I wouldn't be forgotten."

Her words made sense and filled him with happiness.

"Sweetheart, are you sure this is what *you* want? I need to be sure you aren't just making these choices for me."

"Of course I'm making them for you," she said, beaming back at him. "And for me. For us. For our marriage. For our future family. And yes, this is what *I* want, Pres. This is what I want more than anything else in the world."

The waiter stopped by with a basket of bread, and Elise dropped his hands to take a slice, placing it on her bread plate and looking up at him. "What about you?"

His eyes were so loving and tender, it was hard to stay seated and not round the table to sit in his lap, wind her arms around his neck, and breathe in the masculine scent that was Preston, that filled her heart with love and goodness and the sweet, sweet promise of second chances.

"I have to admit, I'm relieved you don't want to move to California, but I want you to know that I was willing." He paused. "I would have relocated for you if it was a deal-breaker."

Her heart clenched, and she swallowed over the sudden lump in her throat. LA, which had been a point of deep and fraught contention two years ago, was something he would bend on now? The very idea overwhelmed her, and she didn't know how her heart could feel any larger or more full.

"My firm has a branch there, so I could sit second-chair on cases until I passed the bar. I looked into it . . . just in case it was really important to you to stay there. But I'm relieved you don't want to." He breathed deep and sighed, reaching across the table for her hand. "Really relieved."

She was deeply touched that he was prepared to move for her and sniffled softly as she took a sip of water.

"And I don't want you commuting to and from New York, so I think—while you're working on *The Philly Story*—I should find us an apartment in Manhattan. My firm also has a branch there, so *I* can commute. Just as you said, it's not bad. I could do three days a week here and two up there. It's manageable. It's even ideal because I had a few clients in New York who were sad to see me go, and this would allow me to work with them again."

She squeezed his hand, loving the excitement and happiness in his voice.

Their dinners came, and they reluctantly let go of each other to eat.

"I loved what you just said about having kids," he said, staring down at his plate, his cheeks coloring just as hers had. "I'd love three. And raising them in New York sounds wonderful to me. Taking our little ones to the Central Park Zoo on sunny spring afternoons and to museums and the theater as they get older. I get season tickets to Madison Square Garden, too. There are fantastic private schools there, and besides, it's central for both of our families. I want our kids to know our families, Elise. Heck, I'd like for you to actually *meet* my family."

She giggled, looking up at him as she wound pasta onto her fork. "I'd love to meet them. Well, actually, I briefly met Brooks and Jessica at the engagement party. Brooks knew about us, didn't he? I could tell by his expression. He looked . . . terrified."

Preston nodded. "He found out a few months ago. He stumbled across the divorce papers."

Her heart lurched at the very thought of them. How close they'd come to throwing something precious away.

"He must hate me."

"He doesn't. If anyone understands the rocky road to true love, it's Brooks. And Jess is pretty excited to have a movie star in the family."

"I hope she'll be just as pleased to have a Broadway actress in the family."

"Knowing Jess, the title of sister-in-law will probably be her favorite of all. It wasn't always a picnic being the only girl of five."

Elise, who already had three sisters, couldn't wait to welcome a fourth into her life. "I can't wait to get to know her better."

"Will you move in with me until we find a place in New York?" he asked.

"Of course. There's nowhere else I want to be." She leaned down, picked up her purse off the floor, and rifled through it. When her fingers emerged, they were holding the silver key ring he'd gifted her on the opening night of *Ethan*

Frome, and she grinned at him with tears in her eyes. "I just need a key."

He stared at the key ring for a moment before lifting his eyes to hers. His voice was raspy with emotion as he said, "I'll have one made after we wake up tomorrow."

"Thank you."

"Thank *you* for giving me my life back," he said.

"Thank *you* for giving me a second chance to be your wife," she answered.

"I had no choice. I love you," he said simply.

"I love you, too."

Preston held her hand as they walked the half block back to his apartment building, his body fully aroused and humming with want. He forced himself to think of something else and realized they hadn't discussed their marriage and the public.

"We forgot something," he said.

"What to name our firstborn?" she asked, grinning up at him.

She was so adorable, so beloved, he paused, dropping his lips to hers for just a moment before resuming their walk.

"No . . . though that's a conversation I can't wait to have with you."

"Me too," she murmured, her bare arm brushing against his and making his blood sluice south.

Mercy. At this rate, he was going to walk into his apartment building with a tent pole under his belt, like some excited teenager. He cleared his throat, willing it to go down until they made it to his apartment. "We, um, we forgot to discuss the fact that you're a public figure."

"So are you."

"And we got married in secret two years ago," he said, pulling open the door of his apartment building and guiding her inside. "If we announce that, there will be a media storm, with every reporter in the world wondering why we were estranged for the past two years. I don't want people mucking through our personal business, Elise."

"Me neither."

"Then, as much as I hate it," he said, "I think that, besides our families and Jax, we should let the media believe that we've just met and started dating."

It rankled because they'd just fought hard to put their marriage back together, and now they'd have to conceal it.

"I wish there was another way," she said softly as he pressed the elevator call button.

"I don't think there is."

The doors opened, and he pulled her into the elevator, into his arms.

"If I could, I would shout it from the rooftops," she said. "I'm Mrs. Preston Winslow!"

"And I would write in the stars," he said, recalling the words she'd used to tell him that she loved him two years ago, "so that every night when you looked at the sky, my love would shine back at you."

"Pres . . ." She sighed, her eyes filling with tears. "Kiss me."

Backing her against the wall of the elevator as it leisurely climbed to the ninth floor, he lifted her into his arms as he had earlier that evening at Chateau Nouvelle, and she wrapped her legs around his hips as his lips smashed into hers.

His tongue broke the seam of her lips, searching for hers, stroking and sliding against it as they were lifted higher and higher. She arched her back, her nipples pinpoints through the flimsy fabric of her romper, and threaded her fingers urgently through his hair, her fingernails digging into his scalp.

The elevator doors opened, and he turned, his lips still fused to hers, moving swiftly through the doors and down the hallway to his apartment. At the door, he sucked her bottom lip between his and finally released it with a soft pop.

"We said the words two years ago," he said fiercely, leaning his forehead against hers. "But our *marriage* begins tonight."

Leaning Elise's back against the door and holding her with one hand, he found his keys in his pocket and quickly unlocked the door, twisting the knob as they barreled into his front hallway. Kicking the door closed with his foot, he adjusted her in his arms briefly, finding her lips again as he strode down the dim hallway, through the massive, sunken living room, through an arched hallway, past his office, past a guest room, to the door at the end of the hall.

Her lips were bright red and glistening when he drew back from her, her eyes dark and languid with arousal, with desire.

"No going back," he said—a warning, a promise.

"We belong to each other," she vowed, her voice thick and breathy as her breasts pushed into his chest with every panted breath.

Spearing her with his gaze and forcing her to return it, Preston pushed his bedroom door open and stepped into the room.

Elise's body had flooded wet and hot when he lifted her against the wall of the elevator, but now her muscles clenched in anticipation as he stared at her, the sheer intimacy of his eyes drilling hers making her feel weak and needy, like if he didn't fill her soon, she'd scream from the high pitch of her arousal, from the intense need to be writhing beneath him, his strong body driving into hers over and over again.

"I've relived our wedding night a million times," she murmured, dropping her forehead to his shoulder. "I'd lie in my bed and touch myself, trying to feel the way you made me feel, but I couldn't . . . I couldn't . . ."

Preston froze, his fingers clawlike, digging into her backside as his breath caught beside her neck. "You're blowing my mind."

The gravelly heat in his voice made her bold. "I'd rather blow something else."

"Fuuuuuck," he groaned. "Are you for real?"

"Try me," she dared him, turning into him so she could lick his throat. Under her tongue, she felt his pulse jumping like crazy, and he gasped as she blew on the damp skin, then pressed her lips against it.

"I need you naked, sweetheart," he whispered in a ragged groan. "Please."

Unlocking her ankles as he loosened his grip on her bottom, she slid down his chest until her sandaled feet touched the floor. She slipped out of the sandals and looked up at him, at the lust that cut his face into angles and made his eyes glitter with hunger.

He placed his palms on her shoulders, staring deeply into her eyes. She leaned her neck back slowly, until her throat was totally exposed, and let her hands droop listlessly by her sides, giving him total control. She felt her breasts push forward, straining toward him with every inhaled breath, but she was still, locked in his gaze, letting him know that she was completely his, that she'd never run from him again.

He smoothed his hands down her arms, so softly, so slowly, goose bumps rose up on her flesh, and she heard the smallest whimper borrow her breath and whisper past her lips. His hands stroked the skin of her arms, all the way to her wrists, which he held with his thumbs over her pulse.

"Your heart is racing," he murmured.

She nodded, her eyelids fluttering but not closing.

Skimming his palms back up her arms, he paused at her shoulders, then lifted all but his fingertips from her skin. Her trailed them—slowly, like a feather's touch—to the elastic hem of her romper, one index finger tracing the border, his eyes still boring into hers, his breathing quick and shallow.

She felt another rush of wetness between her legs and gasped softly, her eyes widening as she realized her body was preparing for his, readying itself, and barely able to keep another whimper from leaving her throat, she gave it permission, watching his eyes as the small sound of want pulled his eyes to her lips.

His right hand—his large, warm palm—slipped under the elastic, sliding slowly to her left breast, his fingers stopping when they found her bare nipple, swollen yet firm, and he covered it with his palm, finally dipping his head and claiming her lips with his.

She moaned into his mouth, a sound of want and fury, as he squeezed her breast, his thumb rubbing mercilessly over her aroused flesh. Inserting his free fingers into the elastic, he raked the fabric down, the friction over her exposed nipple almost unbearable until his palm covered it, soothing it, both thumbs circling her pebbled flesh as she leaned into his touch.

His tongue swept between her lips, exploring the wet heat of her mouth as his hands slid lower, abandoning her breasts and pushing her romper over her waist, over her hips . . . his breath caught suddenly, and he groaned as he realized she wasn't wearing panties. Her romper fell to her ankles, the flowered fabric soft and light around her bare feet as Preston caressed the skin of her back.

He leaned back to look into her eyes, and she'd never seem him so wild, so undone.

"So. Fucking. Hot," he groaned, his panted speech choppy and awestruck.

"Take off your shirt," she demanded, unable to wait for him much longer.

He reached behind his neck, and a second later his shirt was on the floor. As she stared at the chiseled perfection of his bare chest, her fingers smoothed over the ridges and stopped at his belt, quickly unbuckling him, unbuttoning the top button and pulling down the zipper of his pants. He shoved them down his legs, stepping out of them, and Elise dropped her glance to his boxers. Hooking her thumbs in the sides, she pulled the fabric up and over his massive erection, staring at the veins that pulsed and jumped under her perusal.

"You're as beautiful as I remember." She sighed, skimming her eyes from his penis to his flat abs, to his rock-hard pecs, back up to his face.

He stared back at her, his brows furrowed like he might be in pain, his hands in fists by the sides of his gloriously naked body.

"My memories don't do you justice," he said, his words soft like a caress. "I have one soul. No one had it before me, and no one gets it when I'm gone. But in this life, I give it to you. You own me, Elise."

She reached for his face, palming his cheek, and he swept her into his arms.

"I love you," she said. "Everything I am belongs to you."

He nodded, placing her gently on the bed and covering her body with his. Elise bent her knees, making a cradle for him between her thighs, and felt the tip of his erection positioned at the entrance of her sex. But instead of plunging forward, as she wanted him to do, he dropped his head and sucked one of her nipples into his mouth, laving it with his tongue, his thumb and forefinger gently pinching the other as she writhed beneath him, trying to force him to slide inside of her.

"Please, Pres . . ." she moaned. "Please, it's been so long . . . I want you . . ."

Leaning up on his elbows, he looked down at her face. "I love you."

Tears sprang into her eyes as he slowly inched forward, his thick heat stretching the walls of her sex and making her gasp in pain at first, then quickly in pleasure.

"Are you okay?" he panted. "It's been a long time."

She smoothed her hands down the hot, damp skin of his back, landing on his firm buttocks and digging her fingers into his skin to urge him forward.

"I want all of you," she murmured, closing her eyes and pressing her head back into the pillow as he slid forward a little more. "I want to feel so full of you that I don't know where you end and I begin. That's how I want our marriage to be this time . . . with us . . . as one."

Her words floated away on the last of her exhaled breath, and Preston surged forward, burying himself inside of her to the hilt. A strangled groan emerged from his throat, and he drew back, his erection sliding against the hot, trembling walls of her sex only to thrust forward again. Elise moaned, a swelling starting in her heart and spilling over into her belly, making her feel warm and full, gathering and building, tightening around him.

"Again," she panted, and this time as he drew back and pushed forward, she raised her hips off the bed to meet him, and he groaned loudly, the very beginnings of a roar. His arms, which had been bent beside her head, slid under her neck, and he crushed her chest with his.

"I dreamed of this," he murmured, his lips close to her ear, his breathing jagged as his teeth bit down gently on her lobe. "I dreamed every night of you beneath me, sweetheart."

"I love you, Pres. I love you with everything I am."

He pulled back and surged forward again, cupping the back of her head tenderly, capturing her eyes with his. The swelling that had started in her heart had turned into a wave of trembling, quivering anticipation, and she whimpered loudly, holding on to his eyes for as long as she could. As he surged forward again, her eyes rolled back in her head, and her entire body tightened to the point of rigidity. With a cry of delight, she exploded around him in a million points of pleasure, from the tips of her toes to the hair on her head and everywhere in between . . . and all of it, every last bit of who she was, belonged to him. To Preston. To her husband.

"I love you!" he bellowed, sliding forward one last time and pulsing, hot and vital, into the deepest depths of her body, joining them together in every possible way, from now until the end of their days.

Hours later, when they'd made love twice more and showered together, Preston toweled off his wife, then wrapped her in a fluffy, white towel and carried her to their bed. Snuggling beside him, she shimmied out of the towel and pressed her naked back against his naked front. He pulled her against him, his arm over her hip, nestled under her breasts.

She sighed, a sound of pure happiness, and he held her tighter, profoundly aware of the second chance they'd found and taken, and committed to never taking a moment with her for granted.

It was dark in his room and so quiet, he was sure she'd fallen asleep when he heard her voice, soft and low, say, "Pres?"

"I thought you were asleep."

She shook her head against the pillow, and her hair tickled his nose. "Not yet."

"You okay?"

"I'm perfect," she said, "except for one thing."

"Whatever it is, I'll fix it for you, I'll get it for you, I'll slay it for you, or buy it for you, or barter for it, or beg, borrow, or steal. Tell me what you need, sweetheart, and it's yours."

She turned in his arms and faced him, her breasts flush against his chest, her lips a breath away from his.

"I don't want to be someone I'm not. I'm Elise Winslow. That's who I am. That's who I want to be to the whole world."

"But we decided—"

"Marry me," she said, her eyes sparkling with mischief and happiness as she reached for his cheek.

"Did you just propose to me?" he asked, grinning at her, his smile so wide it ached.

"Mm-hm," she hummed, leaning forward to kiss his lips. "And your answer is . . ."

Tell me what you need, sweetheart, and it's yours.

"Yes," he said. "I'd marry you every day for the rest of my life if it would make you happy."

"Tomorrow," she said, invoking his proposal to her, then giggling at his expression. "No. No. Not tomorrow. I'm kidding. But . . . soon. I don't care if it looks rushed. I don't want to sneak around to be with my husband. I want for the whole world to know I'm your wife."

"How about . . . two weeks?" he said, beaming at her, loving the idea of renewing their vows in front of both their families. "Do you think we can get them all together?"

"Will yours be willing to travel?" she asked.

"For my wedding? Nothing would keep them away."

"Lowville?" she asked, her eyes hopeful.

"On the farm," he agreed. "I love it."

They were both silent for a moment, staring at each other with goofy, happy smiles, digesting this new turn of events.

"Do you really think it's possible?" Preston asked. "In two weeks?"

"I'm here in your arms," she said, leaning forward to kiss him again. Her tongue darted out to play with his, making him thicken and swell all over again. "Anything's possible. We'll . . ."

". . . figure it out," he finished for her. "I love you to the moon and back. Writing it in the stars alone could never be enough."

"Then write it every day on the fabric of our lives . . ." she said, borrowing the words that had been spoken at their wedding, "to form a most beautiful tapestry."

"I promise," he vowed. "Every day."

"Me too."

She kissed him again, and he pressed himself against her, letting her know how much he wanted her again.

"You know what we never said?" she asked, a saucy smile on her lips as she rolled to her back and crooked a finger at him, inviting him to follow. "Happy anniversary, Mr. Winslow."

"Happy anniversary, Mrs. Winslow," he answered, covering her body with his and leaning down to kiss his wife. "Happy forever."

Epilogue

Nine months later

"This is Juliana Rankovic reporting live from the red carpet, where we're about to go inside and find out who will be the next Best Actress winner!"

"Right you are, Juliana. And this has been one exciting race. Powerhouse Amy Adams is here with her sixth Academy Award nomination, Sigourney Weaver with her fourth nomination, and Miranda Richardson and Keira Knightley each here with their third."

"Don't forget my personal favorite, Elise Klassan."

"I think you mean Elise Klassan-Winslow!" said Brian Fieldcrest, winking at his cohost.

Juliana giggled, nodding at the camera. "That's right! The entire nation swooned over the story of Hollywood starlet, Elise, falling instantly in love with millionaire Preston Winslow while on location in Philadelphia shooting *The Philly Story* last summer. And that whirlwind wedding after they'd only known each other for a couple of weeks? Talk about *romantic*! Be still my beating heart, Brian!"

"Wasn't she a beautiful bride? And Juliana, we're already hearing quite a buzz about *The Philly Story*. But sadly for Elise's fans, it seems like she and Preston have made New York their home, and from what we understand, Elise is concentrating on her Broadway career for the foreseeable future."

"Don't forget, Brian, Elise actually got her *start* on Broadway, costarring with Maggie Gyllenhaal in *Ethan Frome* three years ago. Now starring in *A Streetcar Named Desire* at the Orpheum, she's back on top! That girl's got theater in her blood."

"It appears so! Now Juliana, have you been hearing those delicious rumors about Elise and Preston starting a family? Her dress tonight sure was roomy, and I have to say . . . that would be one adorable baby!"

"Give her a break!" said Juliana, chuckling at her cohost. "That was a gorgeous Missoni maxi dress, and one of my top fashion picks of the night. She pulled it off like a charm. Was there a bump under there? Only Elise and Preston know for sure, but I have to agree: Baby Winslow will be a cutie pie. No question about it!"

"Juliana, let's go back inside the Haywood Auditorium now where Charlize Theron is about to present the award for Best Actress in a Motion Picture . . ."

The camera panned from the glittering ceiling of the auditorium to the stage where Charlize Theron, dressed in a sparkling, silver-sequined gown, had already greeted the audience and was introducing the names of the Best Actress nominees.

". . . Elise Klassan-Winslow in *The Awakening*, Keira Knightley in *Mansfield Park*, Miranda Richardson in *Julbilio*, Sigourney Weaver in *What Happened in Krakow*, and Amy Adams in *Once Upon a September*." The camera panned to each of the actresses in turn, splitting the TV screen with their smiling, expectant faces. "And the Oscar for Best Actress goes to . . . Amy Adams in *Once Upon a September*!"

The music trumpeted as the camera remained on each of the other four nominees for an extra moment before zooming in exclusively on Elise Klassan-Winslow, who stared up at her husband's enamored face, her eyes adoring and her lips tilted up sweetly.

As Miss Adams made her ascent to the stage, the cameras lingered on Elise, watching as her handsome young husband, Preston Winslow, of the Philadelphia Winslows, beamed down at his wife, cupped her cheeks reverently, and kissed her. *Really* kissed her to the delight of every viewer at home. And when Elise finally drew away from him, her eyes sparkled with happiness like she hadn't just lost the Oscar for Best Actress but had already won the greatest prize in the world.

THE END

The Winslow Brothers continues with . . .

CRAZY ABOUT CAMERON

THE WINSLOW BROTHERS, BOOK #3

THE WINSLOW BROTHERS
(Part II of the Blueberry Lane Series)

Bidding on Brooks
Proposing to Preston
Crazy about Cameron
Campaigning for Christopher

Turn the page for a sneak peek of *Crazy about Cameron*!

Chapter 1

Cameron Winslow pressed the call button on the elevator, checking his watch as he waited for it to descend. Ten thirty. Yet another fifteen-hour day.

Since his brother Christopher had decided to bail on their financial company, C & C Winslow, to pursue a congressional bid, Cameron had been left high and dry and in charge of the accounts they'd painstakingly built up together. Somewhere deep inside, he knew that he couldn't continue on like this, and yet . . . they'd inherited the company from their late father and had worked hard not just to respect their father's legacy, but to make C & C Winslow their own. He couldn't give up yet. He wouldn't.

The lobby door whooshed open, and Cameron turned to see Margaret Story step onto the marble floor. The building super, Diego, rushed to take her wet umbrella, and Margaret smiled at him, her lips tilted up in a demure grin. Cameron's eyes trailed hungrily down her petite body, taking in the short tan raincoat she had belted at her tiny waist and her gorgeous legs in two-inch heels. Sliding his eyes back up, he focused on her dark-brown hair pulled back severely in a smooth bun and black-rimmed glasses covering her cognac-colored eyes.

He felt his body tighten in response and turned away from her, facing the shiny brass door of the elevator as it dinged softly.

Margaret Story was the unaware star of Cameron's filthiest naughty-librarian fantasies.

Always had been. Always would be.

And yet Margaret was a lady—someone who deserved his respect and admiration. He had no business thinking about her like that. There were women you did filthy things with . . . and women you married. He knew plenty of the former, but Margaret was firmly the latter. And since Cameron Winslow wasn't exactly in a position to be considering marriage, his deeply embedded moral code insisted that Margaret Story was strictly off-limits to him.

Not that she was available, he thought, clenching his jaw. She'd been dating some self-important asshole at her father's company for the past several months. Cameron had had the misfortune of being trapped in the elevator with Shane Olson and Margaret once or twice, and he wasn't anxious for it to happen again anytime soon. It was hard enough to see Margaret at all—seeing her with her smug, overconfident boyfriend, when she deserved so much better, was almost unbearable.

Cameron glanced back at her quickly, glad that Shane was absent tonight but hoping that she'd chat with the handyman for a few more seconds so that he could make his way upstairs alone.

"Thanks so much, Diego," she called as the elevator door opened. He heard her heels clack across the marble floor as she rushed toward the elevator. "I'll give him a call tomorrow!"

Cameron turned around just in time to see her step inside the suddenly tiny box and give him a careful smile.

"Cameron."

"Meggie."

She flinched at his use of her childhood nickname, her pretty lips pursing. He knew she didn't like it, but using it kept some distance between them, and Cameron needed that distance if he had any chance of behaving decently around her.

She leaned forward to press the eighth-floor button, and the slight movement released a scent of lilac that made Cameron groan quietly. She smelled like spring, and it made his mind switch from rational thought to spring fever whenever he was close to her.

Margaret turned around to face him, lifting her chin. "Honestly, Cameron, I don't know what I ever did to you."

This was a familiar conversation. She initiated it at least once every couple of weeks when they bumped into each other, and as much as Cameron dreaded it, he sort of longed for it too. It meant that he mattered to her—on some level, insignificant though it may have been, prim, perfect, pristine Margaret Story cared that Cameron *appeared* not to like her.

Cameron did his best to look bored, glancing at her with half-lidded eyes and shrugging.

"Fine," she said, shaking her head, her expression just shy of hurt. "Be that way."

She turned back around, pushing her purse to her elbow and crossing her arms over her chest.

He'd grown up with Margaret Story—their estates separated by the Rousseaus' house on Blueberry Lane in nearby Haverford. And she'd always, more or less, been the person she was now. Even as a child, she'd been bookish and severe, likely to blow the whistle on any misconduct and get adults running over to spoil the kids' fun. Cameron really hadn't paid her any attention until her legs suddenly got long and coltish and her small breasts started to tease him at neighborhood pool parties.

He'd watched her then, studied her, quietly fascinated by her innate serenity. She was more comfortable hanging back, the second of five sisters, perennially in older Alice's shadow and looking after her younger sisters, Betsy, Pris, and Jane. He had a sense that she liked flying under the radar, which made her his favorite target for teasing: the attention, to which she was unaccustomed, always made her red and flustered, and Cam had savored her reaction to him. He loved pulling her braids—teasing her in an attempt to loosen her up—and when it backfired and she stomped away in a snit, he couldn't help wishing he could somehow figure out how to be the boy who could make her loosen up, make her smile.

But at thirteen years old, just when Cameron might have mustered up the courage to steal a kiss from twelve-year-old Margaret, whom his barely teen heart loved desperately, his father died suddenly of a heart attack. His whole world changed overnight, ending in his move to London with his mother, brothers, and little sister . . . and Margaret Story became a dim memory attached to happier days he'd just as soon forget.

Five years later, he moved back to Philadelphia for college, like his brothers, but Margaret no longer lived in Philly, and he heard through the grapevine that she was in finishing school in Switzerland, a tradition for the Story sisters. And from what he gathered over the years from mutual friends, she'd stayed abroad, learning about French and Italian wines from old-world masters.

A few months ago, Cameron ran into Margaret again. While he chatted with Alex English in the lobby of his apartment building, Margaret—Alex's date—suddenly walked back into his life. She'd returned from Europe, finally, and had just moved into the fashionable Newbury Arms. Of all the places in all the world, the little girl whose braids he'd pulled now lived in the apartment directly over his.

And she was stunning. Sophisticated and charming, beautiful and refined, Margaret Story had grown into a modern-day Grace Kelly, complete with an ever-present chignon and elegant taste in clothes. With not a hair out of place and a voice that never raised beyond the honeyed tones of her quiet speaking voice, she was the epitome of grace and refinement.

"May I ask you a question?"

Jolted from his thoughts, he looked up at her. "Why not?"

"Have you ever had any work done on your apartment?"

He shook his head. "Nope."

She sighed. "Okay. Thanks."

The elevator stopped, and the door opened to the fourth floor. Mrs. Stewart took her time getting onto the elevator, her two Pekingese dogs yapping unpleasantly. Margaret moved back a little to accommodate the feisty fur balls, and her elbow brushed against Cameron's forearm. He knew the polite thing to do would be to move back to give her more space in the tiny, old-fashioned elevator, but he didn't want to. He wanted to touch her, even if it was through layers of raincoat and suit jacket.

"Push the L, huh, love?" asked Mrs. Stewart in her light Scottish brogue.

"We're going up, Mrs. Stewart," said Margaret as the doors closed.

"Oh, dear. I want to go down to the lobby." She reached forward and pushed the button for the fifth floor. "I'll get off at the next floor instead."

That strategy made very little sense to Cameron, but he held his tongue, feeling at once annoyed and secretly thrilled to have a little extra time with Margaret's arm pressed against his. The top of her head, which just reached his shoulder, was so close that if he leaned forward, he could brush her hair with his lips. Eager to divert himself from such foolish thoughts, he cleared his throat.

"Are you having some work done?"

"I'm thinking about it," she said without turning her swanlike neck to face him.

He wanted to know more, but appearing interested would be at odds with his usually insouciant demeanor toward her. The elevator dinged at the fifth floor, and Mrs. Stewart's Pekingese pups launched through the door, thinking a walk was imminent, and Cameron felt some sympathy for the fifth-floor lobby carpet.

"So I guess that means it'll be noisy upstairs," said Cameron.

As the elevator doors closed again, she turned slightly to face him. "I'll ask Geraldo to work during the day so I don't inconvenience you."

"Very considerate. Thanks."

"However," she continued, "since you're rarely home before midnight and always out of the building by seven in the morning, that leaves him plenty of time."

This was interesting. She kept tabs on his comings and goings? Why in the world Cameron found this so captivating, he couldn't put into words, but his cool facade slipped, and he couldn't resist teasing her just a little.

"You spying on me?"

She took a step away from him, backing toward the doors as her cheeks turned pink. "N-no. I just . . . I mean, I take a run some mornings and see you heading off, and when I come back from . . . I mean, some evenings when I return late, I notice you . . . you . . ."

"You notice me, Meggie," he rumbled, letting his eyes rest on hers.

"Yes." She lifted her chin. "Yes, I do. I notice that you don't say hello. I notice that you wish you were anywhere but trapped in an elevator with me making small talk. I notice that although you know how much I hate the nickname Meggie, you never miss an opportunity to use it."

She was magnificent with her flashing, light-brown eyes and pink, pillowed lips. If she were his, he'd lunge toward her right now. He'd bury his hands in her hair and send her goddamn hairpins to the floor as he pulled her face to his and—

Margaret shook her head in disappointment and turned away from him, as though giving up on his ability to give an appropriate response to her mini tirade.

"Diego gave me the name of his cousin Geraldo," she said, steering the conversation back to safer waters. "Apparently he does work for other tenants now and then."

Cameron took a deep breath, wishing away the very vivid images in his head, and heard himself say, "Come to think of it, I do have a project that needs attention. Perhaps I should schedule him too, as long as he's going to be here in the building."

She glanced at him over her shoulder. "Oh? I didn't realize you were considering a renovation."

"My master bathroom's too small," he blurted out.

As she stared at him, her little pink tongue darted out to lick her heavenly lips, and her voice was a little breathier than usual when she finally responded, "Oh, I see."

The elevator dinged, stopping at Cameron's floor, but he made no move from where he leaned against the back of the elevator. *What* did she see? She couldn't possibly see what he saw in his head: her small, lithe body all soaped up, her soft skin pressed against his as she leaned back against him, naked in his bathtub, her back to his front, her hair tickling his bare chest, her legs entwined with his, his hands on her slick, pert breasts as she moaned his—

"I can give you Geraldo's information. Hold on a sec." She rifled through her bag, pulling out her cell phone as the doors opened.

Cameron's cock was hardening by the second. He needed to get away from her. Far away. *At least* a full floor away.

"Text it to me," he said, brushing her shoulder as he strode past her through the open doors.

"But I don't have your—"

Looking back at her buttoned-up beauty over his shoulder, he said, "717-555-7172."

And the doors closed.

Look for *Crazy about Cameron* at your local bookstore or buy online!

Other Books by Katy Regnery

A MODERN FAIRYTALE
(Stand-alone, full-length, unconnected romances inspired by classic fairy tales.)

The Vixen and the Vet
(inspired by "Beauty and the Beast")
2014

Never Let You Go
(inspired by "Hansel and Gretel")
2015

Ginger's Heart
(inspired by "Little Red Riding Hood")
2016

Dark Sexy Knight
(inspired by "The Legend of Camelot")
2016

Don't Speak
(inspired by "The Little Mermaid")
2017

Swan Song
(inspired by "The Ugly Duckling")
2018

ENCHANTED PLACES
(Stand-alone, full-length stories that are set in beautiful places.)

Playing for Love at Deep Haven
2015

Restoring Love at Bolton Castle
2016

Risking Love at Moonstone Manor
2017

A Season of Love at Summerhaven
2018

ABOUT THE AUTHOR

USA Today **bestselling author Katy Regnery** started her writing career by enrolling in a short story class in January 2012. One year later, she signed her first contract for a winter romance entitled *By Proxy*.

Katy claims authorship of the multi-titled Blueberry Lane Series which follows the English, Winslow, Rousseau, Story and Ambler families of Philadelphia, the five-book, best-selling A Modern Fairytale series, the Enchanted Places series, and a standalone novella, *Frosted*.

Katy's first Modern Fairytale romance, *The Vixen and the Vet*, was nominated for a RITA® in 2015 and

won the 2015 Kindle Book Award for romance. Four of her books: *The Vixen and the Vet* (A Modern Fairytale), *Never Let You Go* (A Modern Fairytale), *Falling for Fitz* (The English Brothers #2) and *By Proxy* (Heart of Montana #1) have been #1 genre bestsellers on Amazon. Katy's boxed set, The English Brothers Boxed Set, Books #1–4, hit the *USA Today* bestseller list in 2015 and her Christmas story, *Marrying Mr. English*, appeared on the same list a week later.

Katy lives in the relative wilds of northern Fairfield County, Connecticut, where her writing room looks out at the woods, and her husband, two young children, and two dogs create just enough cheerful chaos to remind her that the very best love stories begin at home.

Sign up for Katy's newsletter today: http://www.katyregnery.com!

Connect with Katy

Katy LOVES connecting with her readers and answers every e-mail, message, tweet, and post personally! Connect with Katy!

Katy's Website: http://katyregnery.com
Katy's E-mail: katy@katyregnery.com
Katy's Facebook Page: https://www.facebook.com/KatyRegnery
Katy's Pinterest Page: https://www.pinterest.com/
     katharineregner
Katy's Amazon Profile: http://www.amazon.com/
     Katy-Regnery/e/B00FDZKXYU
Katy's Goodreads Profile: https://www.goodreads.com/author/
     show/7211470.Katy_Regnery

CPSIA information can be obtained at www.ICGtesting.com
Printed in the USA
LVOW10s1614190616

493130LV00002B/2/P